Praise for the TYLER VANCE novels:

"From the quick-clutch first sentence, Harvey establishes himself as a writer possessed of cool control . . . the muscular story zips along in pared-down prose. Tyler is tough, but sentimental enough to avoid being hard-boiled."

—*Publishers Weekly*

"Certainly one of the best thriller debuts in years. We are straight into Raymond Chandler country and *The Big Sleep.*"

—Jack Higgins

"Clay Harvey's *A Flash of Red* is taut, knowing, and headlong. Welcome aboard!"

—Robert B. Parker

"Fast-moving . . . an excellent thriller."

—*Denver Post*

"Elegant prose sets apart this new thriller. Throw in a tightly woven plot and you have yourself a book that will keep you flipping pages furiously into the wee hours of the night. . . . The story's charm lies in Harvey's characters. Multidimensional, sometimes unorthodox, they will pry open your heart and snuggle comfortably inside."

—*Rapport*

"Powerful."

—*West Coast Review of Books*

"Clay Harvey scores with *A F*
mish, this is not the book for

Titles by Clay Harvey

DWELLING IN THE GRAY
A WHISPER OF BLACK
A FLASH OF RED

DWELLING IN THE GRAY

CLAY HARVEY

JOVE BOOKS, NEW YORK

This is a work of fiction. Names, characters, places, and incidents are either the product of the author's imagination or are used fictitiously, and any resemblance to actual persons, living or dead, business establishments, events, or locales is entirely coincidental.

DWELLING IN THE GRAY

A Jove Book / published by arrangement with
the author

PRINTING HISTORY
Jove edition/March 2000

The Penguin Putnam Inc. World Wide Web site address is
http://www.penguinputnam.com

ISBN: 0-515-12747-7

A JOVE BOOK®
Jove Books are published by The Berkley Publishing Group,
a division of Penguin Putnam Inc.,
375 Hudson Street, New York, New York 10014.
JOVE and the "J" design
are trademarks belonging to Penguin Putnam Inc.

PRINTED IN THE UNITED STATES OF AMERICA

10 9 8 7 6 5 4 3 2 1

This book is dedicated to
Nancy S. Fleming
Writer, editor, raconteur.
And, most of all, a lady by any definition.

I gratefully acknowledge the following:

My son, Christopher, ten in two weeks, and who still believes I know everything. Well, almost everything. I love you, pal.

Faye Hiatt, just for being Faye.

Mike Holloway, who everyone knows is really Dave Michaels. And Nancy Holloway, for keeping Mike straight. Kind of.

Susan Cooke. Every author should have such an astute reader; nothing gets by Susan. She's a gem whose exuberance never flags, who is never too busy, and whose friendship never wavers.

Melissa Ann Elizabeth Bergeron Carter, not only for her encouragement and wit, but for her keen insight into the human (condition, comedy, drama, malaise—choose one). She delights everyone. Don't tell her I said so.

Friend Andy Riedell, war vet, teller of tales, former flyer of planes, currently happily retired with his motorcycle boots on.

Sandy Wingate, a jewel whose trenchant critiques are always spot on.

Barbara and Ron Sickenberger, an ennuptialated pair worth emulating. In every way.

Nancy Donnell, who provided peerless pies whenever my waistline showed signs of shrinkage.

Debbie Ortiz, voracious reader, who promotes Tyler

Vance at every opportunity and can't wait for the movie. Me too.

Officer Ed Humburg, who teaches me about sleeper holds, police codes, handcuffs, and other in-stuff. He even knows what he's talking about.

Ms. Emma Laine, who makes sure I dot all my *p*'s and *q*'s, or cross my *i*'s, or something. She's been guiding me with a firm but gentle hand for thirty-five years. I relish thirty-five more.

Dr. David Best, who advises me about folks' insides. And sometimes their outsides.

Tom Colgan, editor supreme, father extraordinaire, a man with a keen sense of humor. And he's a New Yorker!

The past is not over. It isn't even the past.

—WILLIAM FAULKNER

DWELLING IN THE GRAY

PROLOGUE

ALL SHE WANTED WAS ICE CREAM. BUT EMILY JANSEN was pert and pretty, sixteen and filled out, and she was employed at the sheltered workshop with others unable to comprehend reading and writing, and the ice-cream shop was filled to overflowing with gonadal high-schoolers who had no use for "retards."

Well, maybe *one* use. . . .

Circling sharklike came four of them while Emily waited patiently for her cone of butter pecan. They were jocks—big, boisterous, full of contempt. And hormones. Consciences, though, in short supply.

"Hey, cutie," said the fullback, slipping an arm around Emily's slender waist.

"Hi," she said back, smiling, since she was a happy child.

" 'Hi,' she says," exclaimed the fullback to his cronies, clustered about and elbowing each other; then, "C'mere, honey," pulling her close to lick an ear redolent of Ivory soap.

Emily tried to pull away but the gridiron star held her

tightly, tongue thrusting. "Stop," she cried, alarmed now, twisting and turning to break free.

" *'Stop,'* " mimicked her abuser, squeezing so tightly Emily could scarcely breathe.

"Stop!" echoed his trio of pals, falsetto.

"Stop," said another voice, calm and quiet and unemotional, silencing the room as effectively as a cathedral bell.

The fullback turned toward the voice, examined its owner from head to toe, dismissed the threat.

A mistake.

Once again he laved the girl's ear, jerking her against himself, his breath hot and vile. Suddenly a vise gripped his wrist—or so it seemed, the pressure was so intense—and his body was jerked off balance and pummeled rapidly and repeatedly, causing his nose to splinter and air to desert his lungs in a sibilant *whoosh.* Abruptly he was on the floor and in the clutch of the worst pain he'd ever experienced. A shake of his head—golden locks flying from the sudden movement, purpled nose misshapen—and he lumbered back up to tower over his tormentor. "I'm gonna kick your ass!" he wheezed, tossing a massive fist.

Another mistake.

When he woke—minus six teeth and four minutes of memory that were never regained, his friends supine about him, bloody and unconscious—the dummy and Sir Galahad were nowhere in sight. The gaps where his teeth no longer rooted hurt so badly that he soon passed out, but not before thinking: *Someday I'll nail that bastard.*

His propensity for mistakes was apparently inexhaustible.

THE BEGINNING

GREENSBORO,
NORTH CAROLINA
JUNE 1954

NEWBORN

LEIGH VANCE HAD BEEN PREGNANT FOREVER, EIGHT AND a half months as the crow flies, and, it being her second child, knew about what to expect. But that first baby—a December girl six years ago—had come without much drama, unless you counted the discomforts attendant to normally simple tasks (walking, sleeping, sitting, even keeping food down) to be drama. Not that kneeling beside the toilet when your belly's the size of a clothes basket wasn't a trial—to both your stomach *and* your knees—but with this current gravidity had come a heat rash, Lord help her. Never again a summer child; Leigh itched worse than one of Odie's flea-bitten coon dogs.

So, with pleasurable anticipation, since this pregnancy was not living up to her expectations, Leigh decided to go ahead and have the child a bit early—say, a week, ten days. She put it in the Lord's hands at the genesis of her ninth month, after a miserably hot afternoon filled with scratching and sweating and nausea and an unusual number of kicks from within.

The Almighty answered promptly. On the morning of

the third day after Leigh's initial prayerful request for a rapid but healthy termination to her gestation, she awoke besmirched. Not drowning in a pool of blood, or course, but certainly not the spotting she was used to seeing on the sheets of a morning. So she went to find Odie—in the kitchen preparing their breakfast—to show him the bespoiled linen. He nearly swallowed his tongue, but with Leigh choreographing his every move, managed to get the doctor on the phone.

"Leigh's made a mess on the sheets," Odie informed the good doctor. "There's blood all over everywhere."

The MD, inexplicably composed despite such a horrifying development, inquired as to the size of the stain. The soon-to-be-papa-twice responded with an accurate approximation. "Sounds like placental bleeding," opined the medic, who then requested their immediate presence at the hospital, where he would meet them.

And thus came Leigh to be uncomfortably ensconced in a hospital bed, scratching her distended abdomen relentlessly, raising welts, and consuming apple juice by the quart. (She wasn't close to term and there was no significant dilation, so the nurses allowed her to drink all she wanted. Besides, it stifled her complaints.) The heavy consumption of fluids necessitated frequent trips to the toilet, where Leigh would often espy blood in the bowl along with urine, which frightened her. She was closely monitored for twenty hours; the bleeding continued. So, at 3:30 in the morning of June 24, 1954, Leigh's physician induced labor, then scrubbed up while the expectant mother was being anesthetized and the expectant father was choking down tranquilizers. Not long past four o'clock the baby was out, crying and kicking and indignant. Three days later he was home, rocking in the arms of his six-years-older sister, Anne, a bottle in his mouth and contentment in his eye.

During the next few days, the proud parents discussed names for their offspring. Neither favored Tyler, but familial pressure was too great to overcome. Grandmother Vance had been a Tyler, a direct descendant of the tenth president of the United States; her compatriots at the DAR would flip their corsets if she didn't follow through on her avowed commitment to the family moniker.

So Tyler it was, up front. But what for in the center? Odie favored Clairmont, his great-uncle's given appellation, and a grand old Southern name it was, too. Leigh leaned to Cornelius, her maiden name, arguing that since Grandmother Vance had claimed dibs on first names, it was only fair that she be allowed to choose the middle one. Her husband agreed in principle but not in execution; he simply couldn't abide the thought of his only son being labeled, *ugh* . . . Cornelius. "He'd grow up hating us," he insisted to his spouse. Odie's elder brother, Clyde, offered his own name for consideration, but was voted down, for no good reason in his view. So he went fishing. And thus the battle raged until an enterprising relative suggested that the infant be provided only a middle initial, "C." Despite gaping mouths and eyes bulging from incredulity, thc portentious kinsman forged on, explaining that Odie could introduce his heir as Tyler Clairmont Vance while leaving Leigh free to inform feminine friends that her spanking new son answered to Tyler Cornelius Vance. Why, she could even poke "Esquire" on the end to high-tone it for the DAR ladies.

The family took a vote and the idea was adopted, though not entirely without reservation. Great-aunt Louise insisted that she'd simply refer to the child as "TC," which everyone agreed was just like her, the contrary old biddy. Grandpa Cornelius allowed as how he'd always been partial to Cyrus as a fine name for a boy child, but since nobody else seemed to agree, he'd just call the newborn "Bud." That made no sense to anyone but Grandpa Cornelius, whose reputation as an eccentric spread to several counties, including one in West Virginia.

And so did it come to pass that one unnamed, underweight infant with a full head of hair and more than his share of plucky relatives was dubbed officially and legally "Tyler C. Vance." (No one in the family ever called him Clairmont, nor yet Cornelius—just simply "Ty" or "Tyler," depending on the formality of the occasion or the degree of exasperation engendered by the child in whomever was addressing him at the moment.)

The baby Vance weighed five pounds, twelve ounces at birth, and quickly tried to improve on that by consuming his mother's milk at a rate that taxed her ability to dispense it. His diet was bolstered by formula, which gave the baby the nutrients needed to thrive while allowing his mother's production facilities a welcome respite.

"Are your nipples sore, honey?" asked Grandmother Vance at the peak of output and consumption.

"Feels like they got caught in a car door, especially the left one, which he seems to favor," Leigh responded. "But it's a comfort he's a hearty eater," she added, looking down lovingly at her infant, at that moment firmly attached and receiving sustenance. "Means he'll grow big, like his daddy."

But the boy didn't. Despite an appetite appropriate for two lumberjacks, young Tyler never grew bigger than average. Whatever he ingested his metabolism and nonstop nature conspired to burn up before it had a chance to coalesce into fat cells. He grew wiry and lean, and hell for strong, quick as a whip in any kind of game, mental or physical. But large, no.

Lack of stature didn't trouble the boy much until first grade. Having spent little time around children his age except for a plethora of cousins, both older and younger, he had not been exposed to bullies. In minor scrapes with kids his own age or approximate size, he had always acquitted himself acceptably; not an aggressive child, he was nonetheless aggressive enough to take care of himself, until meeting up with Jimmy Phelps and Terrance Twittle. Both were seven, had flunked first grade, and were strapping big bruisers from the rough side of the tracks. They were boys born with the bark on, meaner than a wounded catamount, and encouraged to be so by their fathers, neither of whom could boast steady, gainful employment but who had in common a fourth-grade education and a fondness for white "likker".

Jimmy and Terrance were cousins, though they resembled each other more closely than many siblings. Terrance was afflicted with crossed eyes, Jimmy with a cleft palate; both had prominent ears, noses, and feet. None of the aforementioned conditions improved their sour dispositions nor imbued them with a sunny outlook; the two made schoolyard life miserable for every male child at Ramsay Park Elementary, and most particularly for young Tyler C. Vance. Ty, cursed with a chivalrous nature, never seemed to acquire the knack of staying in the background while some hapless child got a blackened eye or, even worse, endured some form of heinous public humiliation at the hands of the Jughead Twins, as Jimmy and Terrance were called by the other children—out of earshot, of course. Always ready to step forward on a child's behalf, Ty was constantly rewarded with a bloodied nose, boxed ear, or a dunk in the goldfish pond.

And so it went throughout the fall of his first school year, until one fateful day when Uncle Darryl was about to decamp after one of his semiannual visits. Odie's youngest brother had spent four years at Purdue—on a boxing scholarship. A Golden Gloves champion three years running, Darryl appeared bound for the Olympics until a skiing accident ruined his left knee and there went competitive pugilism. On this particular occasion young Ty was just getting off the school bus, fresh from a soaking, courtesy of the goldfish pond—and with a black eye to boot. Uncle Darryl, coming out of the house with suitcase in hand, spotted the boy's disheveled condition, took in the shiner, and spun on his heels. For the rest of that day and seventeen thereafter, Darryl Vance worked with his nephew, introducing him to the manly art of fisticuffs. Ty, with innate speed, strength, and superior hand-to-eye coordination, absorbed it all like a sponge, having to be shown punches and blocks and combinations usually only once. Before returning to his trucking company back up north (in Virginia), Darryl bought for Tyler a heavy bag, a speed bag, and a jump rope. No gloves; the task this budding boxer faced involved bare knuckles, unprotected skin, and guts.

Ty worked hard. Day after day, his daddy—no slouch with his fists, having sparred with younger brother Darryl all through high school—watched and encouraged and corrected and cajoled. Darryl came to town every month or so to spend the weekend and assess progress.

Tyler's initiation to boxing had begun in late October 1960. By late May, he pleaded with his uncle that he was ready, explaining how he could not stand to avoid the Jughead Twins even one more day, to offer no resistance to their taunts and dousings for one more recess period. He'd *had* it; his patience and ability to endure debasement was not worn thin, but vaporous. Uncle Darryl conferred with brother Odie. The two agreed: Ty might not have yet achieved quite the level of skill desired, but continued capitulation to his tormentors might hinder his will to resist such behavior by others in the future. Time for him to try his wings, despite the risk of a sound thrashing from his adversaries. Better damage to the body than to the spirit.

It was arranged. Ty's cousin Vince (a sixth-grader at the same school) would fake a stomachache at 10:20 the following Monday morning, young Tyler's recess time. But, instead of going to the office to phone his folks, Vince would slip out to the playground to observe the fracas and ensure that the contest didn't get out of hand. Odie and Darryl planned to watch from an adjoining vacant lot, unbeknownst to Tyler, who thought he'd be on his own, unaware even that his older cousin was going to be lurking in the wings.

Uncle Darryl brought Ty the news at bedtime; the boy was lying on his bed listening to Little Richard on the radio. He switched it off when his uncle walked in with his serious face on. Darryl told his nephew: "Tomorrow's the day. Now, don't pick a fight, but if the Jugheads start something, you offer to take 'em on one at a time."

Ty was excited. Apprehensive. Ambivalent. But he said, "Okay."

"Remember, stay inside, punch to the body. They're too tall for you to stand-up box, they've got the reach on you. Take the fight to them. Don't play and don't get fancy. And whatever you do, don't show off. This isn't a game. You might get hurt if you fool around."

Ty swallowed, his little Adam's apple bobbing.

"Hit 'em as hard and as often as you can. Try to end it quick. Don't let 'em wear you out. If they grab hold of you, or take you down, don't play their game. Butt with your head, use your elbows, knee them in the crotch, but don't get tied up or smothered. They're just too big to try to outmuscle. Got it?"

"How do you know how big they are?"

"Your daddy and I drove by the school yesterday, to have a look at 'em."

"Can I beat 'em?"

Darryl nodded. "Maybe. Won't be a picnic. They're big and tough and mean, but both of them are soft around the middle. That's where they live. Punch there, over and over, and you can pull it off—*if* you don't let 'em hit you. At least not often. And they probably won't. Kids are grapplers; they generally don't know what they're doing. When one of them hit you in the eye before, it was likely because you didn't know how to protect yourself, not because they were especially good. Anyone can hit a stationary, unprotected target with their fist, even your cousin Velma."

Ty smiled at that, envisioning little Velma, pink and pudgy and practically three. He said, "Okay."

"Fight smart, don't give up, remember to protect your head. I'll be proud of you whatever happens. So will your daddy. You don't have to prove a thing to us. This is for you."

Tyler jumped up to hug his uncle tightly, tears forming

against his will. He held on for a long time so Darryl wouldn't notice the tears and be ashamed of him. He'd have been astonished to learn that his uncle was doing exactly the same thing.

HANDLING BULLIES

MARY LIN BEESON WAS THE CATALYST. PRETTY, GREEN-eyed, and pigtailed, she'd been Tyler Vance's primary distaff interest since he had first cast his gaze upon her at Sunday school. Being comely and quite popular, she was always surrounded by playmates—both genders—and displayed a tendency for staying close to her teacher when outside at recess, thus dodging the incessant torment suffered by other children at the hands of the Jughead Twins. As coincidence would have it, this Monday morning she strayed far afield from her common haunts, wandering innocently into Phelps/Twittle territory. Terrance, not so smitten by Mary Lin as most of the other boys, wasted no time in exploiting this opportunity to exhibit his detachment. He shoved the helpless girl into the dirt, then rubbed her nose in the sandbox for good measure, while she squirmed and struggled.

At 10:31 A.M., Eastern standard time, Tyler Vance spotted—from the elevated vantage point of the jungle gym—poor Mary Lin being tortured by his avowed enemy, and sped to her rescue. His blitz was observed from afar by his father and uncle and from up close by his cousin Vince, not to mention Terrance's cousin Jimmy, who immediately tried to waylay young Tyler en route. A hand clamped onto Jimmy's shoulder. It belonged to a meaty sixth-grader named Vince, thus putting the kibosh to whatever intervention Jimmy had in mind. So he simply stood and watched the melee.

Just before Mary Lin ran completely out of air, her assailant was flung from her onto his back in the sand. The girl sat up gasping for breath, spitting grit and saliva. Her new spring dress was in shambles. To her credit, she did not scream, just sat crying softly.

Terrance, still supine, stared in disbelief at Tyler Vance. Had this punk really tossed him on his keister? Time for a lesson in fealty. He lumbered to his feet, towering a full head (and maybe part of a neck) over his adversary, whom he planned to reduce to whimpering mush forthwith. He said, "Now you're really gonna get it," put up his dukes, and advanced menacingly.

Into a stiff left jab. The punch did three things simultaneously: it startled Terrance Twittle to his marrow; it opened a cut where an incisor punctured the lining of his mouth from the force of the blow; and it bruised Ty's knuckles so badly it brought instantly to mind his uncle's directive to go for the body, a much softer target. Before Terrance had regrouped his defenses, Ty did just that, three times, fast—left, right, left—turning his hips as he threw each punch, using his body weight. The behemoth before him grunted at each blow and, after the third landed, flailed his arms to ward off more punishment. One of them caught Tyler and pushed him backward, off balance.

Although winded, Terrance Twittle knew an opening

when he saw it and threw himself into the fray with renewed vigor, encircling his opponent with his longer arms. Tyler's reaction was to lower his chin onto his chest—to avoid being drawn in too tightly—and pummel Mr. Twittle repeatedly in the stomach and ribs. This tactic seemed to work just fine; Terrance, not being able to suck in much air due to the continuing assault on his midsection, released his grip and lashed out with a foot, catching Tyler on the shin.

Boy, did that hurt. So badly that it made Ty see red, literally, as well as Twittle's unprotected and bulbous nose, hanging right there in front of him nearly out of reach. But *nearly* is not *completely*. Tyler aimed a right cross at the appendage, feeling the shock all the way from elbow to shoulder as he connected. Staggering backward, hands administering to his battered nose, eyes watering up in involuntary reaction, Terrance yelled loudly, "Jimmy!"

Ty swirled about, looking for Phelps, whom he'd overlooked during the intensity of battle. Figuring that Twittle was now out of the picture, Vince surrendered Jimmy's shoulder, saying, "Go on. Help your cousin."

Jimmy Phelps lowered his bullet head and charged like a rhino, all seventy pounds of him. Tyler simply tilted a shoulder and dove forward, aiming low. He hit his attacker just below the knees, causing the larger boy to flip over his back, landing flat and hard.

Over in the vacant lot, Uncle Darryl said, "Where'd he get that move? You teach it to him?"

"Not me," Odie replied, "but it worked pretty good."

Terrance was still yelling, blood smearing his face, but he was not disabled. He started forward with the obvious intent of grabbing Ty from behind. Vince was about to take an active role when Mary Lin etched herself permanently in Tyler's memory by shouting, "Ty, look out!" whereupon the boy spun to catch Twittle in midstride. The two glowered at each other, neither showing fear, until Jimmy groaned, stirred, and tried to rise.

"You give up?" asked Tyler C. Vance, Esq., six (pushing seven) years old and invincible.

"Give up?" replied Twittle. "Shit no, I'll—" He couldn't finish, given the force of the uppercut that clicked his teeth together like a clapper board in some Hollywood studio. On his duff again, not certain how he got there, he rescinded his decision, deciding to quit before he lost some permanent teeth, several of which he'd only recently acquired.

The Phelps faction remained hostile, however, managing to knock the scrappy Vance kid on his fanny twice during the next five minutes. But not without cost. Though Tyler's lip was split from a punch he'd failed to slip, and his chest was sawing in air from a blow to the ribs he'd not deflected with an elbow, his opponent also spent time in the dirt, and bore the beginnings of a mouse under his right eye, the result of a dozen lightning jabs and one jarring left hook.

Tyler was about to suggest calling the fight a draw when Jimmy aimed a kick at his groin—which Ty avoided by backpedaling. Phelps followed up by tackling the smaller boy, taking him to the ground and climbing on top. Spinning like a cat to face downward, Ty got his arms under him and pushed upward onto his elbows and knees, with Jimmy still straddling his back as if on a horse. Ty then captured his rider's right leg in the crook of his right arm, reaching under to lock hands, then rolled forward onto his left shoulder, heaving with all the power in his legs.

Overbalanced, Phelps hit the ground heavily on his left side. Tyler held onto the leg and continued his twisting movement with the larger boy still in place, then released the leg and pivoted his trunk to expose Jimmy Phelps's torso. A short, wicked elbow to the solar plexus ended the battle. Instantly.

Tyler Vance climbed to his feet, looked down for a moment, then walked away. Thirty children trooped after him, babbling happily. Excluded from the revelry were the Jughead Twins, unhappily destined to endure that unpleasant sobriquet openly now that they were no longer feared.

Cousin Vince did go to the office, but claimed that his bellyache had improved, and could he return to class. He did.

Two proud Vance males sashayed home to assure Momma that all was well. "I still don't like it," she grumped, relegating the men to the back porch so she wouldn't have to listen to their interminable recountings.

And so they wouldn't catch her beaming.

A NEW FOE

TYLER C. VANCE DID NOT SUFFER HIS VICTORY WITH APpropriate humility. While he didn't actually embrace belligerence as a philosophy, he took more seriously than was prudent the Don Quixotic role he felt had been thrust upon him by circumstance. Any slight—imagined or genuine, directed at himself or a fellow grammar school inmate—was handled combatively and with an uncharacteristic lack of forbearance for the petty polemics of his peers. He forgot he was a kid. Monitoring the playground for any and all infractions became burdensome, not to mention alienating. He was so often serious, so seldom fun, that most of his former friends eschewed his company. A few stuck with him, for a while; at length even those stalwarts grew weary of his hair-trigger pugnacity.

Ty still had youngsters to play with, cousins and neighborhood kids; around home he felt no pressure to police his environs. But at school, he doggedly played Gary Cooper in *High Noon,* with Mary Lin as Grace Kelly. (The little girl never forgot what Tyler did for her when no one else turned a finger, remaining a loyal friend until her family moved to Dubuque in 1967.)

The second grade flew rapidly but not uneventfully. Odie, his one and only boy having been involved in more than two dozen donnybrooks, was summoned repeatedly to parent/teacher and parent/principal conferences, and even one parent/*custodian* conference since Tyler had treated the son of one of Odie's hunting pals—head handyman at Ramsay Park School—to a goldfish-pond baptism unsanctioned by higher authority. Tyler was, in turns, reasoned with, threatened, punished, cajoled, and, finally, confined to his classroom and the lunchroom, with all recess privileges denied.

The boy, endowed with the stubbornness of J. Edgar Hoover and the resolve of Helen Keller, withstood his ordeal stoically, secretly relieved to abandon his judge-and-jury mantle. Some of his devil-may-care personality resurfaced; he was even more carefree at home. Second grade ended, summer rowed languidly by, and Tyler faced third grade at a new school, a preemptive move on the part of his parents to forestall the possibility of a return to a fractious and dissolute nature.

It might have worked, too, if only Tyler hadn't become so adept at kicking ass. Still not large, just average in stature and heft, he was growing quicker and stronger all the time, and had displayed an inordinate knack for finding a critical weakness in any opponent, no matter how formidable. The school year began badly when Tyler, responding to a negative comment about his marble-playing abilities, whacked a fifth-grader so hard the boy lost his shooter, a gorgeous cobalt cat's eye. The polished orb flew from the child's hand after Tyler decked him with a straight right to the schnoz.

Tyler wasn't booted out of school that day, though it seemed touch and go for a while. The principal—a fellow choir member of his mother's at the Methodist church—gave him a stern warning, then lapsed into tears after the child left. Everyone at Cross of Calvary adored the Vances, and Mrs. Hall—the principal—had baby-sat for Tyler many times when he was endiapered. Genuinely distraught, she wondered what would become of this youngster—the product of a fine Christian pairing—if he continued down the path he was taking.

She needn't have worried. Tyler C. Vance was about to confront the means of his redemption.

Just down the hall, departing room 118 en route to the office with an inoculation record from his family practitioner, strode David Johnathan Michaels. David was also a newcomer to Central School, his family recently having migrated from Georgia, where his mother had taught scuba diving and his father had laid bricks, done carpentry, piloted a crop duster, and taught classes on the side.

Jiu-jitsu classes.

Tyler and David passed in the hall, the latter nodding a friendly greeting, which Ty, miffed at having been called to the carpet this first day of school, dismissed with a glare.

David, rebuking the rebuff, said, "Not very friendly, are you?"

The waxed tile floor squeaked with indignation as Tyler's Keds dug in, reversed direction, and padded over to confront this kid who knew no better than to behave disrespectfully, sarcastically, injudiciously—to *him.* Perhaps a word or two might be in order. Just a simple reprimand, instructions on protocol, not up-close-and-in-his-face, assuming the kid would listen to reason and adjust his attitude.

So, for a good thirty seconds, Tyler C. Vance dressed down this interloper, informing poor Dave of his lowly place in the student pecking order and, further, offering advice on manners appropriate for passing someone in the hall who was in no mood to exchange amenities. David withstood the harangue silently, politely, then asked, "Can I go now?"

Tyler goggled like a guppy, couldn't believe what he'd just heard. All of his speech, eloquent as it was, had been wasted on this bumpkin. Perhaps a more physical reproof was in order. Verbally allowing as how he just might have to box somebody's ears, Tyler assumed his most aggressive stance and countenance, prepared to strike like a mamba at any further sign of disrespect.

Dave Michaels, about to make a lifelong friend, said, "Not mine, I hope."

Then young Tyler committed the most serendipitous mistake he'd ever make; he aimed a fist at David Johnathan Michael's nose. It never landed. But Ty did, on his butt beneath the water cooler. He bumped his head on its lower surface getting up, diverting his attention just enough to slow his roundhouse right, a risky punch under any circumstances but effective when it landed solidly.

It didn't land at all. He reflected, pivoting over Dave's hip, headed for the floor again, seemingly in slow motion as his thoughts coursed ahead of his body. *"Oof!"* from his mouth as the breath left him, which he'd had happen before, several times. Knowing that it wasn't fatal, that it was as easy to catch your breath on the move as sitting on the floor feeling sorry for yourself, he launched an attack, sweeping his leg in a broad arc aiming for his opponent's ankles. *Let's see how* he *bounces,* thought Tyler.

But it didn't happen. David anticipated the ploy and responded with a hard punt to the knee, exploding sparks of pain in Tyler's head. He said, "Ouch," climbed awkwardly to his feet, and punched once more at David's nose. Finding air. Young Michaels sidestepped, avoiding the blow, and now had Ty by the wrist with his right hand, by the elbow with his left. Tugging down on the wrist and up on the elbow, Dave reduced his assailant to a puppet on a string, eliciting howls of pain and impotent wrath, the stridency of which depended on how much pressure was applied.

"Say uncle," he advised.

"I'm not gonna say uncle, just quit it," from Ty.

More pressure.

"Uncle!"

A bit more pressure yet; not much, just a little. Putative pressure.

"Uncle!" quoth Tyler.

Letting go of the arm, David stepped away, out of reach, but remained ready.

Ty rubbed his arm ruefully, all the starch taken out of him. "Nobody ever whipped me before," he tendered.

"Hi. I'm David Johnathan Michaels, from Savannah, but you can call me Dave." He held out a hand.

Tyler looked at the hand, tentatively raised his to grip it, then shook firmly.

Dave said, "I didn't whip you, you whipped yourself. I just didn't let you whip me. Hope I didn't hurt you much."

Tyler shook his head. "No worse than if you'd hit me with a ball bat."

Dave smiled. "You came too close with that last punch. I was afraid you'd bop me one if I didn't do something, and you swing hard. So I took hold of your arm and straightened it a little."

"Like to straightened it the wrong way," said Ty, grinning now. "Where'd you learn to fight like that?"

"From my dad, but it took me a while . . . ," Dave began as the two walked off, shoulder to shoulder, like they would time and time again through the years, good times and bad. Mrs. Hall viewed them from her doorway, partially open, from which she'd observed the entire episode.

Smiling to herself, she said, "Thank you, Lord," and turned away.

NIMRODS

TYLER WAS IN THE FRONT YARD WHEN HIS DADDY brought Granny Vance home from the doctor's office that early fall afternoon. He was culling rocks for use in the slingshot Odie had bought him from "the Bean Shooter Man," a gent by the name of Hussey, over in Asheboro. Hussey made each slingshot by hand—most often from dogwood or maple forks—stripping off the bark then going over the wood with broken glass and sandpaper for a marble-smooth finish. The sling, of pure gum rubber, launched rocks with a satisfying snap. Hussey himself, it was claimed—though Tyler had never seen it—could hit quarters tossed in the air. Regularly. Ty was skeptical; he'd tried it often enough, unsuccessfully. He *had* managed to bag a few score of bullfrogs, for their legs, and more than his share of cottontails and tree squirrels, but airborne coins were safe from his bean shooter.

His daddy came out of the house, looking worried. Tyler walked over, saying, "How's Maw-maw?"

"Not so good, I'm afraid." The Vance matriarch was afflicted with cancer, diagnosed as terminal, and the family had pretty much come to grips with the inevitable when Cousin Will, a student at MIT, raised everyone's hopes with information about a relatively new treatment called boron neutron capture therapy. In the late fifties it had the learned corridors of MIT abuzz. Unfortunately, nearly everyone who'd tried the therapy had died, either from complications arising from the treatment or from the cancer itself. The current outlook was bleak.

Sitting on the porch swing, Ty's head on his daddy's shoulder to offer solace, the pair passed a quiet ten minutes. Then Odie said, "Weren't we supposed to get Dave and round us up a mess o' squirrels this afternoon?"

"Yeah, but if you don't feel like it, it's okay."

"No, it's all right. We'll go. Get us out of your grandmother's hair for a while. You been practicin' right smart with your bean shooter?"

"Some. Not as much as maybe I should," Ty replied.

"What're you doin' with all them rocks spread out on the newspaper?"

"Separating the roundest ones. The rounder they are the truer they fly. At least I think so."

"Analyzin' your misses, are you?" Odie chuckled.

"Well, my release is always the same. I anchor on my chin and let go without jerking, but sometimes a rock'll fly wild. Has to be some reason. So I decided to experiment. As long as my rocks are pretty round, and pretty smooth, too, I usually hit where I aim. About as far as from here to the mailbox, anyway."

"Do the little smooth rocks kill squirrels and frogs as good as the jagged ones?"

"Better, I think. 'Course that might be just because I place my shots more accurate with the round rocks. I usually hit 'em in the head."

"Finish up your rock selectin' and we'll go fetch Dave."

Ty slew four squirrels with five rocks that afternoon, Dave bagged five out of seven tries. After it grew too dark to see well enough to shoot, they repaired to the barn to skin the squirrels. (Skinning is not really the right verb, at least in the traditional sense. Removing thc outer layer from a squirrel is less skinning than peeling. After making a strategic slit beneath the tail, thc hide is pulled off like a sweater, over the animal's head. Performed thus, there is little or no hair left clinging to the exposed meat, where it's the devil to remove.)

The threesome then cooked their catch over an open fire, squirrels spitted and rotated until brown and juicy, then eaten with a pile of roastin' ears drenched with butter, and buttermilk biscuits baked in an old Home Comfort woodstove and slathered with homemade blackberry compote from berries gathered in the thicket behind the dog lot. Hot coffee afterward, in tin cups warmed beside the fire to prevent cooling the liquid when it was poured; black for Odie, ditto for Dave, who had acquired his taste for java on Atlantic coastal trawlers, fishing for mackerel with his ma. Tyler, consuming the brew primarily to be like his daddy and best friend, tainted his with sufficient Carnation evaporated milk and sugar to lighten its hue from dark brown to beige. *What I'd really like is some hot chocolate,* he thought, but kept his counsel. No need Dave thinking him a sissy, because, aside from his pal and a select few family members—not all, by all means—Tyler didn't much give a hoot what other folks thought of him. (Except Mary Lin, of course, but she'd still like him if he grew hair all over his body and bayed at the moon. Which he didn't, but might as well have, he and Dave spent so much of their free time in the woods during the next decade.)

Time passed. The boys received air rifles for their eighth Christmas, quickly developing sufficient proficiency to put four pellet holes in a V-8 juice can every six tries, clear out to fifty-five yards, while standing, not prone in the weeds like some military-academy cadet, and with open irons, not the more accurate aperture sights.

The following yuletide brought Tyler a Winchester Model 52 rimfire sporter, with Dave receiving a hand-me-down Model 12 pump, in twenty gauge so as not to dislocate a shoulder. The inseparable pair took on newspaper routes to finance their prodigious ammunition expenditures, and swapped their guns back and forth while hunting as well as "targeting," until an uncommon level of skill had been achieved by both.

Dave and Tyler became the bane of local turkey shoots, taking turns taking on all comers then walking away with the spoils. Their victories hinged not only on prowess but also on the legendary precision of Ty's little Winchester bolt-action .22. With their families becoming increasingly sick of eating turkey, the boys took to selling the fowls to buy ammo, which they used to win more birds. And so on.

Due to parental vigilance, neither child neglected his schoolwork, though star-pupildom was far from their minds. Solid Bs satisfied the expectations of both sets of parents, who, although apprised annually at term's beginning of their boys' exceptional IQ levels, understood their sons' lack of enthusiasm for the academic world and their concomitant fascination with nature. Besides, both read prodigiously, most often the pages of *Boys' Life* and various outdoor magazines, but also Louis L'Amour, Jack London, Max Brand, Frank Gruber, and Robert Louis Stevenson. They were adept in math as well, having worked in Odie's snack bar at the lake—and at the golf shop in winter—since they were nine, counting out change like a born shopkeeper.

Aside from each other's company, hunting, shooting, reading, their girlfriends (the object of David's affection was a lass named Jill, normally as placid as the splash of spring rain on a mountain lake, but who occasionally displayed a tartar's temperament), and tennis (the duo reigned as state triple-A doubles champions for three years running, garnering glory and gilt frippery for their alma mater, athletic letters for their wool jackets), Ty and Dave paid close attention and devotion to only one other thing: martial arts. They delved deeply into various karate styles, savate, competitive wrestling (briefly, in their sophomore and junior years, when they beat all comers but found the sport tame), judo, and other hand-to-hand disciplines. Finding sparring partners—aside from each other—proved difficult after tenth grade; their reputations preceded them. As one of Ty's maternal uncles put it, "Them two boys can kick ass and take names." Indeed they could, and did, as the years flew.

The boys hunted and fished even more often during their senior year, bagging game of varying sizes and descriptions, living off the meat while in the woods, jerking prodigious quantities of venison in the heat of the autumnal sun, so near the earth you'd swear you could touch it. It was a fine time, full of japery and adolescent male posturing. Sunsets and mallards. Moccasins skimming over algaed water, heavy brown bodies producing S-shaped ripples. Whitewater sounds near a falls-fed pool, clear and cold and unpolluted, too gelid for swimming but teeming with bluegill full of pluck and succulence. Fall colors; restless hearts lulled to slumber by youthful ponderings, both shared and unspoken; frosted ponchos in the lightless risings, too early for dawn, too late for campfire luminance; the morning ablutions of a raccoon, prelude to its climbing a den tree to disappear into the hollow sheltering confines; red fox curled beneath a persimmon tree, nose buried deep in its coat against the dawn chill. The final halcyon days of a resplendent, shared youth.

And then disaster at the ice-cream parlor.

UNCLE SAM

ONE WEEK AFTER TY'S BOUT WITH THE FOOTBALL OAFS, Odie and brother Clyde were hosing out the concrete dog pens in back of Odie's house, as always, nearly gagging from the stench. Ty was unloading fifty-pound sacks of feed from the International Harvester pickup. Dave Michaels sat on a nearby stump and watched, his nose shoved deep inside his shirt against the smell.

"Son," Odie began, "seems you're in a pickle."

"I didn't start the fight," Ty objected.

"You think I don't know that? Don't matter, though. I own lots of property, pay plenty in taxes, and I know a bunch of folks, but them boys you whupped come from serious money and you don't. That one you put in the hospital is Strobe Roundtree's only son. Strobe has a heap of influence in this burg."

"Just because he's a lawyer."

"Yep. And because he does lots of favors for lots of people nigh as rich as him. He plucked the DA's daughter out of a manslaughter rap last month, the very DA who's chompin' his bit to stick you in front of a jury on assault and batt'ry." He paused, then said, "Maybe even with intent to kill."

Ty said, "That's ridiculous. What about witnesses? Surely someone will come forward who—"

"Forget it," Odie interrupted. "That time of the day the Sweetery's full of high schoolers. Most of them run with the Roundtree boy and his crowd, not kids from our side of town. Word I get from Judge Parker is that only one adult is known to have seen the fight." He paused to let the implications of that sink in. The silence grew heavy as Clyde and Odie finished their malodorous task and recoiled the hoses.

"The ice-cream shop owner," Dave speculated from his seat on the stump.

"Yep," said Odie.

"And what does he say?" Clyde asked.

"What do you think? He knows where his bread is buttered."

"But it was four on one," Dave protested.

"I know that. But like it or not Ty has a reputation as a scrapper. Truth is, you both do. Them poor little footballers claim Ty started the fray, and there's no one to say different."

"Except me," Tyler said, then brightened. "How about Emily?"

"Not much help from that quarter," answered Odie. "I hear her father won't let her testify. Besides, the DA'd eat her up on the stand, her being a bit slow and all. Mustn't count on the girl."

Ty plopped down on the ground beside Dave's stump, crossing his legs lotus fashion. A fly buzzed, in search of a place to light. "So what do I do, Daddy?"

Clyde propped up a tree with a shoulder as Odie

walked over to his son and lowered himself to the ground, then leaned back against Dave's stump. He grinned at Tyler.

"What?" said Tyler.

"Nothin'. It's just that you haven't called me Daddy in quite a spell."

"Sorry, didn't know you missed it. Always thought that was for kids."

Clyde snorted. "Where'd you come up with a fool notion like that? We called your grandpaw Daddy 'til he died, and we were both in our thirties then."

The fly zoomed again, narrowly avoiding Ty's ear. As it flew past, he snagged it with a flick of his hand. "Hungry?" he asked Dave, who grinned and replied, "Ate already." Ty opened his hand to release the insect. It droned drunkenly toward the dog pens.

Odie observed all this with amusement, then said, "So here's the plan. Judge Parker—me and him go way back, y'know—has agreed to docket your case. June twentieth, in fact. You'll still be seventeen, and if you plead guilty to assault it won't show up on your permanent record. 'Expunged' is the word the judge used. Meant to look it up.

"Anyway, as punishment you'll get a choice of six months in juvenile detention—some of which could turn into real jail time when you hit eighteen—or joining the military."

"The army?" Ty was incredulous.

"Considering the circumstances, I doubt any other branch'll take you. They'll have to know the situation."

"But the army *will* take him?" Dave asked.

"Probably," Odie said.

"They need people to stop bullets over in 'Nam," Tyler commented.

"Son, I'll go along with anything you decide, long as it's not runnin' away from this thing, which I know you won't do."

Quiet again for a while, broken by Dave: "Well, if you join the army, I am too. We'll enlist on the buddy plan, do basic and AIT together. After three years, we'll come home flush with G.I. Bill benefits. Go to college, be doctors, or lawyers, or Indian chiefs."

"Or something," Clyde said.

And it was decided.

KOREA

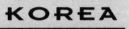

ONE

THE PLANE BANKED, MADE THE TURN FOR ITS FINAL APproach, and touched down at Pusan, Republic of Korea, just after noon on May 18, 1973. PFC Tyler Vance deplaned, stood on line with 157 fellow soldiers, duffel bag slung over one shoulder, military records in the opposing hand. In front of him stood a redheaded redneck from Barstow, Georgia, shifting his weight impatiently from foot to foot. The lad ultimately put down his duffel, dug a coin from the depths of his dress greens, and tossed it in the air, catching it deftly on the back of a hand. He repeated the toss, the coin twisting in flight, scattering the refracted sunlight that filtered into the quonset through its many windows. The heat was oppressive.

"Where you from?" This was directed to Tyler by the ruddy rube up front, who had turned about, obviously intent on palaver to while away the time.

"North Carolina."

"No shit. I was stationed at Bragg for basic. You from near Fayetteville?"

"Not far, hundred miles or so. Greensboro."

"Hell, I been to Greensboro. One weekend. Went to see a buddy's girlfriend at W.C., I mean UNCG. Wasn't called Women's College no more like when my sister-in-law went there back in '59. Nice town, Greensboro."

"I like it."

"You at Bragg?"

"First few days, at the reception station," Ty said, "being issued my clothes, taking tests, suffering shots."

"Them shots is a bitch, ain't they? Heard tell we ain't seen nothing yet compared to these here gamma-goblin shots we're in for today, and soon I suspect. Poke you in the ass, both cheeks, and they tell me right after it comes to feel like you got a golf ball lodged in there. I ain't looking forward to it, I surely ain't. Rather have the hepatitis or whatever the shot's s'posed to keep you from getting. Wouldn't you?"

"I don't think I'd want hepatitis, no. But whatever kind of shot you're talking about doesn't sound like much fun, either."

"For a fact. Where'd you do basic?"

"Fort Polk."

"Louisiana? Heard that place's a bastard, worse'n Fort Jackson, South Carolina. Was it?"

"Can't really compare, since I've never been to Jackson, though I had several friends in AIT who had been there. None of them seemed to miss it much."

"Ain't that the truth. I ain't been nowhere in the army I miss. At all," responded the redhead, looking around, absorbing the ambiance. "Don't reckon I'll pine for this place none neither, once't I'm gone. Fort Polk cold in the winter?"

"Not especially. And the DI's weren't as bad as you've likely heard, either. The mosquitoes, however, lived up to their reputations. Must've lost a quart of blood playing war in those infested swamps."

"Where'd you do AIT?"

"Fort McClellan, Alabama."

"Thought that was special for reservists and NGs, them who was going home right after."

"That's partly true. Half my company were National Guard. The other half were bound for Armored OCS, me included."

"You?" The redhead grinned, looking Tyler up and down. "What, you in disguise?"

Ty grinned back. "Nope. Decided against going to OCS, unfortunately after I'd already signed up. One of my drill sergeants opened my eyes. When I was at Bragg, taking the battery of tests, my scores must've lit somebody's flame because—"

"What'd you get on the GT?"

"One hundred forty-nine."

"The hell you say. I heard 152 was the highest score you could get."

Tyler simply shrugged.

"That right, 152 is tops?"

"That's what I've heard," Vance responded.

"So how the hell'd you miss three points, 'stead of getting 'em all right?" Mildly sarcastic.

"Math section did me in. I left the third from the last question blank and gave the wrong answer on another one."

"You got all the other part right, English, or grammar, or whatever?"

Ty nodded.

"Hell, I didn't even finish, let alone get 'em all right. You must be pretty smart."

"Good looking, too. Anyway, when I tested out so well on the GT, they gave me another type of test, with questions like, 'If you had to steal a loaf of bread or shoot your mother, which would you choose?' I must have made the right choice, because next thing I knew some officer's leaning on me to go to OCS, become a gentleman and all that. Being an ignorant hick from the sticks, I fell for it. Signed up. Was assigned to Armored OCS right after AIT.

"That's until my DI took me aside and enlightened me. 'You want an extra year?' he says. 'No,' I tell him. 'Want to be a target in 'Nam?' he goes on. 'Reckon not,' I admit. 'Then you better reconsider.' So I did. Quit before I even started. As punishment, I lost the special school I'd signed up for and got stuck with Infantry. And here I am."

"What a sad story. Learn anything from it?"

"Oh, yeah. Don't fuck with Uncle Sam. Never volunteer to do anything, except type. Don't—"

"Type?"

"Sure. A leg from Bragg used to swim at my dad's lake on weekends, came to stay with his uncle or something. He advised me—I was fifteen or so—to tell everyone I met in the army, God forbid I should have to go—he was Jewish—that I could type, whether I could or not. Fortunately, I took typing in junior high so I didn't have to fake it."

"What good did it do you?"

"In basic, I was trucked in from training sites like the firing range—after I'd finished up, of course—to do paperwork in the orderly room. The other guys'd have to march out to the range, then march back. I'd usually get to ride in the cab of a deuce-and-a-half. And I was relieved from some boring classes, too."

"Bet that made you right pop'lar with the other fellers. Them having to hoof it all the while you was riding."

"Funny you should mention that," Ty laughed. "They did act miffed, for a fact. Of course, a lot of them resented me anyway, so I didn't feel I was losing much."

"Resented you for what?"

"I enlisted on the buddy system with a guy I grew up with. We'd hunted, played sports, done martial arts, lifted weights, that sort of thing, for nearly ten years. We were in pretty good shape. For example, our platoon had to make like monkeys on the horizontal bars—once across, then back—before each meal. A lot of guys couldn't handle it. Dave—my pal—and I found it no trial, nor yet the push-ups, or the running. The PT test was a joke, so far as Dave and I were concerned, and I don't mean to brag. Our company's first sergeant and the CO were fond of us and used us as examples to 'encourage' the other boots."

"You're hell on push-ups, huh?"

"I can do a hundred, easy. With one arm."

A Spec-4 behind Tyler in line had been kibitzing. This last statement was more than he could stand. He put a hand on Ty's shoulder, turned him around roughly. Sticking his ugly mug in Vance's face, he growled, "Twenty bucks to see you do that. If you can't, I keep the twenty and kick your ass when we get to Camp Casey."

Tyler looked the man in the face for five seconds. The man removed his hand from Ty's shoulder and stepped back. Tyler said, "Let him hold the money," indicating the redhead. The SP4 handed over the sawbuck.

Tyler dropped to one knee, leaned forward onto his right hand, then looked up. “Which arm?”

The SP4 replied, “You a southpaw?”

“No.”

“Then do it lefty.”

Tyler switched hands, spread his legs a bit for balance, then knocked out a hundred one-armed push-ups with his new friend from Barstow, Georgia, counting them off one at a time, aloud. Upon reaching one hundred, Ty looked up—still holding the push-up position—and said, “How many more for a buck apiece?”

The Specialist Fourth Class simply shook his head.

Standing up, Tyler once again looked his antagonist in the eye. “You can still look me up at Casey, kick my ass. Anytime. Bring a friend. Bring three.”

SP4 Benson—or so it read on his name tag—shook his head, no thanks, and left the queue.

“Beats all I ever saw,” said the redhead, handing Ty the folded twenty.

“Keep it. I’d have done it for nothing. Didn’t like the guy’s attitude.”

Pocketing the greenback, the redhead offered his hand. “I’m Lucas Kinney. You can call me Flipper.”

“Flipper? Why?”

“ ’Cause,” answered Private Lucas Kinney as the line moved forward, slowly but inexorably, and the men were introduced to army life overseas.

TWO

AFTER EXCHANGING THEIR CURRENCY, GETTING PUNCTURED in their derrieres, and enduring a few other necessaries, Vance's group loaded onto the beds of several military two-and-a-half-ton transport trucks—the vehicles affectionately dubbed "deuce-and-a-half" by the grunts, without which they would have had to walk wherever they went while training. They motored northwest from the port city of Pusan, through Seoul, and on to their destination, Camp Casey, adjacent to the Korean hamlet of Tongduchon. Just around the mountain from Casey was a smaller military post, Camp Hovey, home of the Second Battalion, 3d and 32d, a part of the Seventh Division. It was to Headquarters Company of this battalion that Tyler Vance and Private Lucas Kinney were attached. Ty, having informed the paper pushers at Casey of his typing ability, was promptly assigned to HEADCO as an assistant company clerk, an MOS that did not appear in the official TO&E, an oversight that hadn't prevented the company's First Sergeant from requesting one. He moved his gear into the Quonset hut that served as home for the Headquarters Platoon, including in its number such support personnel as supply clerks, armorers, cooks, and the like.

Next morning, after an unpleasantly warm night in a strange environment, insomnia exacerbated by severe posterior discomfort courtesy of his recent inoculations, Ty sat with his new friend Lucas (assigned to Headquarters Platoon as driver for the CO) in the mess hall and consumed real eggs, pancakes, sausage, coffee, and milk. Greedily. It was 0517 hours, of a Tuesday, and already seventy-eight degrees outside.

Around a mouthful of egg, Lucas said, "You wasn't shittin' about that typing business."

"Nope. Works every time."

"Heard we was headin' north of the Imjin soon, to shore up the Second Division, who's sendin' a battalion south for a rest-up."

Ty nodded. "I heard that, too. We'll not be far from Uijongbu, maybe ten, fifteen miles east. Tent city. Only Quonset hut is the mess hall, though they're building a latrine-bathhouse now."

"Be hot as hell under all that canvas."

Tyler agreed, dipping his chin as he masticated a sausage link, adding, "And since this company—hell, this battalion—is undermanned, we'll all have to pull patrol duty, have our names on a roster just like KP in basic. Except a few chosen ones, of course."

"Whaddya mean patrol duty? Like maneuvers, field exercises?" Lucas queried, beetle-browed.

"Field exercises? You wish," answered Tyler.

"We're not goin' into the 'Z, are we?" asked a concerned Lucas Kinney.

Ty just looked at him incredulously. "Why do you

think we're going up there? You think they rotate a battalion every ninety days to get relief from *training?* They want relief from getting their tails shot up, their legs blown off by mines while they're out gathering wood. Sure we're going to patrol the DMZ."

Lucas put down his fork, said, "I ain't hungry no more," and swallowed his last mouthful of egg, leaving a smear of grease on his chin. "Guys do that draw combat pay, same's in 'Nam, don't they?"

"You bet," agreed Tyler Vance, sipping at his coffee, adding sugar, tasting again, grimacing. "Things heat up, especially in the spring and summer. Anyone going into the 'Z deserves combat pay.

"This Spec-5 over in supply," Ty continued, "told me that every year some North Koreans cross the MDL, jump or cut through the fence on our side, then shoot up some mess hall or barracks. Then they skedaddle back across, thumbing their noses. Our guys can't go after them, legally, anyway. They have to catch them on our side, in the mile-wide stretch between the MDL and our boundary fence."

"What's a MDL?" from Kinney.

"Military Demarcation Line, a little wire strung across the Korean peninsula, separating the North from the South. The DMZ is two miles wide, half ours, half theirs, and each of us is supposed to stay on his own turf. We patrol one-square-mile sectors on the south side of the MDL. Six-man squads, including one katusa who speaks the lingo. Sometimes we go out three days at a stretch. Live off K rations, sleep on the ground. Set out claymores after dark and shoot anything that moves unless it has hair all over it. Maybe even then. The idea is to interrupt a North Korean fireteam on its way south to wreak havoc, or coming back through after raising hell on our side."

"You don't sound scared."

"Why be scared?" Tyler teased, not really taking all this shoot-'em-up nonsense seriously. "There'll be six of us, with all our advanced training and weaponry. We'll outgun the bastards."

"Great. I can't wait."

"Worry not, Flipper. Why *do* they call you Flipper, anyway?"

" 'Cause," said Flipper, who was nervously tossing into the air his silver dollar, sometimes catching it on the back of his left hand, sometimes the right.

"That a Peace dollar?" asked Ty, who had been somewhat of a numismatist in his preadolescent days.

"Heck no, it's a whole dollar."

"Not *piece* . . . never mind. Can I look at it?"

"Catch," said Kinney, flipping the coin to his pal.

It was a Peace, all right, dated 1919 and in virtually uncirculated condition. Ty examined it, obverse and reverse.

"This coin's worth a chunk. Only a little over a million were minted. I'd be careful with it," he said, handing it back to Flipper, who received it then tossed it into the air, catching it on the back of his left hand.

"Over a million seems like a lot to me. My paw give it to me when I was born, and another just like it to give my firstborn when he comes. It was made the year Paw was born. His daddy give him a gold dollar when he was born. Little bitty thing, no bigger'n your fingernail. Hard to flip one like that. I tried it. I like this'n here better. Got some weight to it."

"Aha," said PFC Tyler Vance.

"Whatcha mean, 'aha'?" asked Private Lucas Kinney.

"Flipper."

Lucas, grinning, said, "You ain't altogether dumb, are you?"

"Not altogether," Ty laughed, and finished his coffee.

THREE

THREE WEEKS INTO JUNE, TYLER VANCE, NOW NINETEEN and counting, labored up a steep slope, firing his M-16 issue rifle at imaginary enemies, empty blank-cartridge casings flying from the ejection port of his rifle, a sheen of sweat attracting dust to his body. Reaching the crest first among his comrades, he sat on a rock and looked down, breathing raggedly. Several hundred feet below, his platoon picked its way through the rice paddies, gingerly in most instances though a few gung-ho soldiers splashed along, often stumbling to sprawl full-length in the murky water. Ty laughed when he noted that Clyve Davidson, his squad leader, was one of the enthusiastic men who took a paddy dive, acquiring a snootful of water and relief from the heat.

Such heat. Heat Tyler had never experienced—105 degrees in the shade, humidity like the inside of a laundry room. Heat that woke you at 1330 hours on a Sunday afternoon—your body bathed in perspiration, sheets soaked from it—when you were just trying to catch a little snooze after noon chow.

Wiping his forehead, Tyler laughed again. James Southern, a bozo from Winter Park, Florida, was charging up the hill, toting his ever-present M-60 machine gun, ammo belt swinging to and fro as he ran, whapping his thighs. James—for goodness' sake, *never* call him Jim—was a hoot. Serious as a Mormon undertaker, he couldn't take a joke, let alone participate in one, and hated army life with a passion bordering on fanaticism. Here he came, trademark red bandanna covering his poll, fatigue cap in his pocket (it wouldn't fit over the bandanna), dirty up to his hips from slipping and sliding all over the mountain. He arrived and sat down heavily beside Vance, wheezing. After devoting a minute to regaining his breath, he said, "How'd you get up here so fast?"

"Took the shortcut."

"What shortcut?" James asked suspiciously, having been the object of Ty's warped sense of humor on several occasions.

"Over yonder." Ty aimed a thumb aft, where the hill took a sheer drop out of sight. "There's a road zigzagging up the back side. Wide enough for a jeep and only half as far to the top due to the steep angle of the slope. Without that road, no one could make it up. But the road makes it a piece of cake."

"Yeah?" Still dubious, but hopeful. James hated hard physical labor. "Too bad I didn't know about it. How'd you—"

Ty interrupted, "Here comes Lieutenant Kosicsky. Now we're in for it, being first and all. We'll have to set up the mess tables and all the chairs when the trucks arrive. Just me and you, good buddy. Look down there. Nobody else'll make it up here for a half hour, maybe more."

"Dammit!" James opined. "Wish I hadn't pushed so hard to the top."

"Maybe the lieutenant hasn't spotted us. Believe I'll sneak around the side of this little promontory, circle around back, and come up the road again in an hour. Might dodge a load of work that way. See ya." Ty climbed to his feet.

"Wait!" Southern grabbed his arm. "We'll go together."

"Oh, no. He might spot two of us, but he won't spot me, alone, by myself. You dig?" Ty made as if to leave.

"Wait a minute!" James Southern swiveled his head, looked around, formulating a plan. "I'll go that way," he said, pointing north toward the wooded section of the hilltop, "and shag it to the bottom. We'll meet and come up the road together. How's that sound?"

Tyler pretended to ponder the question. "Well . . . okay. But you'll have to get down quick. I intend to climb about one-quarter of the way back up the hill, then settle under an overhang I spotted on the way up, just off the road. Take a short nap."

Southern liked it. "You shifty bastard. Sounds fine to me. See you at the bottom." He jumped up, took two steps, stopped, turned, and said, "Is the road hard to find?"

"Can't miss it."

"Right," said Southern and took off. Ty made a big show of gathering up his gear until James was out of sight, then he settled back on the rock, mopping more sweat from his face. He looked over to where James had disappeared into the brush and grinned. "Have fun."

In a few minutes, Lt. Bobby Kosicsky huffed and puffed to the top of the hill, flopping down on the exact spot James Southern had only recently vacated. "Didn't . . ." (gasp) "I see . . ." (wheeze) "Southern . . ." (huff) "up here . . ." (puff) "with you?"

"Southern? Doubt he'll get up here for an hour, sir, carrying that heavy machine gun. I was waiting for you. We going to set up the mess tables, same as yesterday, grab an extra plate of chow before the others join us?"

Pointing, Kosicsky said, "Why not? The mess truck's on its way." In front of them, halfway up the hill, on a road not readily seen from any angle except theirs, chugged a deuce-and-a-half. In its bed was a huge quantity of hot food, cooked back at base and transported out to the troops in the field. A half-dozen tables and a suitable quantity of metal folding chairs, stacked haphazardly behind the rocks where they rested, had been trucked up earlier.

"Too bad," offered the lieutenant, "that Southern's not here to enjoy the food while it's both plentiful and hot."

"Right, sir. Too bad."

"Wonder where he might be. I could have sworn I was just behind him coming up the hill."

"Dunno, sir, but I wouldn't be surprised if he came up the back way."

Kosicsky stared, dumbfounded. "The back way? There *is* no back— You mean that way?" He leveled a finger, pointing toward the precipitous rear slope.

"Wouldn't be surprised, sir."

Incredulous, the lieutenant said, "A mountain goat couldn't make it up that way."

"PFC Southern is a tenacious man, sir," Tyler said.

Kosicsky stared at the drop-off and shook his head. The two put up tables, assisted the mess crew in setting out the food, then sat at one table and consumed hot beef stew, fresh loaf bread, and blueberry cobbler. Five hundred feet below them, on the face of a sixty-degree slope, James Southern slipped and slid and ate dirt, not stew, all the while plotting revenge.

• • •

Ty sat with several other soldiers, watching the sun set over the beautiful Korean landscape, distant mountains purple in the dying light, the peak he was on still suffused with golden rays. A sheltered dingle ran off to the south. Out of the sun's reach, it lay in shadows, heavily foliated, mysterious. Several Korean children sat nearby on their haunches, waiting for him and his buddies to finish dining and put down their plates. Then they'd scramble after the leavings, not gleefully like kids in the States eating hot dogs on a picnic, but intent on quieting hungry bellies.

Clyve was saying, "Where'd you say you were from, cowboy?"

"Not no cowboy. I'm a timber man. Born and raised in Moscow."

"Idaho, right?"

"Tha's right," agreed the timber man, whose name was Devon Faust. "I can ride and rope better'n most cowboys, I'll allow, but can't none of them top a tree." He'd arrived at Camp Hovey yesterday, fresh from AIT at Fort Knox, Kentucky, APC-drivers' school. Since there were no APCs (armored personnel carriers) in this neck of Korea, he'd been assigned to Headquarters Platoon as armorer.

"Where'd you get that there name—Devon?" asked Lucas Kinney.

"Well, us being Fausts and all, and my daddy being a western fan, and Max Brand being his fav'rite writer, he named me after a gambler in one of his books."

"One of whose books, your daddy's?"

"Shoot, my daddy never wrote no books. In one of Max Brand's books, *Timbal Gulch Trail*. Had a gambler in it by the name of Walt Devon. Daddy studied on calling me Walt, but his uncle was named Walter and he didn't want nobody saying I was named after *him.*"

Clyve Davidson asked, "What is the importance of you being a Faust?"

Tyler spoke for the first time. "Frederick Faust was Max Brand's real name. Brand was a pseudonym."

"Why, tha's right," said Devon Faust, delighted.

"Suit of what?" piped in Lucas.

"Pseudo*nym.* Means pen name, nom de plume."

"Forget I asked," Lucas said.

"Does that mean you're related to Max Brand, or Faust, or whoever?" Davidson questioned.

"Sure like to be, but it ain't so," Devon replied. "If it were, I'd be too rich to associate with the likes of you."

Just then James Southern stomped up to the little group, grim as Calvin Coolidge at a wake. "I didn't find any road."

Tyler, the epitome of innocence, responded, "You didn't?"

The other men, unaware of what was going on but all too aware of Ty's penchant for practical jokes and James Southern's lack of empathy for same, sat still. Silent. Listening. "You know I didn't," Southern continued.

"How could I know?"

"Because there is no road."

"There isn't?"

"You know damn well there isn't. You knew it all along. That's why you sent me down there."

"Sent you?"

"Do you have any idea how long it took me to climb back up here?"

Ty looked at his Seiko. "Well, you left around—"

". . . how much trouble it will be cleaning that M-60?"

"Try using a toothbrush. You can really dig out the dirt if—"

"Shut up! You're not funny, Vance. Not funny at all. Someday, I'll have rank on you, and I'll . . ." He closed his eyes, obviously picturing that glorious day.

"You'll what?" Lucas asked from the sidelines.

Southern looked upon him as a socialite might view a glowworm atop her Waldorf salad. "I wasn't talking to you."

"Yer right," said Lucas, standing up. "But I'm talking to you."

"It's okay, Flipper," Tyler said, standing now to put an arm around Kinney's shoulders. "He's just irritated. He'll get over it in a month or two."

James Southern spun on his heel and walked away.

Clyve called after him, "See ya, Jim." They all saw Southern's shoulders hunch as Clyve said "Jim," as if he'd stopped a spitball with the back of his neck. But he didn't break stride, just stomped away.

"Whorehopper never could take a joke," Lucas said, easing back into his folding chair. "Here," he yelled, flinging his plate to the Korean youngsters, all of whom had stayed put during the drama, watching, inscrutable and expressionless. Like chicks after a handful of corn they attacked the plate, scrambling for what was left: a crumb of bread, four peas, some ham fat.

"Wish we could give them something substantial to eat, not garbage," Tyler said.

"The Old Man won't let us," Devon said, "says it encourages 'em to foller us around."

Ty sighed. "I suppose he's right. Still . . ."

"Still, what? There's nothing you can do. Nothing at all. If you gave them your whole plate of food, then you'd just have to go hungry. There's no PX out here to run to and grab a burger," Clyve said. "Try to ignore them."

"Doesn't work. They're always there."

"Then live with it."

"I reckon."

And the men moved off to the staging area, assembling for a moonlight stroll.

Eighteen miles. Four hours. Full gear. After a long hot day in the field.

Tyler Vance led Headquarters Platoon. Near the end, he fell in beside Sergeant Davidson, taking an arm. His friend was flagging.

Just short of their bivouac, Clyve faltered, couldn't continue. Not a step. Everyone but Ty and Lucas and Devon Faust kept going. The latter two milled about uncertainly; then they too marched on, knowing the CO would be pissed at those who fell behind and couldn't finish.

Really pissed.

Tyler draped his squad leader over his shoulders, took both rifles by their slings, held Davidson in place with an iron grip.

And carried him the last half mile.

FOUR

VANCE AND JASWINDER RAHMAN, A SHORT-TIMER FROM Groton, Connecticut, were teaching Kim Park, their squad's katusa (Korean national soldier), to play poker. Kim was doing right well; he was ahead sixteen bucks. The game was five-card draw, quarter ante.

VANCE: You going to bet or what?

PARK: I thinking.

RAHMAN: Think faster.

PARK: Need catchee king.

VANCE: (Exasperated) Don't *tell* us what you need. (Throws up hands) It spoils the game.

PARK: Bet one dollah.

RAHMAN: That's more like it. Call. (Coins clink as they are tossed into pot)

VANCE: I'm in. (More clinking) Whatcha got?

PARK: (Gleeful) Ha-ha! No needo king. Havo three al-leady. (Lays down hand)

RAHMAN: Shit! (Throws cards into pot)

VANCE: Shit! (Throws cap onto floor)

PARK: (Raking in money) You fellas teachee Kim play pretty good. Ha-ha. No needo king.

RAHMAN: You're going to need a doctor, you keep rubbing it in.

PARK: (Angrily) You bad sport. I no play.

VANCE: He's joking, Kim.

PARK: No jokee too muchee. I win. Who deal?

RAHMAN: Yours. Remember to let me cut.

Sergeant Davidson and Private Kinney arrived from the PX and unloaded their acquisitions (soap, socks, shampoo, Hersheys) onto their footlockers. Davidson, short, slender, blond as a hay bale, opened his locker and took out a letter. "Top gave me this to bring you, since you weren't at mail call." He tossed the missive to Tyler, saying, "Still at Benning."

"Hmm?" from Vance.

"The postmark. Your buddy's still down in Georgia."

"Oh. Yeah, he'll be there 'til the first week in August, at least. That's when he graduates from 'shake 'n' bake.' "

"From where?" asked Davidson.

"Instant NCO school. We both made PFC out of basic. He opted for the last shake 'n' bake class, to nail his stripes down early, maybe snag a slot in Intelligence. I'd already made my choice, OCS, but reneged. So he's there and I'm here with you mugs, maybe soon to rub elbows with Kim Il Sung. Ain't life grand."

To Park and Rahman, "I'm opting out, guys. Gotta read my mail."

Park said, "Okay by me. I shine buckle." He swung his stocky legs off the bunk, picked up a can of brass polish, cast about for a clean cloth.

Ty tore open the envelope, removed its contents—several sheets of paper, covered heel to crown with a fine sprawling handwriting, green ink—and started reading. Lucas walked over, peered down, watched his friend reading the letter. Put a big, pink-freckled mitt on Ty's shoulder, saying, "Why don'tcher mouth move when yer reading, like mine?"

Across the room someone snorted derisively. Tyler darted the snorter a withering look.

"Because my lips get too tired, Flipper," he said, smiling up at his big bluff amigo. Then he finished the letter, stowed it in a back pocket.

Lucas picked up his boots while Rahman boxed the cards and tossed them into his nightstand (Korean manufacture, purchased used for twenty bucks from one of the contract KPs—a Korean national named Choi but whom everyone called Papa-san—and delivered atop the rear rack of the old man's bicycle, to which it had been secured with bungee cords), draped his swarthy, lanky, very hairy body across his undersized bunk. Took out his wallet, withdrawing a photo of his smiling six-month-old daughter, most recent of three, the one he'd never seen. She'd been born three months after his departure for Korea, lithe and dark and handsome, like her mama and papa. He kissed the picture, then yelled, "Fifty-three days and a wake-up."

Devon Faust, asleep on the floor beside his bed until Rahman cut loose with the short-timer's cry, bolted upright and shouted, "Shut up, Jas!" then reclined onto his left side and promptly went back to sleep. Within three minutes his rhythmic, muted snoring resumed.

"That boy could sleep through a clogger's convention," commented Lucas Kinney, who then returned to spit-shining his combat boots. Spit, rub, dab of Kiwi; spit, rub, and so forth. The Quonset reeked of shoe polish and Brasso.

Into this pleasant milieu strode Cpl. James Southern, of First Platoon, newly acquired stripes freshly sewn onto the sleeves of starched fatigues. Rahman glanced over, took in the nascent insignias of higher rank, and asked, "Been to the vill', Jim? See your yobo?"

"I told you not to call me Jim. My name is James."

"Sure it is, Jim," answered Jas. If he was intimidated by Southern's rise in rank, it didn't show.

The new corporal turned his gaze on Tyler. "I'm going to find a way to get you, Vance. Soon. I promise."

Vance appeared to be amused, which bothered Southern.

Kinney glanced up from his boot polishing. "You making E-4 don't buy you much, Southern. Least of all, respect."

"Corporal!" snapped Southern. "Not just E-4. I'm an NCO now," he added, puffing up like a pouter pigeon.

"Just a glorified E-4, Jim, no different than me," from Rahman.

"You're a Specialist-4. I'm a noncommissioned officer. I can go to the NCO club. You can't."

"Now there's a perk," responded Rahman. "You get to swill liquor with other noncoms and boss the troops in your squad. But you have no rank on any other E-4 unless he's specifically placed under your command. Besides"—he yawned, covering his mouth with the back of a hand—"I have time in grade on you."

"I've got rank on *him,*" said Southern, aiming a bony finger at Tyler.

"How you figure?" asked Lucas, still sitting on his footlocker, polishing essentials in hand.

"Shut up, plowboy."

Lucas put down his boot and rag, stood up, sauntered toward Southern, who said, "That's right, Flipper, take a swing at me. Assault on an NCO. That'll get you time in the stockade. Come on."

"My name ain't Flipper."

"*He* calls you Flipper," Southern said shrilly, again pointing at Ty.

"I tolt him he could, dunderpate. Never tolt you. Telling you now not to."

Ty got up slowly, indolently, and stood beside Lucas, patting the big man's back soothingly. "It's okay, Flipper. Don't give the brand-new NCO a hard time. Let me." He grinned at Southern. "Jim, you're entirely too serious, which is not only bad for your health, it's bad for *our* health. Puts us off our feed. However, with your new rank and all, maybe you can spend more time with us headquarters boys, let us absorb your homespun wisdom. It'll be a real plus for those of us with plebeian backgrounds."

Lucas whispered, "What's plebeian?"

Cpl. James-not-Jim Southern nearly choked. To Tyler he said, "Listen, you piss-drinking son of a bitch, I'll have you cleaning toilets with a spoon!"

Lucas whispered, "You drink piss? It got any kick to it?"

Clyve Davidson spoke for the first time since Southern had inflicted his presence on the assembly. "James, you better reexamine your hole card."

"What are you talking about?"

"You're not speaking to a PFC."

"I'm talking to *him*!" Once again the thin angry digit was directed at Tyler.

"I know that."

"He's a PFC!"

"No, he's not."

"What?" Southern's certainty dissolved.

"Have you noticed his sleeves?"

"He's wearing a tee shirt!"

Lucas Kinney opened Ty's locker. In plain view were a half-dozen fatigue shirts, a pair of khakis, a set of dress greens. All bore corporal's stripes. Kinney grinned his best shit-kicker grin.

"Since when?" sputtered a deflated Southern.

"Orders came through Monday. A day before yours."

"He should be a spec-4, not a corporal!"

"Normally would be," Davidson said, "but Top thinks Ty's a leader—what does he know—and we're short one E-5 in this platoon. He intended to go ahead and give Vance a third stripe, but the CO wouldn't let him, it violates regulations. But Ty'll be up for review shortly, and likely get his sergeant's stripe then. I'd walk softly if I were you, or you might be the one cleaning shit-bowls."

Still irate, Southern retreated, slamming the door as he went.

Devon Faust sat up from his feigned slumber. "That guy's got a real hard-on. Someday you're gonna have to thrash 'im good, Corporal Ty, sir, your honor, your holiness. And that's a fact," he predicted, then lay down and immediately went back to sleep.

Lucas looked at Faust with awe. "Don't he beat all?"

FIVE

"WHAT DO YOU THINK OF THIS?" DEVON FAUST ASKED Vance, handing him a short, well-used shotgun.

"I'll be damned," answered Ty, peering into the open chamber, then poking a finger inside to be certain no shell lurked. "A Winchester Model '97 riot gun. Where'd this come from?" he queried.

"Found it back in the stacks aside another'n just like it, maybe not quite so clean. Sarge and I figure they been here since the Korean War, prob'ly twenty years or more," Faust explained. "My gran'daddy carried one like it when he worked as guard down the state pen. Showed it to me when I was a yonker, even let me shoot it once. Thing kicked the shit outa me," he went on.

Ty laughed and said, "I fired one, too, on a deer hunt in Hyde County. I was eight, maybe nine. Picked off my deer using number one buck, two-and-three-quarter-inch, not magnums. Picked myself up out of the mud afterward. Didn't shoot it again for two or three years."

"When we due to leave for up north?" Devon asked.

"We start packing day after tomorrow. In a week, we'll

be ensconced in tents fifty miles from here, on North Korea's front porch."

"What's company strength now?"

"Nowhere near enough," said Ty. "Around 140 men, including katusas."

"We'll all be pulling patrols, I reckon."

"I reckon. Shouldn't be too bad, just hot."

"You bet, and K rations, shaving in cold water, the trots . . ."

"Timber Man, you telling me you haven't had it worse?"

Faust grinned. "It'll be a vacation."

"So what're you complaining about?"

"Getting shot at."

"Phooey."

"Them stories about tunnels ain't real?"

"I suppose there are tunnels, all right, and some North Koreans sneaking around on our side shooting at folks and raising a ruckus. So what? Me and you can handle them by ourselves. Throw in Lucas and they better head for Pyongyang with their tails between their legs. And I," Tyler continued, "shall strive to convince our beloved Top sergeant that this"—he hefted the shotgun—"is just what I should tote whilst defending freedom, apple pie, and South Korea. It's even got a sling."

Then, glancing at his watch, he added, "Nearly chow time. Let's beat the line."

They did.

• • •

The move north proved uneventful. Irritating, time consuming, troublesome, hot, dusty, fraught with delay—but uneventful. Headquarters Company settled into their new environment with little fanfare, less enthusiasm. After a week to acclimate themselves to their new surroundings—PX, movie theater, watering holes, ladies of solace—patrolling the DMZ became a reality. Even Kinney, who piloted the company commander's jeep, was scheduled time in the 'Z.

To provide as much stability and continuity as possible, the first (top) sergeant allowed his platoon NCOs to choose their own five-man teams, and did not shift the roster unless serious conflicts arose. Tyler picked Jas, Flipper, Devon, Kim Park (each squad included an NCO and one katusa in its composition), and a short-timer named Jack Jackson for his squad. After the squad had pulled two three-day patrols, separated by a week in camp performing their MOS-indicated duties, a cluster of men arrived from the States, rotating Jackson out of the group and back to "the World." In his place came Sergeant Adderson, a New Yorker with a nasty attitude and subereous skin. Sergeant Davidson, seeking to avert a mutiny, bearded the first sergeant in his den, requesting a shift in squad makeup. Clyve took over Ty's group (Vance was still an E-4), with Adderson now in charge of recent rotatees, none of whom had formed long-term alliances among their fellow soldiers. Adderson groused about being circumvented until Top (about three sheets in the wind) buttonholed him one night at the NCO club and berated him for ten minutes in front of his peers. Things went smoothly thereafter.

No one had seen much while patrolling the 'Z except a few ring-necked pheasants and a pair of the strange, homely little tusked deer that frequented the unpopulated areas of central Korea, and some booby-trapped grenades left over from the war, trip wires still attached. No evidence of tunneling, no land mines, no sudden attacks at dawn. Just heat, mountaintop observation posts where eagles soared, and the grating, omnipresent loudspeakers that spewed haunting (and strangely unsettling) Oriental music, propaganda, and monologues in Korean that made Kim Park grind his teeth.

"Communists number fucking ten," Kim mumbled one evening over cold K rations (beef with potatoes), while a speaker blared just around the next ridge.

"What are they saying?" asked Jas Rahman, ten days away from rotation stateside.

Park just shook his head.

"He won't never tell," Faust said. "But whatever it is makes 'im madder'n hell."

After chow, the men moved to a different location within their square-mile area of responsibility, set up claymore mines, spread out in a rough line—with one man facing rearward to cover the back door—and settled in for the night. As NCOIC, Davidson was in charge of the PRC-10 radio, their communications link with the nearest OP, and other patrols in their sector.

Tyler tied a string to his left wrist and passed it on for the others to do the same, a silent alarm should a "situation" develop. Twenty feet off to his right, Rahman took a swig from his canteen, wiped his mouth, and commented, "I know this breaks your heart, but after our next patrol you won't have me to kick around anymore."

"I'll be scared out here in the dark without you, my trusty grenadier . . . watch where that M-79's pointing. Where's the LAW?"

"Right here beside me."

"Good. I need to know in case you're slain in the dark and I get charged by a tank."

"What'll you do if the LAW doesn't stop the tank?"

"Whisper, 'Feet, don't fail me now.' "

Rahman laughed. "Such initiative."

"I'm a trained soldier."

"What about my poor, bullet-puckered body?"

"Fret not. I'll come back for it later," Vance promised.

"That's real comforting."

"After all, you've got that big bag of M&M Peanuts in your fatigue jacket."

"That's all I am to you, a bag of M&Ms?"

"Of course not, Rahman. What do you think?"

"Well, you had me concerned there for a minute."

"There's also the Milky Way in your pack, and . . ."

"Asshole."

"Camel jockey."

"Grits eater."

Ad infinitum.

• • •

Just before dark, on the east wind there drifted in a muffled explosion. Everyone looked at everyone else, instantly alert, then checked their gear. Was tonight the night? Not for them.

A mile away, just south of the DMZ, Pvt. Wilson Bennett, returning to his truck with an armload of tools and following a well-used, well-marked trail—the same one he'd taken that morning—stepped on an antipersonnel mine. It blew off his heel, leaving his toes undamaged. The entire foot was later amputated; without an Achilles tendon, the appendage wouldn't do the boy much good.

He was nineteen, fresh out of high school where he'd made all-state as a lightning-quick tailback. Distraught at the abrupt curtailment of what might have been a promising football career, subsequently abandoned by a fiancée unable to deal with his handicap and its resulting deep depression, he plied himself with sufficient Smirnoff and amphetamines to kill a horse. He left a note bequeathing his Purple Heart and disability check to his brother, Billy, who pawned the medal in Miami, cashed the government check at a Winn-Dixie, and took his girl to Disney World, where the pair had a high old time.

Billy didn't think of his brother once.

SIX

TYLER AND JAS WERE DISCUSSING THE DIRECTION OF contemporary music when Lucas Kinney returned from the village, having had his ardor banked. "Crocodile Rock" emanated from a transistor radio nearby. Kinney sat on his bunk and monitored the discourse, offering no opinions of his own. Being a country music buff, he had no idea who Elton John was, so he simply lit his pipe, puffed, listened to the talk and the music, tapping his foot in time.

Directly the disputation abated. Ty and Rahman gathered their towels, soap, and flip-flops for a trip to the showers. Kinney mused. "How come," he asked, "you two never go to the vill'?"

"Not just us," said Ty. "Davidson doesn't. Devon has been maybe twice, but not for the same reason you go. He likes *maeuntang,* if you can believe that. Stuff burns my tongue out by the roots."

"So why don't you guys go? Get a woman, have some fun?"

Tyler sat down beside his friend, who was obviously

troubled. "Jas is married, you know that. He sticks his kids' pictures under your nose often enough. So is Sergeant Davidson. I have a girl back home. Been going steady with her since June a year ago. Name's Brenda."

"Got me a girl, too. But she ain't here, and I am. I get the urge."

"Who doesn't? We're not dead, you know." Ty laughed.

"So? Why don't you? Go to the vill'?"

"I promised Brenda I wouldn't fraternize with any other girls, and that includes fallen ladies of exotic origin."

"Fallen ladies?"

"Prostitutes."

"But Brenda'd never know."

"I would. I gave my word, and I don't do that unless I intend to keep it. If I went back on my word just because nobody'd find out, I'd have trouble looking at myself in the mirror when I pluck my eyebrows."

Lucas mulled things over. "Is it the same with Jas and Davidson?"

"I suspect so. We've never discussed it, but I've noticed that they don't go to the vill' to get their pipes cleaned. I've always assumed it's because they're committed."

"I never tolt Sharlene I wouldn't have no truck with other women. She never did to me, neither, about other guys."

"Then you're covered." Tyler slapped his buddy on his broad, honest back.

"I ain't doin' wrong?" asked Flipper, face lit like a jack-o'-lantern.

"If you are, I'm as guilty as you."

"You been with hookers?"

"Not hookers, but girls I wasn't committed to except for the night."

"You feel bad about it later?"

"Sometimes. Sometimes not. They were all willing participants. I never coerced anyone."

"Coerced?"

"Talked them into it. Lied to them, told them I loved them when I didn't, that they were prettier than anyone I knew, bullshit like that."

Kinney absorbed what he'd heard, felt better about living by the sword. He said, "Yer a good friend."

"Be sure you check for crabs," Vance responded, then went to take his bath.

• • •

Jas Rahman lathered up, hot water cascading off his balding pate, running in rivulets through his matted chest hair. He sang, "Nine days and a wake-up," in a rich baritone, somewhat off-key but mellifluous nonetheless. The shower room, bathed in steam, smelt of rubber sandals, Dial, shampoo, and—indistinctly—Brut.

"Why do you use Prell?" Rahman asked Tyler. "My sister uses Prell. You a little light on your feet?"

"Come here, sweetie, and I'll tell you," Ty said in a falsetto vaguely reminiscent of Fanny Brice.

"Not me. After this patrol tomorrow, I'll be back in camp for good, then back to the World. I'm staying away from you. We might fall in love."

The pair finished bathing, stepped out of the shower stall and into the drying area. Ty carried his zippered case over to the sinks, placing it atop a shelf beneath the long shaving mirror. His Prell shampoo was clearly visible as it lay in the open case.

A katusa entered the bathhouse, shirtless, towel draped over one shoulder, and stepped over to the sink next to Tyler. Washed his hands and face, drying them carefully on the towel. Noticed the Prell in its soft plastic tube. Looked at Tyler standing there shaving, and pointed to the shampoo.

"Catchee cold cream?" he asked.

"That's not cold . . ." Vance started, then caught himself. "Sure, help yourself," he said, and continued shaving.

The Korean picked up the Prell, squeezed a healthy dollop into his waiting palm, replaced the shampoo where he'd found it, rubbed the liquid into his hands industriously, then onto his face. Examining the result in the mirror, he appeared puzzled. He added water from the faucet, getting lather. He scrubbed harder; more lather. Additional water; even more lather. Recognizing a ruse, he cut loose with a string of profane invective—in Korean, of course, since he knew little English.

Ty undiplomatically doubled over with laughter.

Jas looked at him sternly. "How do you come up with such things on the spur of the moment?"

"His idea," Ty blurted, leaning against the shower stall for support, tears streaming down his partially shaven face.

Trying unsuccessfully to avoid it, Jas began to giggle, then chortle, then guffaw. He sat down on the concrete floor holding his stomach. "Stop," he pleaded, "I can't get my breath."

The katusa departed in a huff, his frothy countenance

resembling a cotton ball with hair and eyes.

"Did you see the look on his face?" Ty howled.

"No more! I can't stand it!"

Tyler retained a place in his heart for Prell the rest of his life.

• • •

Jas was still going on about the incident the next morning while the men drew arms, ammo, and grenades, were issued flak vests, secured three days' worth of K rations.

"Franks and beans, yuck. Hope I got hot chocolate in some of these," grumped Faust.

"If I get any, I'll swap you for coffee," Kinney offered.

"And me," said Kim Park, "no likee hot choklit."

"Okay by me," agreed Faust. To Tyler, "You carrying that riot shotgun again? That gun's a fav'rite of yours, ain't it?"

"We spend most of our time in the woods. If we get in a firefight in such cover, I'd rather have this than one of those M-16s spewing little bitty bullets."

"Not me," Davidson joined in. "With two magazines taped together I have forty-one rounds at my disposal, quicklike. That thing holds just six shells."

"Sure," countered Tyler, "but each round I trigger spits nine .33-caliber balls. I can saturate an area with fifty-four projectiles faster than you can fire twenty-one shots and stop to change magazines."

"Right, but then it takes you an hour to reload," countered Davidson.

"Shee-it," said Kinney, in two syllables, Southern style, "you ever see Tyler stoke up that hopper? He shoves in shells faster'n a possum eating goober peas."

And thus they bickered, the six amigos, as they loaded onto the back of a deuce-and-a-half bound for the DMZ.

Only two of them would return.

SEVEN

THE DEUCE-AND-A-HALF DROPPED THEM OFF AT THE gate, where Sergeant Davidson uscd his key to pass them through the southernmost barrier to the DMZ—a tall chain-link fence—then double-checked his map, noting the assigned coordinates, and moved the squad out, heading northeast. Faust, taking point, jacked a round up into the barrel of his M-16, dropping its mag to replace the cartridge. (He didn't favor the two-magazine approach preferred by some of his colleagues, claiming it ruined his rifle's balance.) Tyler brought up the rear, walking backward much of the time with the Model '97 twelve-gauge slung inverted under his left shoulder, a hunter's carry that provided quick access and didn't fatigue his arms unduly as he walked.

The patrol passed beneath a stately, towering pine, one of its lower branches smacking Vance in the back of the head as he glanced rearward, covering their backtrail.

"Thanks, Rahman," he said, twisting his neck, assessing the damage. "Good thing I have on a helmet."

Rahman chuckled. "Sorry, thought you saw it. If you

were royalty, like old King Sejong, the tree would have lifted its branches for you to walk under. Lineage will tell."

"It's for certain you're royalty. A royal pain in the ass," Tyler rejoined.

"Peasant."

"Serf."

"Vassal."

"Would you guys shut up," interjected Davidson. Then, "Who the hell is King Sejong?"

"Fourth ruler of the Choson dynasty. Nice man. Ruled Korea not too many years before Columbus took his little trip to the New World," answered Tyler.

"What's this about a tree?"

"When he visited Mount Songni, a tall pine raised its branches for him to pass underneath, a magnanimous gesture for an evergreen, don't you think? Stood it in good stead, though. Sejong made it a minister."

"Baptist?" queried Lucas.

"Of state," said Tyler.

"Where do you get all this shit, Vance?" Davidson asked.

"From Jas," said Ty.

"Where does he get it?"

"From Tyler," Rahman averred.

"What's 'magnanimous' mean?" Devon asked as the little group entered a copse and disappeared from view.

• • •

"Those clouds look like rain to you?"

"Those clouds look like rain to me."

"Seem like it's getting chillier to you?"

"Seems like it's getting chillier to me."

"Will you two shut up?" said Davidson. "Damn, I'll be glad to see you go stateside, Rahman."

"Me too," Jas agreed.

"Not me," said Tyler, "I'll miss you."

He threw his arms around Rahman, who grimaced and whispered, "Not in front of the others."

Devon Faust shook his curly head. "Surely won't be the same around here."

"Thank God," said Davidson. "You guys want coffee with lunch?" General murmur of agreement. "Then we need wood for a small fire." He looked around. "Stuff here's too green. We'd make enough smoke for a tire factory. Vance, you and Park skip over that rise and scare up an armload apiece. We'll build it over there, under the branches of that strange-looking tree. The smoke'll get lost in the foliage if you guys collect the right kind of wood."

"Think I need you to tell me that?" Tyler replied. "I was building smokeless campfires when you were still cruising Main Street in that 396 Chevelle you're always bragging about."

"Then skedaddle."

"Can we roast marshmallows when we get back?"

"Go!"

"Come on, Kim." Ty picked up his shotgun, saying, "I won't have to suffer this abuse much longer."

"What, you gonna quit?" Flipper said, enjoying the persiflage.

"No. I'm getting my sergeant's stripes. Then I'll be the squad leader and get to order you and Faust around."

"Unless you get court-martialed for telling lies about pine trees," Clyve called as Park and Vance started over the hill, helmets bobbing as they climbed. He grinned at their departure. "You can't help but love the guy," he added, dropping on one knee to dig out lunch.

• • •

When Vance heard the first explosion he was a quarter mile away piling bone-dry wood onto Park's outstretched arms. At first the two weren't alarmed; they'd often heard muted blasting as the North Koreans built their nonexistent tunnels. But on the heels of this hollow *crump* of detonation came the angry stutter of several AK-47s, then another blast, probably a grenade. The two men dumped the load, grabbed up their weapons, and double-timed it back toward their companions.

Too late.

EIGHT

WHEN THE MORTAR ROUND EXPLODED BESIDE HIM, SGT. Clyve Davidson was fiddling with frequencies on the PRC-10 radio, supporting it on his lap as he sat cross-legged atop a protruding stub of shale the size of a billiard table. The force of the blast burst his right eardrum instantly and showered him with shrapnel, most of which impacted the PRC-10, protecting his vitals. His exposed right hand was severed at the wrist and flung thirty feet to whap wetly into a tree trunk then fall to the ground. Clyve was blown backward off the rock, landing hard but rolling quickly to his feet. As he did so, an AK-47 opened up from his left, five slugs slicing through his body almost simultaneously, one of them bursting his heart and coursing on through his spine. He fell to the ground limply; within two minutes he was dead.

From the north another assault rifle opened fire on Jas Rahman, who had turned to look for the source of the explosion. The first of twenty rounds fired at him in a couple of seconds ripped open his neck, luckily missing the carotid artery, then sped on to strike Lucas Kinney low in the back as the young man from Georgia snatched up his M-16 to return fire. Two more bullets found flesh, one smashing Rahman's right femur, dumping him to the ground as the leg gave way, another passing through his middle right side, beneath the lung. For a moment, he was out of commission.

Kinney, undeterred by the hole in his lumbar, swung to the attack, spraying the nearby brush with a magazineful of ammo. His efforts kicked up dirt divots, sent flying splinters of wood, whined menacingly off rocks, but let no blood. As he ducked behind a log to switch magazines, a third AK-47 bore down on him from the right, at fifty yards, riddling his body. He lunged away from the hits to fall heavily then writhe on the ground spitting blood from ruined lungs, racked with pain from a jaw smashed at its hinge by a bullet. Hit seven times, Lucas managed to stumble erect, recharge his weapon, and open fire just as Rahman, propped on one knee, entered the fray with his M-79, launching a grenade at the unseen enemy.

A spate of withering fire was the response. Jas hit the dirt, avoiding the deluge, but Lucas Kinney, swaying defiantly on his feet, caught the brunt. Dust and blood flew from his body as the slugs impacted, causing the big man to jerk spasmodically like a maniacal marionette. Abruptly he collapsed, shot to pieces, and lay still.

Rahman stuffed a fléchette round into his M-79, rising to survey the carnage. Only Devon Faust was left, over behind a rock unloading his M-16 at something only he could see. Jas clicked shut the grenade launcher with a snap of his wrist, sensed movement to his rear, spun to confront an enemy soldier running at him, rifle to the fore, bayonet extended. *Idiot,* thought Rahman, as he fired the fléchette load, watching the man take the hit, disintegrate into shark bait, drop like a stone, all in the space of a heartbeat. The mangled heap didn't even twitch.

"Rahman! To your left!" shouted Devon Faust, reloading from a pouch on his web belt. A pair of North Koreans was flanking them, intent on getting a more open shot from eighty yards away. Ignoring the pain in his neck and leg, Jas recharged the M-79, sat down to take aim at the two men who'd just taken refuge in a little grove of trees, and was dealt an excruciating blow to the back. He dropped his weapon and rolled over to a shielding log, gasping for breath.

This is it, he accepted. *Vance and Kim will never make it back in time, assuming they're still alive.* Fumbling at a back pocket—bloody fingers trembling from shock, feeling thick, clumsy, cold—he passed out.

Devon Faust, seeing Rahman fall, said to himself, *Old Hoss, you plan to get outa this mess, you can use that M-79.* So he set off to get it. He tossed two grenades, thirty degrees apart, then low-crawled toward Jas, cradling the rifle across his forearms as he went, making it, no problem. The only sounds were an angry *boom! boom!* when his grenades detonated. As he retrieved the grenade launcher, he wondered aloud, "Why'd they quit shooting?" He peeped out from behind the log and took a hard-toed boot in the face. He tried to scramble upright, but a second blow found his lower spine, paralyzing him for an instant. Then they swarmed all over him.

• • •

When Tyler Vance peered over the lip of the little draw by which he and Park had made their approach, he nearly vomited. The bodies of Clyve Davidson and Lucas Kinney had been stripped and laid one atop the other. A North Korean was preparing to burn them. Another enemy soldier, wearing a helmet liner from one of the dead Americans, sat on a stump watching three of his men torture Jas Rahman. Jas was crawling slowly in a circle, as if blinded, while the three men stabbed bayonets into him in various nonlethal areas. Rahman screamed at each penetration, then lapsed into mindless moans. The soldiers laughed.

Twenty feet away, Devon Faust had been tied to a tree in a sitting position, his boots removed. Three North Koreans were attending him, too, using bolt cutters to remove his toes, one at a time. Tyler heard a sodden *snap* as they cut through the last toe of Faust's left foot, followed by a soul-wrenching shrill from Faust. Tyler's jaw set like granite. Fresh out of toes, the three soldiers conferred a moment, one of them gesturing at Devon's groin. The other two began to remove the American's pants, their intentions obvious.

Ty shifted his attention to Rahman; one of the North Korean soldiers was trying to force open his right hand. Jas was resisting. The soldier tried harder, twisting and jerking, placing his boot on Rahman's wrist, to no avail. He stomped Jas's outstretched hand, then bent to grab it but Rahman tucked the injured hand into his stomach protectively, covering it with his other hand. Then, oddly, Jas raised the hand to his lips and kissed it. One of the soldiers spoke harshly, tried to pull the arm down from Rahman's face, then suddenly grabbed up a rifle and skewered the man at his feet with a bayonet, right in the center of his chest. Rahman's body heaved upright convulsively, twisted sideways, wrenching the rifle free of the soldier's grasp, then curled into a fetal position and slowly relaxed, one foot twitching spastically. The two other soldiers yelled at the one who'd finished Rahman, gesticulating, shoving him roughly away from the body.

Annoyed that their sport was over.

One of them glanced at Faust, as if deciding whether to join that trio of fun lovers.

"Like hell," Ty said under his breath. The soldiers ambled over to where Faust was being tormented. They laughed and pushed each other playfully. Only the one wearing the helmet liner remained aloof, still perched on his stump, viewing the barbarity like one of Satan's overseers.

"Kim, I need for you to nail the one with the helmet liner," Tyler said. "He's about a hundred yards or so. You'll have to take him because I can't take my attention off the others."

"You no worry 'bout him. I takee. No worry. He dead man."

"Okay. I'm going to drop back below the ridgeline, swing down there"—he pointed—"and come up to them along that dry wash. When I reach the head of it, I'll be thirty, thirty-five yards from them. You'll be able to see me from here. When I raise my arm over my head, you'll have five seconds to shoot that son of a bitch. Soon as I hear your shot, I'll open up. Got it? Five seconds from when I raise my arm. That enough time?"

Kim nodded. "Man dead. You no worry. What about rest?"

"My problem."

"You havo only six shot."

"I'll improvise. Don't worry, they'll be close. I'll take all seven."

Kim looked dubious, but said, "Okay."

"Ready?"

"Fucking A."

Ty gave Park a thumbs-up and melted down the slope.

• • •

Vance took a quick one-eyed look from behind a boulder, then tucked his head back. Faust had been giving the North Koreans a hard time getting his pants off, kicking and twisting and crossing his legs. Two or three of them would hold him down, then one would have to let go to try to jerk down the pants and he would roll his hips and cross his ankles, bloodied stumps of feet coated with grit. One of them took out a long, slim knife and held it in front of Devon's face, then with a quick flicking motion sliced off the end of the American's nose. Blood spurted everywhere. Faust brought a knee up into his molester's crotch as Ty raised his arm to signal Park. The North Korean doubled over, grabbing himself, then plunged the knife into Devon's neck just as Kim opened fire.

Seven Oriental faces swung toward the sound of the shot, clustered together like a covey of quail. On more than one occasion, Tyler had taken three bobwhites on a covey rise.

These targets were much larger than quail.

He took the nearest first, dumping him with a load of buckshot to the chest, seeing the pellets rip into the man, the horrified expression on his face, a button fly from his shirt. Blood from the first man speckled the second—a short, fat grub who threw up his hands to deflect the crimson spray. Tyler shot him in the face, the lead balls destroying the upraised hands as they bored on through. Leaping backward, runty legs splayed, a third soldier exposed himself—the one who'd been making preparations to incinerate Davidson and Kinney. Ty shot that one in the liver as the man dove sideways. A fourth jumped to the right, intending to use Faust as a shield. Vance led him a little and cut loose, the whizzing shot pattern taking the man in midstride, snapping his upper arm bone like a stick and coursing on through the rib cage to lacerate heart and lungs. One kamikaze charged straight at Tyler, rifle coming up to firing position. Vance removed the guy's face and most of the back of his head, then swung on a sixth man darting to his right toward a rifle leaning against a tree, blasting him in the back of the neck. The force of impact so overbalanced the man that he slammed into the tree, careened off, and alighted in a pile of rocks.

Tyler, advancing as he'd been firing his shotgun, was now within twenty yards of Faust. The last North Korean soldier stood at Devon's bloody feet, the long slim knife held in front of his chest. Ty stopped. Smiled. Laid down his gun. The Korean came toward him, manipulating the knife in front of his body cobralike, in a figure-eight motion, cutting edge up. Ty went to meet him. Fifteen yards. Ten. Seven.

At five paces, Ty plucked from his flak vest a grenade, clamped the handle in his teeth, and moved. Very fast. He parried the knifeman's thrust, caught the wrist as it went by with his right hand, grabbed the man's elbow and applied leverage. The soldier raised up onto his toes, the blade clattering to the rocks at his feet.

Tyler braced the man's hyperextended elbow over his left shoulder while maintaining the viselike grip on his wrist, freeing up his own left arm. Removing the grenade from his mouth, he spun the Korean to his front, off balance, jerked out the pin while holding in the handle. Grabbing his surprised antagonist once more, he slammed him in the stomach with the grenade hand, pulled out the Korean's waistband with the other, deposited the grenade in the man's shorts, then lifted him overhead and flung him through the air. The soldier was clawing frantically at his trousers when the grenade went off, splattering Tyler with bloody cloth, gristle, intestinal contents, and bone chips.

• • •

"Neat move with the grenade." Devon's voice was hoarse.

"Just rest now."

"Kinda turned him into a Roman candle, didn't you."

"Let me stop this bleeding."

"Too many holes, old son."

Tyler, face streaked, looked at his friend.

"Hey, cowboys don't cry. Everything's gonna be all right," Faust said.

Ty wiped his face. "Thought you weren't a cowboy," he said huskily.

"Don't you tell, but I been in a rodeo every year since I was seven, one event or another. I'll allow I won't be riding in any more." He winced from the pain.

"Sure you will."

Faust gripped Ty's hand hard. "It's okay, good buddy. Really it is. I was hurting bad 'til that guy stuck me up high, then things sorta went numb. I knowed I was a goner after they clipped them last toes. Too much blood. Sure am cold."

Ty took off his shirt to cover the dying man.

"Anyone else make it?" asked Faust.

Ty shook his head.

"Thought I heard someone yelling a while back."

Striving mightily to clear his throat, Tyler said simply, "Jas."

"Oh." Now Devon's eyes misted over. "That's a damn shame. He was a good man. A really good man."

"The best. Like you."

"Don't know about that. Done a few things I ain't so proud of."

"We all have, Devon."

"Where you reckon I'm heading?"

"Before today is over, I believe you'll be meeting Jesus, face to face."

"You reckon?" Faust smiled.

"I reckon."

"Hallelujah," said Faust.

Then he died.

• • •

Park was standing off to one side, as if he didn't want to intrude on Tyler's grief. He held his helmet in his hands. Ty walked over to him, looked down at the little katusa, then placed both hands on his shoulders. "Thanks for taking that soldier out."

"Thankee no ne'ssary. My job. You do most workee. Damn good, too."

"Thanks anyway."

Park nodded solemnly.

"Will you check the North Korean soldiers, make sure they're dead?"

"Fucking A."

"And then put some clothes back on Sergeant Davidson and Private Kinney? Get the hand out of the sergeant's mouth?" The North Korean soldiers had retrieved Clyve's severed hand and stuffed it into his mouth.

Park nodded solemnly again.

"I'll check on Rahman."

Park looked even more solemn. "Muchee too bad. He havo fam'ly."

Tyler walked over to Jas Rahman, short-timer.

Eight days and a wake-up.

He'd never wake up again.

Ty turned the body over carefully, respectfully. Looked at the tightly clenched right fist. He rubbed the side of Rahman's face with the back of his hand. "Will you open it for me, pal?"

He pried open the dead fingers with surprising ease, as if Jas wanted him to.

There, in the opened palm of the outstretched arm, lay a crumpled photograph of an adorable, happy little girl.

Who would never meet her daddy.

Tyler wept.

And seethed.

And vowed that one little girl in Groton, Connecticut, would never want for stories of her papa.

NINE

ONE OF THE IMMUTABLE RULES OF PATROLLING THE Korean DMZ was that no squad ever entered another squad's patrol sector without radio communication or direct orders from the OIC (officer in charge) of the nearest observation post. Thus, despite the fact that another small group of American soldiers was less than a half mile away during the firefight and its aftermath, no one came to investigate or assist. The incident was reported to the closest OP, but since nobody knew what was happening, the OIC reluctantly ordered everyone in the area to stay put until further notice. So everyone sat back and waited. To hear something.

Nothing came.

Two hills away from the spot where Kim and Tyler Vance were laying out bodies, covering each with a poncho, Sgt. Gerald Sizemore voiced what everyone else was thinking. "Some poor bastards got hit, hard. Command sure as hell ought to send someone to check it out. There might be wounded that need tending to."

"Sure, Sarge, but who'd go? I sure wouldn't."

Sizemore looked at the man who'd spoken as if his face were crawling with maggots. "Baker, there's five American soldiers over there, and one Korean national. Some or all of them are likely hurt, maybe dying, and possibly some could be saved. If it was you, you'd be pissing your pants and crying, 'Help me, help me,' so shut your cowardly fucking mouth."

On that note, the conversation faded.

Meanwhile, Ty and Kim Park had laid out their companions and turned their attention to the stricken Prick-Ten. After a cursory examination, Ty proclaimed the radio unusable and tossed it into a gully. Then, realizing he'd have to turn it in, damaged or not, he stomped over and retrieved it. His state of mind was bleak. He took a deep breath, striving to override his emotions—which, if heeded, would have taken him over the MDL into North Korea on a suicide mission—and sat down in the dirt. Rested an aching head on quivering hands, propping his elbows on wobbly knees, legs crossed at the ankles. Never in his young life had he felt so deeply useless, angered, hurt, depressed, overwhelmed.

Park pulled him out. "Not you fault you not dead." Crystallizing it. "Sergeant send you get wood. Me too. Not know sojures come. Not you fault. Nothing you can do bring back friends. You kill sojures, talk to friend before he die. All you can do. Go forward now. Looka back jus' makee you sad alla time."

Head still cupped in his hands, Tyler nodded, ran his fingers over his close-cropped hair, and sighed. "With no radio, we'll have to walk down to the road and hump to the closest OP for help. And hope we don't get shot by our own troops."

"Why we wait?"

"Okay." Ty climbed to his feet, took up the Winchester pump, looked over at the still bodies.

"They be okay," said Kim.

Vance nodded once, tiredly, and set off for the road.

• • •

Three days later Vance had been thoroughly debriefed, his story cross-checked with Park's—the two had been kept apart—and a multitude of investigators had visited the scene, examined footprints, run forensic tests, ad nauseam. The physical evidence indicated that the occurrence had happened exactly as Private Park and Corporal Vance had detailed it, making the pair heroes for avenging the U.S. Army's casualties and punishing a blatant infraction by North Korea of a multitude of conventions and accords. North Korea denied everything, of course, proclaiming the dead Orientals to be ROK soldiers serving as sacrificial lambs of the American imperialists intent on creating an international incident.

Vance had talks with the chaplain, was given a psychological examination by a specialist, and confined to the base for observation. He was sullen, withdrawn, morose. The only person he spent time with was Kim Park. His former loquacious, jocular nature had transmogrified into something else.

Something less.

Something dangerous.

One night he and Park were in the snack bar after seeing a movie, enjoying chocolate shakes and desultory conversation. James Southern strolled in with two of his cronies, stinking of beer, cigarettes, and the NCO club.

He spotted Vance, and, being in his cups, decided to dig in the spurs a bit.

Swaggering over to the table, his two supporters close at heel, Southern stopped, looked down at Park, and said, "Move your ass, gook. I wanna siddown."

Park took a sip of his milk shake through a straw, one striped longitudinally like a barber's pole.

Tyler said, without looking up, "Don't call him a gook."

"Whaddyew say?" Southern challenged, swaying slightly.

Ty looked up, repeated, "Don't call him a gook."

"The fuckyew mean, don' call 'im gook? I'll call 'im any fuckin' thing I wanna."

Park took another sip. Ty took one too, no straw, acquiring a thin rime of chocolate on his upper lip. He wiped it on the back of a hand. "Not for long, you won't."

Southern grabbed Park by the back of his fatigue jacket and slung him from the chair to the tile floor, bumping the table with a hip. In shoving the table aside, Southern exposed his midriff. Before Park touched the floor Tyler kicked Southern in the solar plexus, twisting his foot on impact, booting the surprised corporal backward over a folding chair.

One of Southern's compadres stepped up, snarling; Tyler met him with a stiff jab, then a right cross to the chops. Down he went. The second subordinate—a sergeant from C Company—swung a roundhouse. Vance saw it peripherally, shifted his head to port—getting rapped lightly by three knuckles as the punch blew past—then spun, tossing an uppercut to the sergeant's windpipe. When the man dropped his guard—mouth wide, sucking air—Tyler smashed his upper lip with the heel of a hand, drawing blood and frothy spittle. When the sergeant tried to backpedal, Tyler applied a straight right to the bridge of his nose, putting another down for the count.

Southern was back up, gasping for air, so Tyler stepped in close to sink a fist into his stomach, then ducked as the vomit came, projectile, spraying four chairs and all thereon. James went to his knees, from which position the rest of his stomach contents were directed at the floor—except for a chunk of wiener that landed on a staff sergeant's toe.

Startled onlookers sprang clear, scattering furniture as they went. Park yelled for Ty to look out. The first of Southern's pals was on his feet, legs spread, the blood streaming from his nose ebbing and flowing with each heartbeat. In his hand was a stiletto. He looked as if he knew how to use it.

Tyler said, "So far, this has been a friendly fight. I haven't used anything serious on you guys, mostly boxing. Nobody got hurt badly that way. But, pal, if you don't drop that knife I'm going to shove it so far up your ass you'll polish it every time you brush your teeth."

"Talk's cheap," the man replied, then made his move.

It took Tyler thirty seconds. When he was through his adversary had three broken fingers, two cracked ribs, six missing teeth, and a stainless steel suppository that required professional assistance to remove.

TEN

TYLER WAS IN THE MESS HALL DRINKING COFFEE, CONfined to company limits. No movies, no PX, no library, no milk shakes. He didn't give a flip. It was 0947 of a beautiful early-fall day and he had a letter from Dave in front of his nose, posted from Pleiku, wherever the hell that was. Far from Saigon, Dave wrote, where he'd been attached to Army Military Intelligence, II Corps, as a courier, flying in and out of Dak Pek in a Beaver, collecting Intel photos. Dak Pek was the northernmost border camp in II Corps, formerly held by the French before their pullout. Its runway, at the bottom of a heavily forested valley, was of red brick. Climbing the adjacent hillside was a stairway of sorts, fabricated of spent 105mm brass shell casings. Negotiating that stairway could get pretty hairy, Dave reported. Yesterday his pilot had been shot in the knee by a sniper, necessitating an overnight stay in an area in which Dave figured ten minutes was too long. Such were the pleasures of Vietnam.

The screen door opened and a captain walked in, removed his cap, and looked over at Vance, who slowly got to his feet and stood more or less at attention.

"At ease, soldier," said the officer. "I'm Captain McElroy. You're Corporal Vance, I take it."

"Says that right here on my name tag. Sir."

"Ah, a badass with a bad attitude. Just what I'm looking for." He walked over and nudged out a chair with his toe. "Mind if I sit down?"

"You're an officer. Doesn't make any difference whether I mind or not."

"True. I was just being polite."

"Not necessary. Sir."

"Sit down, Corporal, and let's palaver."

Ty sat, folding the unfinished letter and placing it in a shirt pocket.

"Heard about your little fracas the other night," McElroy said, chuckling, "Did you really ram a sergeant's knife up his rectum?"

"Yes. Sir."

"Good thing you retracted the blade first. Why would you do such a humiliating thing?"

"To teach him a lesson. Besides, I told him I would. Sir."

"You always do what you say?"

"Usually. If I can. In this instance, I could. So I did. Sir."

"Drop the 'sir'. It's straining you. We'll just be two old buddies chewing the fat."

"Whatever you say."

"I've been talking to the first sergeant, who views the fight as not of your making. It's why you haven't been busted and tossed in the stockade. Any number of witnesses state that you did nothing to initiate hostilities."

"That's correct."

"Nonetheless, two of the men you assaulted were E-5s. Makes things a little sticky. CO over at C Company is after your scalp. But your first sergeant is in your corner, and he's got plenty of clout. More than some shavetail first looey, CO or not."

"We call him Top."

"I know what a company first sergeant is called, Vance."

"It's a sign of respect, sir."

"You trying to piss me off?"

"Not especially. Just like to hear the man referred to as Top, that's all."

McElroy took a deep breath. "Maybe I won't be able to work with you after all."

Tyler shrugged and sipped from his cup.

After a lengthy pause, the captain said, "What's your biggest gripe at this point in your military career?"

"They won't let me go back on patrol. I'm confined to the company grounds until further notice."

"You want to go back into the 'Z?"

"Yes, sir."

"Why is that?"

"What the North Koreans are doing isn't right. I'd like to help put a stop to it."

"You lost four good friends, didn't you?"

"Yes, sir. Two had families. Now they're looking at grass from the underside. It's not right."

"Lot of things in life aren't right, Corporal."

"Correct, sir, but I figure I can do something about this particular inequity."

"By killing gooks?"

"I don't use the word 'gook,' Captain, nor others like

it, such as greaser, kike, wop, mick, nigger, slope, spic, ad infinitum."

Grim-faced, McElroy said, "You're too good for ethnic name-calling, that it?"

"No, sir. The folks I'd be referring to are."

"So what do you call people you don't like?"

"Assholes."

"Now there's a definitive term."

"I think so. Genderless, multiracial, not age biased, and it crosses class lines. Anyone can be an asshole regardless of the other aspects of their persona. Those three guys I danced with the other night? Assholes, every one."

"And one was Hispanic, one black, and one Caucasian. Nice little ethnic blend."

"I rest my case."

"That thing out in the 'Z—why'd you handle that all alone?" McElroy went on.

"I wasn't alone, sir. Private Kim Park was with me, in fact made it possible."

"How so?"

"He shot the one man I couldn't take out, not and pull it off the way I did. Without Kim, I'd be dead."

"Not necessarily. If you'd been alone, you could have simply avoided a confrontation and made your way back to an OP."

"Alone or not, I'd have gone down that hill."

McElroy was aghast. "You mean to tell me you'd have done the same thing and taken the risk of having the odd-man-out knock you over?"

"Yes, sir."

"Why?"

"I watched two of those men die. Slowly. Specialist Rahman had three children, one he'd never even seen.

When I went over to him afterward, he had a photo of that little girl balled up in his . . ." Ty paused, tried again. "I couldn't let them get away with it, sir. Couldn't, not wouldn't."

McElroy digested it. Made the decision. "How'd you like to get a little special training, in another country, then come back and run some covert ops? On your own. Stay in the 'Z as long as you like?"

Tyler bolted upright. "When can I leave?"

"Just like that? No questions?"

"I asked one. When can I leave?"

"How soon can you pack?"

• • •

"What'd you think?" asked the first sergeant.

"That kid's really something," answered McElroy. "He doesn't think he did anything special, just moseyed down a little old hill, flanked seven North Korean regulars and wasted them all, splattering the last one all over the countryside."

"That's about the size of it," agreed the first sergeant.

"By the way, I referred to you as 'first sergeant,' " McElroy added, grinning.

"So?"

"He didn't like it. Told me to call you Top. Said it was a sign of respect."

The first sergeant put a smile on his face, or at least what he probably thought was a smile. It more closely resembled the expression a bulldog gets before dinner. "Not all my men hold me in such high regard."

"Nor do you hold all your men in such high regard."

The first sergeant nodded, his slick, massive head

bobbing like a plastic pooch in a car's rear window. "Vance is the best I got. For what you want, likely the best anyone's got. It's in his blood." He paused, examined his fingernails, cut short and straight across. "What troubles me is that he's got such a hate on. Way he feels now, he'd charge North Korea with an ice pick and a string of firecrackers."

"I agree. I want to channel some of that anger productively."

Top stood and held out a paw the size of a hubcap—hairy knuckles, thick wrist, blunt digits. McElroy took it carefully, shook. He said, "I'll take care of the boy."

The first sergeant looked him straight in the eye and said, "You damned well better."

And that's the way it was.

ELEVEN

TYLER VANCE ARRIVED IN THAILAND OCTOBER 2, 1973, attached TDY (temporary duty) to an Army Special Forces unit that trained troops from a half-dozen countries in clandestine operations. Five days a week he arose at 0430, ran fifteen miles with full gear, returned to his billet for a shower, and breakfasted thirty minutes later. His days were filled with physical training, hand-to-hand (with an emphasis on silent killing, blades of all descriptions, the garotte, snares, et al), demolition training, small-arms practice, even lectures by a CIA operative out of Langley, a specialist in that agency's "dirty tricks" division. On the weekends he devoted himself to his own katas, plus more running, jumping, climbing and rappelling, push-ups, chin-ups, and leg raises than a whole platoonful of stateside Marines.

One day he was being introduced to the M-3A1 "Grease Gun," a short, compact, lightweight submachine gun taking the stubby .45 ACP pistol cartridge. Corporal Vance had adapted himself to the effective little arm quite handily, eating the center out of a man-sized silhouette at twenty-five meters. The gun's magazine held thirty rounds and Ty was hosing them into a cluster the size of a soccer ball, the sluggish staccato of the Grease Gun disturbing an otherwise quiet Thai morning. *Bum-bum-bum-bum-bum-bum-bum*, not the ripping *bbbuuurrrrpppp* of most SMGs, due to a relatively slow cyclic rate of 350 rounds per minute. What the M-3A1 lost in speed it more than made up for in controllability and punch.

McElroy stood off to one side, muff-type ear protectors in place, talking to a training NCO. "How's Vance been doing?" he asked.

"You kidding, sir? I've been a range officer for six years, shot Master Class on the pistol team at Fort Lewis, won more trophies in small-bore rifle competition as a teenager than would fit in a bushel basket, was a sniper in Vietnam. Two tours. He shoots better than me, by a factor of maybe twenty percent."

McElroy nodded, watching Vance reload.

"Been doing tae kwon do twenty years, teaching hand-to-hand to Special Forces personnel the past three, won three state championships wrestling in high school, could bench-press three hundred pounds while weighing 148. He's stronger than me, faster than me, more disciplined than me, and can kick my ass."

McElroy arched a doubtful eyebrow.

"Yes, sir. I know a trick or two he doesn't, acquired through painful experience in kill-or-be-killed situations, and if I tried one and he didn't anticipate it, I might put him on the ground. The key to the scenario would be his not anticipating me. If he did, he'd eat my lunch. Given his awesome speed, eye, and reflexes, he probably would.

By the way, he benches 350, though he does weigh a little more than I did."

McElroy watched as Tyler ran through an assault course, pop-up cardboard "enemies" snapping into view, then disappearing abruptly as Vance nailed them.

"See how quick he is?" the noncom went on. "Almost impossible to take him by surprise. He seems to know what's going to happen before it happens. In the ring, too. I can't find anyone to spar with him. Vance started off taking it easy, but some of my Green Berets fancy themselves and didn't pull their punches. So Vance stopped pulling his. After the third guy got sent to the infirmary, my volunteer pool sort of dried up."

Three targets popped up simultaneously, none farther than forty yards from Vance, who took down the first. Then his submachine gun ran out of ammo. Tyler dropped the SMG, drew a .45 automatic from its holster so fast his hand was a blur, and popped the other two targets. Elapsed time for the draw and two shots was about one and a quarter seconds, and that from a flapped holster.

"Sonuvabitch!" exclaimed McElroy. "Did you see that?"

"Nothing unusual about it. He's faster out of the leather than my top men are when they have the gun in their hands."

"Can he move well in the woods?"

The sergeant pointed at his fatigue shirt. "See this Ranger insignia? I'm one of an elite group, highly trained, motivated, physically endowed with uncommon stealth. And, like I said, I was a sniper in 'Nam. I'm a silent, experienced, deadly motherfucker."

"Yeah?"

"In games we play in the bush, Vance sneaks up on me. All the time. I have never sneaked up on him. Not once. The man blends, Captain. Simply disappears. Then . . . there he is. It's uncanny."

"You like him?"

The man shook his head. "Admire him, sir. But he's distant, reserved. Holds everything in, not friendly at all, to anyone. It's like he doesn't want to make friends. Weekends? He works out, runs, keeps to himself. He doesn't mix. At all."

"So you don't like him?"

"Wouldn't say I dislike him, either." Thinking. "Picture a big shepherd that's been abused badly and often. Dog doesn't bother anyone unless they bother him, but he takes no delight in living. He's just there. Eats, sleeps, shits. No fun. Just existing. That's how he is," he finished, pointing with his nose.

"He'll get over it."

The noncom looked at him. "I don't figure he will, sir."

"Will he kill gooks?"

"As long as you don't throw them at him in groups larger than ten."

McElroy glanced at the sergeant, smiling to let the man know he was in tune with the humor.

But the noncom looked serious as he stared down the slope.

• • •

The night was clear and the moon was yellow. Stagger Lee was nowhere in sight. Several soldiers—gussied up in khakis—escorted almond-eyed ladies to and from the

NCO club, the movie theater, the snack bar, where Tyler occupied an outside table nursing a coffee, black. He'd abandoned cream. Not sugar; the brew was sweet as honeysuckle.

His mood was somber, lugubrious. Brenda Ames, his sweetheart back in the World, had Dear Tyler'd him, proclaiming undying friendship and affection and all that, of course, but, if it was all the same to him, she'd like to back out of her betrothal, no animadversion intended. Seemed she'd always had her eye on the football captain, but after considerable prayerful reflection had settled for the captain of the chess team instead, what with her gridiron hero now married and all, and a baby on the way, if you can imagine that impecunious lout being a daddy, not even having a real job, just tossing pizzas at Fat Slim's greasy dive. Anyway, write and keep in touch and take good care of her favorite portion of his anatomy, she might want to use it again if things didn't work out. XXX, OOO.

Shit.

Then there was the letter from Dave Michaels, which had him worried. Dave's plane had been fragged just before touchdown at Dak Pek, and the landing had been iffy as hell. In the end the plane had remained upright, despite only one operative wheel, but he'd had to spend two days on a cot in the team house—listening to things going bang in the night—before he'd been airlifted out of there in an Otter. Aside from that, things aren't going so bad, so how're they hanging?

Ty was no fool. Dave was striving to keep the anxiety out of his tone, but reading between the lines took no special cognitive skills. Trust Dave to make light of his own situation to try to keep Tyler from worrying.

Looking around at the night—streetlamps wreathed with vapor; wet weather on its way—Tyler sipped his coffee and mused. When he'd taken creative writing in eleventh grade, Miss Shebore made him write a poem. How embarrassing. Prose he could handle, but "Annabel Lee" was not in his makeup. Nonetheless, since the whole class had to participate in a national scholastic contest, Miss Shebore had been insistent. A poem. Period.

All he'd ever attempted were inanities like Roses are red / Violets are blue / You look like an aardvark / And smell like a gnu, which he'd penned in Kelly Smythe's yearbook their sophomore year. So, taking the bull by the headgear . . . he had wimped out. Decided on blank verse, short and sweet, but pithy and profound as hell. He wrote:

> The blood-soaked
> Bayonet
> Lies debased on the ground.
> Its duty
> Fulfilled,
> It is forever left
> To the wrath
> Of its conscience.

Such horse apples. He'd won no prize, of course, although he suspected that someone somewhere had suggested awarding him a booby prize. Not only did the poem stink, but the premise behind it was ridiculous. He'd killed seven men some months ago. If remorse lurked, it was buried so deep in his psyche a shrink would have to use dynamite to dig it out.

A sip of coffee; tepid now. He looked around; more couples spooning, as his mother called it. And there he sat in full self-pity mode. *Taking in the moonglow, bereft of remorse / while mankind around him / ran love o'er its course.* He stared into his cup, thinking: *Where the hell did that come from? I'm a poet and don't know it. What a mood. Wish someone would come over and fetch me a rap with a lighter knot, as my daddy might say.*

Thoughts of Mom and Dad, for gosh sakes, maudlin hashing and thrashing, all because my girl cast me adrift and there's a lover's moon and I'm seven thousand miles from home. What a wuss.

He relinquished his spot. Meandered back to his barracks. Tried to sleep. It took him two hours to drop off, and his dreams dripped with disillusion.

• • •

After his run and shower, Tyler surrounded a plate of French toast, then another, chasing it with bacon, a large glass of milk close at hand. His appetite seldom failed him.

Correction: Never failed him.

McElroy spotted him and came over.

"You ever have company for chow?"

"Sure." Tyler pointed to an open book beside his plate, *The Godwulf Manuscript,* by Robert B. Parker.

"Human company," said the captain.

"Parker's about as human as you can get."

"You know what I mean."

"Yes, sir."

"So why don't you? Eat with someone?"

"Hard to read and make conversation, sir."

"Dammit, you know what I mean."

"Yes, sir."

McElroy gave up. "Anything I can do for you before I wing it out of here?"

"Yes, sir, there is."

"Shoot."

"I've got a pal over in 'Nam." Ty gave the name, unit, APO address. "I'd like you to check on him for me, with all your connections. Keep me posted on his situation. He sends letters once a week usually, but sometimes they're delayed. I get concerned. I'd like to know if anything . . . happens. If he's taken prisoner, anything like that, I want you to let me go in after him."

So, McElroy thought, *the lad does maintain a human connection, albeit long distance. That's a plus.*

"Sure, no problem. I'll buzz you once or twice a week, keep you posted. Happy to."

"I'd appreciate it a lot, sir."

McElroy finished his coffee and left the mess hall.

Three months later, Ty left for Korea.

TWELVE

TYLER, ON HIS FIRST SOLO PATROL IN THE 'Z, SAT CROSS-legged beneath the sheltering bows of a Korean fir, a mature specimen perhaps forty feet tall. A fine misty rain fell, but the fir kept him dry; his poncho was still rolled up at the back of his web belt. Naught stirred within his purview.

Before him was a well-worn footpath used daily for the past week by a detail of GIs searching for a tunnel someone with shoulder boards and a sofa butt insisted was in the vicinity. The KPA (Korean People's Army, as the North referred to its military) liked to slip into an area frequented by American patrols and plant a mine or two to sort of liven things up. Tyler had been sent in to chaperon the troops.

He'd been watching the dim trail for a little over an hour, long enough for an American group to walk by at spitting distance without spotting him and for his legs to fall asleep. Sucking a Tootsie Pop, he shifted his buns for comfort and waited for more traffic, communist in nature. So far, nothing.

Putting the binocs to his eyes, he ranged slowly back and forth, searching in sections, starting in close—where the immediate danger was—and working his way out in sweeping arcs. More nothing.

He dozed until his head dropped, startling him awake. Extending his limbs to encourage circulation, he grimaced at the resulting pins and needles. Flexed his fingers—stiff from disuse, not the spring chill. Visual search again, aided by the Zeiss 10X glass. A pair of ring-necks strutted by, lovers. He watched them court a moment, then continued his sweep.

Froze. Three hundred meters away someone was looking at *him* through binoculars. Or appeared to be. Ty sat still as road kill, glasses glued to his forehead. Finally the other man moved, taking the binocs down from his eyes and pointing in Tyler's direction, but not *at* him. ROK uniforms. A typical ploy of the KPA—dress like South Korean soldiers to infiltrate, then lower the boom on some hapless GI or Korean national. Nice guys, the North Koreans.

Here they came, all in a row, following their leader like ducks.

Sitting ducks.

Easing the sniper rifle from its resting place beside him, Ty flipped up the rifle scope's protective lens covers, placed his cheek against the stock. The backs of his upper arms rested against his shins. No elbows on knees; that would be too wobbly. He centered the crosswires on the lead man's thorax, waited to see how many there were. *Three, four, five, . . . That's all, five?*

(*Let 'em come, let 'em come, don't commit until they stop or veer off*) . . . closer, closer, step, right, step . . . closer, closer . . . (*whoops, there go the pheasants, the*

KPA boys caught them by surprise) . . . approaching . . . step, right, step . . . (*two hundred meters, coming right along, lockstep, march*) . . . except they weren't in lockstep, just ambling, taking in the scenery, laughing at the cock and hen they'd just kicked up, enjoying the cool spring rain, uniforms glistening wet . . . step, right, step . . . a gentle breeze stirred the pungent branches of the tree enveloping Vance as he waited in ambush, tickling his neck . . . (*"Raindrops keep falling on my head"*) . . . step, right, step . . . (*pay attention, don't let your mind wander . . . column, halt*).

One hundred twenty meters, give or take a yardstick. Ty waited until they'd dropped their gear, then moved his finger to the trigger, only three pounds of pressure needed, half of that gone already, crosswires in place chest-high (*why go to the chest?—close enough for a head shot*), switched point of aim as the sear released—*boom!*—down the man went as the rifle butt nudged Ty's shoulder, rocking him slightly on his buttocks as he worked the bolt to chamber a 168-grain match hollow point, loaded for him by the company armorer on a little Lyman Spar-T, unbeknownst to his superiors since it was illegal for use in combat, as if the North Koreans play fair—*boom!*—there went the second man, never even unlimbered his AK, the smell of burned nitrocellulose acrid in the heavy humidity, the bolt flashing again as his prey scattered for cover—scarce over where they were—one tossed his rifle up and looked for a target—*boom!*—he'd never find one, jacked the bolt, hand cupped on the upstroke, bolt handle in the thumb-forefinger vee as a round slammed home, two men left, one down behind a skimpy dead tree limb—*boom!*—right through the limb, long pale splinters flying, tumbling slow motion to the ground (*can't believe he thought that would shield him*), bolt open and shut, snick-snick, final cartridge sliding in with a reassuring metallic sound (*look at that last guy, down on one knee wondering who the hell's shooting at him, not going prone to make a smaller target*)—*boom!*—too late (*don't these guys get any training?*).

After checking for wounded (none) and confirming his kills photographically, Sgt. Tyler Vance jotted in his logbook the map coordinates then quit the area, running, putting a half mile behind him in a matter of minutes should the deceased soldiers have friends nearby.

Supping on cold K rations before dark, he prowled until midnight, slept in a hollow tree until the sun pried his eyelids open, then worked his way out to the barrier fence, where he was picked up at a prearranged time. He was transported by jeep to a shower, hot food, and Captain McElroy, who debriefed him thoroughly.

• • •

After the lengthy debriefing, Tyler and McElroy strolled inside the camp's perimeter fence, purple twilight blurring the mountains around them.

McElroy asked, "You comfortable without a Prick-Ten?"

"I wouldn't mind stowing one somewhere, but I don't want to carry it wherever I go. If I walk into something, it'll slow down my response."

McElroy nodded.

Tyler went on, "I'd like a Grease Gun, four extra mags, and two hundred rounds to go with my sidearm and shotgun. I can stash what I don't want to carry, be freed up to hunt in different ways. If I get caught up close with only a heavy five-shot boltgun and a .45 auto to fight with, I'll be at a considerable disadvantage."

"What about grenades?"

"I don't like grenades."

McElroy chuckled to himself. "Yeah, well, you certainly used one to good effect."

Ty said nothing.

"Okay, I'll get what you want. Anything else?"

"Some beef jerky, dried fruit, extra canteen. K rations are cumbersome. I'd like to cache the bulky food with my radio and weapons, eat there once a day. Munch on the fly the rest of the time. Keeps me more mobile, less dependent on my stash in case I get cut off. And I need more K rations to begin with. Three a day isn't enough by half."

"Eat a lot, don't you?"

"I burn it off."

"Okay." McElroy hesitated. "You killed five men today. Bother you any?"

"No."

"No?"

"No."

"You sure?"

"I'm sure."

"Okay. When you want to go back in?"

"I'd like two days off, catch up on some of those tapes my sister sent me without worrying about my teeth getting blown out my fanny should I fall asleep. Read. Write a couple of letters. Enjoy more hot chow, store fat for winter. Take in a flick."

"You mean relax, just as if you weren't Superman?"

"I never claimed . . ."

"No, but the guys who've watched you train or who've

been unfortunate enough to have sparred with you do."

"Two days then?"

"Sure. Take three."

"Two're enough."

"Sure."

As they reached a corner of the fence and turned ninety degrees to their left, an ROK sentry stepped out of a pool of shadow near an ammo bunker. An Ithaca M-37 twelve-bore riot gun hung from his shoulder, complete with handguard and bayonet. He watched stoically as they sauntered past.

"Don't see bayonets on shotguns often," Tyler said.

"Winchester M-97 Trench Guns had them, and the hammerless Model 12s. You want a Trench Gun instead of that riot version you carry?"

"No, thanks. Too heavy. If I need an edged weapon, I want it at the end of my arm, not the end of my gun barrel."

And so they continued through the pleasant dusk, talking of this and that as men do far from home and kith. At that moment, two thousand miles away, Dave Michaels, alone and in the dark, was being ambushed on the pockmarked hillside at Dak Pek.

THIRTEEN

TYLER WAS LYING ON HIS BUNK PLUGGED INTO A SMALL tape recorder, Bob Dylan wailing "Tangled Up in Blue" in his ears through a headset. Vance tapped his toe against the foot rail with "*. . . the sun was shinin', I was layin' in bed . . .*" The upbeat tempo mirrored his mood, uncommonly blithe for him lately. In his hands was the latest *Handloader* magazine, Jan.–Feb. 1974; he was reading an article on the .348 Winchester. Pretty good piece; the writer obviously had done a lot of shooting for the article, listing a lot of personally developed load data, unusual these days when more and more gun scribes seemed reluctant to spend time at the range. *Where have you gone, Townsend Whelen, a shooter turns his lonely eyes to you,* he sang in his head, paraphrasing Simon and Garfunkel.

McElroy came in and sat on Ty's bunk. Tyler took off the headset. The captain said, without preamble, "Your friend in 'Nam was ambushed last night. Took a hit from a fragmentation grenade, not mortal, I'm told. He was evacuated to an infirmary near Saigon. Far as I know, he'll be fine."

Ty let out the breath he'd been holding. "Where was he hit?"

"Butt, I think. Details are sketchy. I'll have more later."

McElroy continued. "We're sending you in at noon tomorrow, eight miles east of your normal haunts. Two medics in a jeep were machine-gunned en route to an OP where some lieutenant cut his finger off with a straight razor trying to sharpen it. The dickhead.

"Anyhow, we expect that success will breed success, at least thinking like a KPA commandant, and they'll try it again. We want you to work that sector for five days, try to catch them on the move. Take them out. But be careful. They used a .50-cal. Whatever range you can reach with that heavy-barreled .308 sniper rig is a piece of cake for a .50. Hit and run, Vance. Hit and run. No John Wayne stuff."

"Sure. They only killed two American medical personnel, noncombatants on the way to assist the wounded. I'll just scare hell out of them, then let 'em go."

McElroy looked at him a long ten seconds, but didn't know what else to say. So he said "So long" and departed, wondering if he'd made a mistake, picked the wrong man. The boy was good, real good, but he bordered on foolhardy. If he was, he'd never make it in the 'Z long-term. They'd ship him home in a body bag.

If they recovered the body.

• • •

Tyler had been back in the DMZ three days and he didn't like it much. Too many evergreens in the new area, too much rocky ground. While that made silent walking easy for him, it did the same for his enemy. On this third day there sprang up a twenty-knot wind, gusting to thirty. It was nearly responsible for his death.

He'd stopped just below the crest of a ridge—not so careless as to skyline himself—to shrug out of his pack and lean his sniper rig against the fork of a stunted pine. Bending over to remove a twisted piece of jerky from the pack, the gusty wind knocked over his canteen. It clanged to the rocks at his feet, making more racket than a one-year-old with a plastic bucket and long-handled spoon, or so it seemed to him. He stood up, suddenly apprehensive, looking to his left.

And there appeared the heads and shoulders of three North Korean soldiers, rifles slung, mouths agape, obscured by the rocky ridgetop from their chests down—a natural defilade, however unplanned. They were unsure what to do next.

Tyler wasn't.

Without a conscious thought, a millisecond's hesitation, he slipped his right thumb beneath the flap of his holster to pop it up, driving downward then, thumb high and reaching for the safety lever, the gun cocked-and-locked in violation of regulations and thankful for it during the split second it took him to complete his draw, snap off the safety, and shoot the three men, each in the head, at a range of thirty-one feet, *bangbangbang,* right to left, using the unique counterclockwise torquing recoil of the slab-sided .45 to his advantage. One man took a 230-grain full-patch slug under the left eye; a cohort received his through a sinus cavity.

The third man—unluckier than his mates—was struck on the chin, resulting in a huge loss of mandibular material and adjacent teeth and tissue. His demise was neither quick nor pleasant; but let it be known that he was the trigger man in the shooting from ambush of the American medics, at which time he had laughed gleefully when one of them fell from the jeep screaming and writhing in agony from a .50-caliber bullet to the groin. The North Korean had waited until the man lay still—holding himself, making sounds not identifiable as human—before he finished the job with a twenty-round burst that so mangled the body it was buried in a closed casket.

Ty took a quick look-see as his targets tumbled down the escarpment. What he saw heightened an adrenaline surge. Five more KPA soldiers clustered at the bottom of the slope, one carrying the barrel of a Big Fifty over a shoulder, the machine gun's base at his feet. Ty was outnumbered, outgunned, outsurprised.

Foolish to be outflanked as well.

Feet, don't fail me now.

He gathered up his gear, pack in one hand, rifle in the other. Five minutes later he couldn't even see the hilltop where the battle, such as it was, had taken place.

• • •

For the next two days, Tyler played cat and mouse with the agitated North Koreans. They hounded him unceasingly, called in another squad to assist, making thirteen in all. Vance did not radio for help, nor did he make his way to the perimeter fence. Instead he thinned their ranks just before dark the first day—his fourth in the 'Z—by taking out their apparent senior officer, who wore no insignia but was given to order giving, hand wringing, pacing, shouting, and gesticulation.

One shot, six hundred fifty meters give or take, dead calm, solid rest over a rock, rolled-up poncho for a pedestal, using another rock as a stool. No easy mark, especially under catch-as-catch-can conditions and estimated range, but not Camp Perry material either.

On the morning of the fifth day, he radioed the nearest OP for instructions, apprising them of the situation. They changed his pickup time from 1700 hours to 2200, figuring the cloak of darkness wouldn't hurt, what with a twelve-man machine gun team on the prowl. Three American squads were moved into the area, told to be on the lookout for a lone American sniper but not to interface with him in any way unless he obviously needed help.

Tyler trekked to his cache, traded the bolt-action sniper outfit for his twelve-gauge '97 and Grease Gun, then set a little trap for his pursuers.

They walked right into it.

Overhanging a well-traveled trail that he had watched his seekers employ on three occasions was a flat rock. Anyone perched on it—about twenty feet above the ground—was invisible from the trail for at least fifty meters. The North Koreans had used the trail only to travel south, although one would think that they'd vary their routine occasionally. Betting they wouldn't, Ty took a chance and climbed into place, arranging his gear around him. Luck had better be with him; if the troops appeared *from* the south, Vance would be as exposed as a festered fistula when they rounded a bend seventy-five meters to his front.

Old habits die hard. Here they came, heading south,

passing under him single file, as he'd once had thirteen cow elk do in the Idaho Bitteroots. That time, he'd waited until the fourteenth animal—a big six-point bull, which now hung on a wall back home—brought up the rear. A simple neck shot had fed the camp—ten men and two women—for nine days.

Here came the twelfth soldier, canteen clanking against his rifle, slung over a shoulder as always. Did these guys get *any* training?

"Where you boys heading?" Ty called out, frightening the tag man so badly he fell—a wet stain soiling the crotch of his trousers—ten meters from the muzzle of Ty's shotgun.

Unslung came a bevy of AK-47s as the KPA insurgents scrambled to mount an offensive. Ty opened the ball, pumping six rounds through the shotgun as fast as he could acquire targets. For him, that was very fast. Rather than recharge the scattergun when it ran dry, he laid it aside to take up the Grease Gun, four mags close at hand. The mountain pass echoed with the deadly staccatto tympani initiated by enemies who'd never met face to face, a microcosm of enmity. Proving what? That men die for no reason other than hate and pigheadedness.

Seven did that day. Some struggled to find cover, escaping the withering fire from above even as they bled to death. Three more were horribly wounded; one died as he made his way toward home, assisted by a comrade so severely wounded he would lose the use of one arm.

Tyler, in a position to finish them off to a man, did not, but gathered his possibles and quit the scene after tossing a canteen and all the food from his pack to the stricken men below.

• • •

"You didn't what?" the portly, florid major shouted.

McElroy winced.

"I didn't kill them all," Tyler answered.

"Sir! You didn't kill them all, sir!" yelled the major, becoming even more florid.

Tyler just stared at the officer.

"Say it!"

Nothing from Ty.

"By God, you'll call me sir or I'll bust . . ." Florider and florider.

A gasket, thought Tyler.

"Major, may I have a word with you? In private?" McElroy interrupted.

"Not until this pissant son of a bitch calls me sir!"

"It won't take a moment, sir," McElroy insisted.

Vance left the room.

"Why the hell are you taking up for that . . . ?"

"Major?" McElroy's voice was calm.

"What?"

"I have something to say and I'd like to say it uninterrupted if I may."

"Well, fucking say it, then."

McElroy closed his eyes, stood, teeth clenched, for a count of ten, then opened them again.

"That young man just came in from the DMZ after spending five days alone, two of them while being hounded by a multitude of KPA regulars. Not only did he elude them, he laid in wait and virtually annihilated them single-handedly. Before that, he killed three men who had him dead to rights. Several days ago, he wiped out a five-man patrol intent on a little mine-planting expedition. He recovered the mines, brought them to me. All this he did alone. No backup. And he's just a kid, never been in combat until Korea.

"What I'm saying to you is that he's special. That he's not to be fucked with, or talked to like you just did. Ever. Not only do I insist—don't say a fucking word until I'm finished—that you leave him alone, but so does the Division Commander, a good friend of the Army Chief of Staff, who, if you piss him off even slightly, will ship your out-of-shape West Point ass to fucking Alaska! Am I clear?"

Mumbled response, blood-pressure 180-over-118, dry mouth. Beet-red.

"Am I *abso-fucking-lutely* clear!"

"Yes."

McElroy stepped closer. Very close. Real close. So close that if he'd scratched his nose, he'd have had to scratch the major's, too. "One more thing. Don't ever cuss me again, for any reason whatever, justifiable or imagined. Comprende? Sir?"

The major turned on his heel, stumbling, bowels rumbling noisily, and scurried out of the room.

Vance passed him in the doorway. "Good-bye. Sir." Ty looked at McElroy and shrugged. "Didn't want him to think I had hard feelings."

• • •

"Why didn't you wax those men?"

"Couldn't, Captain. They were helpless, all the fight gone. It would have been murder, not to put too fine a point on it. I'm not a murderer. I thought about taking them prisoner, but doubted I could handle them in the dark, which was closing fast."

"Call in next time. For assistance."

"Yes, sir."

"That's all, Corporal Vance. Oh, I appreciate the 'sir.' "

"You deserve it."

"I appreciate that, too."

Vance simply smiled.

"Five days before you go back in. No argument. Take a three-day pass if you want, in mufti. Go to Seoul. Eat some good grub, maybe see a movie in a decent theater for a change. They've got a fine library, too, and a great weight room."

"Yes, sir."

"By the way, there's a letter on your bunk. From Michaels."

Tyler rushed out the door.

FOURTEEN

THE LETTER FROM DAVE MICHAELS, NO EXPLETIVES DEleted, read thus:

Dear Tyler Cee,

Okay, go ahead and laugh. Who cares if it's two or three thousand miles, you think I won't hear you? So I got hit in the backside, big deal. I wasn't advancing to the rear. It was so damn dark I didn't know where the incoming was incoming from, so I unloaded my old Remington-Rand .45, two clips, all I had, in most every direction I could think of except up. Sergeant York with a handgun I'm not (shut up) so if I hit anything except trees, the world didn't come to a halt. Then, after expending my ammo supply, with nobody nearby (I was all by my lonesome, the pilot still down at the plane jerry-rigging some damn thing in place when he took an AK round through the upper lip, talk about an overbite, not funny, Vietnam does that to you) anyway, since I had nothing else to throw at my enemies, I lifted my feet and put them down again, over and over, darting through the puckerbrush like Brer Rabbit in the briarpatch, when all of a sudden such a whump did I take to my sit-down parts that I'd have let out a whoop if I wasn't so damn tough. Plus I figured you'd hear me and I'd never hear the end of it. Do I need to start a new paragraph, you're the writer?

So here I am, lying on a slope so steep the rain was falling sideways, and I hear soldiers moving through the brush all around me. Not knowing the color of their colors, like Brer Fox I lay low.

Directly, one of them comes so close, and with a flashlight, that I take a chance and give a little whistle like we've worked out among ourselves. I get the correct whistle back, so I yell out, "Over here," just loud enough for Mom to hear it back home, and this guy whose name is Bart something, a medic from Lansing, Michigan, studied music at a big school in Indiana, plays the bassoon or the bass fiddle, no, trombone! the bass trombone, anyway he comes up and looks me over all the while I'm saying how glad I am to see him, and he starts prodding my ass and I tell him not THAT glad, and he tells me to clamp it and let him see what's what. So I, not in all that good a mood what with the bleeding and all, say something like, "It's my ass, that's what." And he says, "Yeah, and it's got so much metal in it that if I don't get it out soon you'll never be able to walk past a magnet." (Smart alecky bastard reminds me of someone else I know.) Anyway, he asks me can I walk and trying to hold my own in the exchange I tell him, "Hell, no, I can't walk, but I can sure as hell

FIFTEEN

JUNE CAME AND WENT, THEN HALF OF JULY. SWELTERING heat. Vance spent more and more of his patrol time in the woods, dodging the sun. So did the KPA. So did the bugs. He was easing quietly through such dense cover now, searching out a tunnel entrance that rumors placed in his vicinity. No luck so far. Hardly ever was; the North Koreans were adept at concealing their burrowings. Stopping, he removed his fatigue cap to mop his sweaty dome with a handkerchief, then took a long pull from his canteen. Another, washing down a salt tablet. Damn, it was hot.

A piercing ululation from the northeast, high-pitched, terror-stricken. Feminine.

There were no women in the 'Z.

He moved quickly toward the sound, or at least as quickly as he could given the carpet of dried leaves he had to traverse and the circuitous path dictated by caution. He'd feel really foolish walking into a trap, drawn in by a recorded wail of distress like a bobcat homing on a dying-rabbit call.

No, that wouldn't do at all. So he zigged, zagged, and backtracked, finally making his way to the edge of a small clearing, there to behold a harrowing sight.

A young Korean woman was being batted about by a quartet of KPA soldiers, all present stripped to the navel. From the bottom up. One of them slapped the girl—probably no older than sixteen—rocking her small head back, drawing blood from the corner of her mouth. She struck at her attacker and missed, eliciting hoots and hollers from the other men as they encircled her. While her attention was elsewhere, the tallest of the group, a towering six-footer, grabbed the back of her remaining garment and ripped it free. She fell to the ground, trying futilely to cover her nakedness, in no time pounced upon by two of the men, who dragged her back to her feet. There she stood, on display to their lust, panting and panicked but stoutly defiant, facing her tormentors.

The men, quite obviously aroused, argued among themselves about who would go first. The tall man won after a lengthy, heated debate enlivened by pushing and shoving, profanity, and halfhearted threatening gestures. The young woman, having followed the argument to its inevitable conclusion, screamed and scratched and tried to bite, grabbing one man's object of intrusion and twisting it so vigorously he shrieked like a banshee and clutched the offended organ. Despite her spirited defense, she was overwhelmed, slammed onto her back, head held to the ground by one man while two others splayed her legs and held them so. The tall man towered over her, smirking, preparing himself for entry.

Of all the offenses humans inflict on one another, only child abuse was more heinous than rape in Tyler Vance's reckoning. Having no intention of standing by and allowing this one to proceed, he'd spent the last thirty seconds deciding how best to handle the situation. Since none of the men were armed, or even had their pants on, he could simply blast them all with his .45 before they knew what hit them. But shooting four unarmed men, even such scum as these, went against the grain. So he stepped from the sheltering treeline and into the arena with the shotgun held by its pistol grip at arm's length, muzzle down near his ankle, and cocked its hammer. The resulting *click* captured everyone's attention.

The first man to spot him—a wiry, gnarly-legged specimen not much over five feet tall—yelled a warning, then jumped for his rifle, on the ground fifteen feet away. He'd covered one-third of the distance when Ty's blast took out his kidneys and most everything else below the diaphragm, piling him in a bloody heap at the base of a rock. Nothing else moved. Well, that's not entirely true. Three erections abruptly lost interest in the proceedings and drooped suddenly southward, shriveled like slugs on a griddle. Their hosts seemed neither to notice nor care, so intent was their regard of the shotgun that now covered them collectively.

Tyler said, "Howdy, boys. Having fun?"

No response.

He motioned with his left arm for the girl to join him. She did so, trying to cover herself with the sundered clothing she gathered up quickly. When she drew near, he saw that in addition to the bloody lip, she had the beginnings of a black eye. Her arms and breasts bore multiple contusions; there was a bite mark surrounding one nipple. He grimaced. Indicating the bite mark, the bruising, the black eye, then sweeping his hand at the soldiers, with his gesture he asked, Did they all do this?

She shook her head.

Arching his eyebrows, he inclined his head at the trio, all simply standing there, six heads hanging. Which ones? he wanted to know.

She pointed at the tall one.

Ty gestured with the gun barrel. Any punitive action in mind?

She nodded, a bit hesitant at first, then emphatically.

He motioned with the gun barrel again, separating the two smaller soldiers from their associate while making sure they were well clear of their firearms. He walked over to the tall drink of water, put the muzzle of the shotgun to the man's temple, not caring if he had to use it.

The girl joined them, then kicked the tall man on the inside of each ankle, outward, not hard, indicating that he should spread his legs. The man resisted. Ty poked him with the shotgun barrel. The feet moved outward, a little. The girl motioned, farther. The tall man was reluctant. Ty aimed the shotgun downward, at the juncture of the man's legs. Swallowing hard, quaking in his boots, the man's legs came apart, wide, wider, until he resembled a giraffe about to drink at a watering hole. The girl put her hands behind her head, clasping her fingers, nodded at the tall soldier. He followed suit, slowly, shaking so much he nearly staggered. The girl barked something in Korean; the man shook his head in stout refusal. She looked at Tyler. What? he indicated. She closed her eyes, squinting tightly, then popped them open, looking at the man, who shook his head, adamantly. No, he wouldn't do that. Ty motioned for the girl to step back, obviously not wanting to see her splattered with blood when he separated this man from his tender portions. It was a bluff, but Tall Job got the message and closed his eyes, stood there vibrating like a tuning fork, spraddle-legged, hands at the back of his head, trouserless, uncovered and unprotected. Like she had been. He waited for the inevitable. The two KPA soldiers held their breath.

Stepping up close—too close, Ty thought—the young woman, bleeding, bedraggled, humiliated, took in a lungful of air and bit one of the tall man's nipples so fiercely his scream was heard at an OP a mile away.

• • •

"Why are those men naked from the waist down, Vance?" the lieutenant asked.

"Way I found them, sir."

"Without their pants on? What the hell were they doing?"

"Crime against nature, sir."

"No kidding?" the lieutenant curled his lip, disgusted. "While on patrol?"

"KPA are an undisciplined group, sir," Vance reported.

The lieutenant leaned close, whispered into Vance's ear, "You see the bite mark on that big guy? His left nipple's hanging by a piece of skin."

"Licentious bunch, sir."

"Disgusting."

"Yes, sir."

"Take them away."

"Not me, sir. I have to head back down the hill, look for that tunnel."

"Send in Specialist Witherspoon."

"Will do, sir."

"And Vance . . ."

"Sir?"

"Next time you bring in some prisoners, make sure they have their pants on."

"Certainly. Now you mind that straight razor, sir."

The lieutenant glanced at his finger, now healed. "Oh, right." Straight razor, hell. He'd tossed that in the weeds the next day and bought himself an electric, the twice-daily sounds of which emanated from his cramped quarters at the oddest of hours. Anything he hated it was five o'clock shadow.

• • •

Ty returned to the spot where he'd left the girl tending her wounds, tincture of iodine in one hand, cotton swab in the other. Aspirin, canteen, some jerky—she'd appeared hungry. Through his limited Korean and her almost nonexistent English, paired with moderately innovative sign language, he learned her story.

She was eighteen, not so young as he'd guessed. Her name was Sook Moon, and those men, however badly they'd mauled her, had not, emphatically *not,* violated her. She was still a virgin, thanks to him, and inordinately proud of the fact. He nodded, indicating his understanding and appreciation. She went on and on about his heroic rescue; he kept discounting it as of little import. She mistook his reluctance to take credit as an indicator that she was of scant value in his estimation, creating a rift that took some jockeying to get around. Eventually the misunderstanding was smoothed over.

How had she come to be their prisoner?

She'd been traveling to her sick grandmother's home, to nurse her for a few days while the rest of the family was busy in the paddies. Waylaid and whisked over the line by the patrol—probably returning from a scouting mission farther south—she'd found herself in a most horrible predicament. Had the men succeeded in their violation of her, she'd have committed suicide, assuming they left her alive, of which there was certainly no guarantee.

She owed Ty her life.

He didn't view it that way; there was no obligation on her part. He cautioned her against traveling alone this near the DMZ. She claimed to have little choice; the males in her family were too busy to escort her. After an hour of animated, gesticulating conversation, she departed, peering coyly back over one shoulder before stepping into the woods. She waved once, a delicate flip of her wrist.

Then, like a wisp of smoke, she was gone.

SIXTEEN

SIX DAYS LATER, TYLER STEPPED CLEAR OF THE JEEP, BID good-bye to its driver, shouldered his pack and shotgun. This particular entrance to the DMZ was four hundred meters farther along the fence line from where Tyler had last disembarked. His driver parked in a different spot each time, and they never used the same gate more than once a month. It was early morning, not so steamy yet, with the magpies out in force, their raucous racket not entirely unpleasant. Ten meters this side of the gate, Sook Moon materialized from a patch of weeds, startling him so thoroughly he nearly made a lump in his shorts. She smiled shyly, apologetic for her sudden appearance and his obvious discomfiture.

If she'd been North Korean, I'd be spitting up blood about now. Better vary my routine more, get dropped off a half mile away, approach the fence through heavy cover, not amble along the road like a tourist, he thought.

She had a basket with her. Invited him to come, sit, commune.

Eat.

The magic word. No second invite necessary.

The basket was redolent; his nostrils detected the Korea staple, *kimchi*, which he'd had before and not especially liked. Yep. There it was: fermented cabbage individualized with salt, red-hot ground peppers, pickled turnips, radishes, what appeared to be cucumbers, and a few oddments he failed to recognize. Each family had its own additives.

He tried a bite. Gag.

She giggled. He smiled in spite of himself.

Well, you see, sir, I was on this ambush patrol a couple thousand meters south of North Korea—but who's counting—when this lovely Korean lass invited me to lunch, picnic style, no less, sir, so there I sat, my riot shotgun close at hand in case of attack by communist troops, and . . .

What's wrong with this picture?

They'd hang him, *then* court-martial him.

Hmm, what's this? Smells nice. *Kalbi,* she says. Looks like short ribs of beef. Yum. Tastes like short ribs of beef. And in this little bowl? *Saengson chigye,* she calls it, a thick stew. Ummm, fishy taste . . .

And so on, until the containers held naught but air and liquid leavings.

• • •

"Now I'm too full to go on patrol," he said. "Have to wait here three days, 'til they come pick me up. With a winch."

She looked at him quizzically, not understanding.

He patted his stomach, rolling his eyes and making bellyache sounds.

She giggled again, a fine tinkling sound in the still air. He reached over and brushed aside a tendril of black hair. She didn't recoil as he half expected, but leaned into his hand.

Uh-oh.

He sat up straight. Embarrassed, she began to gather dishes; the spoon and chopsticks with which they'd eaten; tiny silk napkins, barely soiled. Then an awkward silence, the result of hormonal anxiety. Opposites attracting powerfully, overwhelmingly.

They sought refuge in conversation.

How had she deduced when he would return? he wanted to know. Even he hadn't known for certain when, until yesterday.

Simple answer.

She hadn't known.

So she'd waited for him all day, every day, for six days.

What did one say to that?

As ladies often do, she resolved his dilemma, relieving him of having to say anything. She must go now, her parents would be worried.

Would he see her again?

Probably.

Where?

She'd find him, on this side of the fence.

Soon, he implored, trying not to show urgency and failing.

Soon, she agreed, then left him, this time not looking back.

He felt like a dork.

• • •

Around lunchtime of his second day back in the 'Z, Vance received a radio transmission ordering him to return to base. He wolfed down K rations, gathered his stuff, and hoofed it to the pickup point, where he was met an hour later by his usual driver.

Sook Moon was nowhere to be seen.

• • •

The problem was Kim Park. He had been reassigned to Camp Kitty Hawk, just south of Panmunjom, the mission of which was to staff guard and observation posts in the Joint Security Area (JSA), a compound within the DMZ in which the North and South held talks. It was an island of intrigue and violence, possibly the most dangerous spot in Korea.

It was within this area that the infamous Poplar Tree Incident was to take place on August 18, 1976, nearly two years after Tyler Vance left Korea. Two American officers were beaten to death by North Korean soldiers in full view of American troops manning Checkpoint 5, barely a quarter of a mile away but too far for intervention. A truckload of KPA soldiers, roaring unexpectedly across the notorious "Bridge of No Return" from the northern side, assaulted the American officers, an ROK army captain, and five civilian workers from the Korean Service Corps (who were pruning a large poplar tree) with pipes and ax handles. After the attack, the KPA troops fled back across the bridge to sanctuary in North Korea.

It was into this deadly and volatile environment that Kim Park had been thrust. On his third night of guard duty, he'd left his post to check out a minor disturbance that had been reported. Caught away from assistance, and with orders not to fire unless fired upon, Park had tried to handle an obviously inebriated KPA soldier alone, laying down his rifle. Suddenly three more North Koreans had appeared and beaten Kim Park so badly he might not recover. If he did, he would never father children.

Tyler read the report, balled it up, and threw it, followed by his footlocker, against the wall of his Quonset in a rage. McElroy, waiting patiently outside, let Vance vent his anger for a few minutes, then poked his head through the door. "It safe to come in now?" he asked.

"Probably not, Captain," Vance answered from the bunk where he sat, shoulders hunched, exhausted by the emotional frenzy.

The captain took the bunk opposite, watching the young man carefully. Tyler said, "It never ends, does it? You think life's sunk as low as it's going to, then it rises up and kicks you in the balls."

"That's about the size of it, son."

"I want to do something about this particular kick in the balls, sir."

"Thought you might."

"Can't shoot them, can I?"

"Not without allowing for World War III."

"What then?"

"You got any ideas?" McElroy asked.

Vance thought a minute. "Matter of fact, I do."

"Let's hear them."

"A change of duty station might do me a world of good, sir. So this is my official request for a temporary transfer to . . ."

They worked on their plan for an hour.

• • •

"Watch out for man with knife scar ear to chin," advised Kim Park, under the influence of morphine to dull his pain. "Ver' mean, ver' good, ver' fast," he continued. The pain, undimmed by distance from its time of origin, might yet drive Kim insane. His scrotal sac was missing, with all its hopeful contents—physical and numinous—denied; dreams of marital delight, simple pleasures of fatherhood, ripped out, cast into the river.

By one man.

"Bad scar. You watchee. Ver' fast." Merciful sleep, then. Healing the body, perhaps not the mind.

Tyler stayed by the bedside for a long time, watching his friend in troubled slumber, wishing things were different. So many things, so very different.

The scarred man's name was Lee Jin Ku. It was claimed that he'd done such before, and worse. Reputation as a kung fu demon. Or maybe just a demon. Ty'd never fought a demon. If he had anything to say about it, he would.

Soon.

And thus did Sgt. Tyler C. Vance, Infantry, come to be reassigned, TDY, to one of three platoons responsible for manning OPs and guard shacks in the Joint Security Area, near Panmunjom, out of Camp Kitty Hawk, smack-dab astride the Military Demarcation Line between the Republic of Korea and its northern counterpart.

And thus did he come to stand guard at Checkpoint 3, located at the southern end of the Bridge of No Return, across which in December of 1968 had marched the crew of the American ship U.S.S. *Pueblo,* after spending nearly a year in captivity.

And thus did he come to be sent out alone one night to investigate a disturbance near the bridge, possibly a drunken soldier.

• • •

No drunk, this one, though he wanted Tyler to think he was, weaving and tripping and pissing on shrubs all the while singing loudly in Korean. Vance approached as if he bought the whole package, drawing nigh until the "drunk" came up from a poorly faked spell of dry heaves with a ten-inch bayonet and stabbed at Ty's throat. Vance dodged, stepping back from the blade, and grabbed the arm, hyperextending it over his shoulder, then snapping downward. In order to keep his elbow from breaking, the Korean followed the arm over Ty's shoulder and onto the ground. Still holding the arm, Vance twisted it just so, causing release of the bayonet and considerable pain, then hit his attacker in the temple with an extended-knuckle punch. And another. So much for him. Tyler turned his attention elsewhere.

The night produced three more assailants; Tyler produced a .45 automatic. The click of its safety as he drew stopped the men in their tracks. Everyone looked at everyone else.

Ty broke the silence. "Anybody speak English?"

No response.

"I'm going to shoot you," he pointed the pistol at the largest man, "if someone doesn't answer me."

No response.

Tyler shot the man in his left forearm, above the wrist,

the ball of flame as the gun discharged doing nothing good for his night vision. Theirs either, he suspected. The North Korean's arm jerked from the bullet's impact, and one of his compatriots reached out to support him, but nothing else happened.

"Next one goes into his belly," said Ty. "Now, does anybody speak English?"

One of them nodded, saying, *"Skoshee,"* Korean-modified Japanese for "a little."

"Do you know Lee Jin Ku?" Ty asked.

The two healthy KPA soldiers exchanged looks. The wounded one was near to passing out, but he held his head up, teeth clenched in pain, and looked Vance in the eye. Ty aimed the gun at the man's stomach.

"We know," one of the men said quickly.

Ty nodded. "Good. Give him a message. Tomorrow night. Me and him. Right here. You understand?"

"Just you?" asked the same man, a squat number with *kimchi* breath and a broad nose. He was incredulous.

"Guns"—Tyler waved the .45 for emphasis—"knives, bare hands, whatever he wants. You understand?"

A slow smile spread across the Korean's face. He understood all right, and obviously relished the thought. He bobbed his head rapidly. "Unnerstand," he assured.

"Tomorrow night. Right here." Ty tapped his watch with the muzzle of the .45. "Same time. Me and him, nobody else."

The man, grinning openly now, said, "No needo nobody. You find out soon. *You* needo somebody."

"Sure. Now get this one out of here before he bleeds to death."

The party was over.

• • •

McElroy said, "You shot him in the arm, Vance. Why?"

"No one would fess up to speaking English. Used him as a lever."

"I understand that, Sergeant. What I *don't* understand is why you didn't kill the motherfucker."

"Shooting him in the wing seemed like a good place to start. Why kill him if I didn't have to?"

"It's likely you killed the first one."

"He tried to do a tracheotomy on me."

"And you thought the other three came to dance?"

Something in Ty's eyes changed. "Anything else? Sir?"

McElroy saw it. "You think this discussion is over now? Just like that?"

Tyler was still, cold, mentally isolated despite the presence of four other soldiers. Focused inward. "Unless you have something important."

McElroy said, "Who decides what's important, Vance? You?"

"I'm tired, sir. May I go now?" Eyes like ice.

"Get out of here."

As Vance turned to go, McElroy added, "Can I still count on you tomorrow night, or should I send someone in your place? Someone with more steel and less compassion?"

Tyler looked at the captain very hard and very long, then said very softly, "I don't think it would be wise for you to send someone else," and left.

SEVENTEEN

GOOD GRIEF, HE LOOKS LIKE ODDJOB IN GOLDFINGER, thought Tyler, as he removed his boots. *Glad he's not wearing a derby.*

The formidable North Korean martial arts demon, having just stepped out from behind a tall shrub, stood shrugging his massive shoulders like the Incredible Hulk. Or a constipated crab. As Kim had indicated, a livid scar traversed the guy's jawline. What Kim had *not* said was how big he was; if Ku missed six feet and two-forty, Ty'd have to give up his future as a weight-guesser with the carnival.

Well, thought Ty, *the bigger they are, the harder they . . . hit. Ha-ha. Hope I still feel like joking ten minutes from now.*

Time to squelch this line of thought, Tyler C. Concentrate. This is the guy who rips balls off. Probably with his teeth. Pay attention, boy.

So he did, moving closer to size up his opponent. Lee Jin Ku stood his ground. At close range, Ty realized Ku was not as tall as he'd first thought, perhaps only five-ten or so, but was built like a buffalo—not to mention being older, more experienced, meaner . . .

Check that. Tyler was going to be meaner; he had a score to settle.

Time to settle it. He assumed a conventional forward stance.

Lee Jin Ku laughed.

Laugh at this, Tyler thought briefly, and launched an exploratory *jun-zuki*—a snap punch, much like a boxer's jab—at Ku's chin. Ku blocked it swiftly, as if snagging a fly as it buzzed past.

Quick bastard, thought Ty, following up with a second snap punch aimed for the same spot. Ku blocked it with a rising hand and attempted a reverse punch of his own, which Ty blocked with his punching arm before snapping a reverse to Ku's ribs. While the Korean was moving away under his own momentum, Tyler landed a roundhouse kick to the back of his head. Good solid kick, too. Perfectly timed.

To no effect.

Ku simply lowered his head, going with the kick, then spun around as if it hadn't fazed him and hit Tyler a double punch—jab, reverse, in very rapid succession—that knocked him on his butt. The Korean did not press his advantage, letting Tyler reclaim his feet while he eased into a tiger stance. Such a stance is useful in protecting the lower body, and allows quick kicks with the leading foot, but is primarily a defensive postion.

He was inviting Tyler to bring it to him.

For the next five minutes the pair dodged and parried, threw knife-hands and side punches, front kicks and hooks—even one marvelously executed spinning hook by Ty that would have finished the fight if it had connected solidly. Alas, Ku deflected it with an X-block, sparing his face but numbing his left arm for a moment.

Momentarily, the fight abated while the combatants caught their breath. Much wheezing and spitting, bent over, hands on knees. Each had received his share of punishment. Ku's lip bled profusely and a swelling was starting above his right ear; Tyler's right eye was nearly closed and his ribs ached from several punches to the wind. Nothing decisive, just chinks in the wall. Sufficient chinks could make a hole.

Lee Jin Ku tried for one now, suddenly snapping into position and advancing, sending Ty backward to avoid a faked rear-leg kick, then launching a rear-leg front kick. Tyler, guessing the intention, took another step to the rear and changed his covering position to block the kick. Ku hesitated a millisecond, checking his kick, the first major mistake of the evening. Tyler delivered a rear-leg roundhouse to Ku's unprotected midsection when the man hesitated.

At the moment of connection, Ku was inhaling. The kick, with all Ty's weight and strength behind it, took his breath and spun him half around. Ty enhanced his advantage with a spinning back kick that impacted Ku's jaw hinge and dropped him to his knees. Hammer-hand to the neck, knuckle-fist to the temple; Ku's head sagged, down on all fours, unaware of his surroundings, resistance gone.

A cross kick then, the finisher, Tyler starting the blow with his left leg extended, foot high off the ground, swinging the foot in a sweeping arc across the front of his body, striking Ku's skull with the blade edge of the foot, following through as the Korean's head snapped sideways and his body collapsed.

Ty turned the heavy man over, grabbed his scrotum with a clenched fist, breath coming in ragged gasps of rage and fear and exhaustion. "This is for Kim Park, you son of a bitch," he gritted, prepared to pull.

He couldn't do it.

Down the hill to McElroy (who had watched it all through the night-vision scope of a sniper rifle, just in case) he plodded, bone weary, strangely bereft of the expected euphoria.

It'd had to be done, for Kim, but he took little pride in it. Relief mostly.

That he hadn't had his ass handed to him.

EIGHTEEN

TY HOVERED NEAR THE ENTRANCE TO THE 'Z FOR TWO hours before entering, waiting for Sook Moon. Three days later, ditto on the way out. Same result both days. He asked McElroy to send him in a day early the next time, when he waited three hours before chiding himself, "This crap has got to stop. I'm supposed to be in the 'Z, not mooning around out here. Ha-ha. 'Mooning' around, I get it."

So he'd stood, grabbed his gear, and was heading toward the gate when Sock Moon appeared in a clump of weeds not large enough to hide a hedgehog. He gaped at her, then waved tentatively. No wave in return. He went over to her, looked down. She wore a simple white gown-like garment, gathered at the waist with a plaited belt. Her hair was so clean and black and newly combed it brushed his eyes with all the hues of the spectrum in reflected radiance. He was glad to see her.

Couldn't tell if the sentiment was reciprocal.

She made an angry gesture, pointing to his watch, the sun. Where have you been? He tried, successfully, to look forlorn. Ashamed. He was. "Panmunjom," he said, receiving a look of instant consternation as her reply. Had he been transferred? No, he shook his head, no time soon. It was just a temporary assignment, and all over now. What had he done? Ty made fighting motions, then their sign for North Korean soldiers. Again a sharp inhalation, You fought North Korean soldiers? He nodded. They hurt a friend, a South Korean soldier friend, very badly, so Ty was returning the favor. That she understood, but why did he have to fight alone? No other way to bring them out into the open; they hide like jackals. She understood that, as well. Was he okay? She fingered the bandage on his cheek. Cut myself shaving, his attempt at levity. Not amused, she peeled the corner of the dressing away, her lips firmly set, angry, eyes smoldering. "I'll tell people I got it in a sword fight," he joked again, "enhance my image." She didn't understand and didn't care that she didn't, knowing he was making light of something serious and having none of it.

He explained to her that they could no longer meet like this; either they'd be shot by the KPA, or he'd be reported to his superiors and be shot by the U.S. Army. She smiled at that, despite herself. Could he meet her a bit farther south, maybe at her village? She considered. Perhaps, if her parents would allow it. She didn't know if they would. She'd meet him here in three days, when he came off patrol, to give him an answer.

Okay, he said, and they parted.

• • •

On the last day of his patrol, wandering through a thinly forested area, he espied some steam rising from the ground. That was odd as hell. Investigating, he found a hole in the earth where none should be, at least judging by geological indicators. He radioed in, seeking assistance from specialists within the Corps of Engineers. Two hours and some serious excavation later found Tyler and several fellow soldiers inside a North Korean–built tunnel traversing subterraneously the South Korean side of the MDL. Surprise, surprise. A railroad track ran down its center, capable of handling ore carts for removing rock and other impediments to underground travel. A regiment of KPA troops could negotiate this passageway three or four abreast. It was an important find, courtesy of Sergeant Vance, who received a pat on the back and an unctuous handshake while a certain major landed all the credit. (That is, until McElroy got wind of it and relayed to the Second Division commander the facts of the matter. The upshot was a letter of commendation in Sergeant Vance's permanent record and a two-year tour of duty for the major. In Greenland.)

Tyler managed to sneak away from the digging party long enough for Sook Moon to find him on the south side of the fence and arrange a rendezvous at her village two days hence. Then Ty slipped back into the 'Z and radioed for his pickup.

• • •

Their "date" didn't go especially well at first. Her family didn't appear to like American soldiers, nor did they offer much gratitude about Tyler's having rescued their only daughter. Ty pondered this awhile, until it hit him: she hadn't told them. When he mentioned it, she sheepishly admitted as much. She'd been too ashamed of what had happened to her to tell anyone, she explained. No problem, he countered; he didn't blame her. It would be their secret. She was obviously relieved.

The foregoing accounted for her family's barely concealed animosity toward him. Tyler was obviously viewed as a threat since no one could figure out how the two had met, with her not being a hooker, nor yet working in a large city like Seoul, nor even on a military base as support personnel. Sook's contact with American soldiers had been minimal. This interloper could be interested in but one of two things, deflowering her or betrothing her (the latter would result in her being spirited away to the United States), neither of which the family viewed with enthusiasm. So not only did he receive cold rice and beef, but the cold shoulder as well, totally out of character for typically affable and generous Korean families, which normally welcomed new friends into their homes.

He and Sook laughed about this unusual state of affairs during a postprandial constitutional. At first she was embarrassed on his account, a little ashamed of her family. Forget it, he reassured her, brushing the whole thing off as being perfectly understandable given the situation. They were merely being protective. His exotic demeanor, rugged good looks, easygoing manner, and boyish charm set her at ease, and they walked and talked and enjoyed each other's company until the evening darkness sent them in search of light.

Tyler returned to base that night as pleased with life as he'd felt since leaving home nearly two years before.

• • •

McElroy was waiting for him, serious of mien.

"What is it?" Ty demanded.

"Michaels," answered McElroy.

"What?" Ty insisted.

McElroy told him that his friend's plane had taken a direct hit after leaving Dak Pek, was diverted to a radio relay site—code-named Langhorn—on the Cambodia/Laotian border for an emergency landing. It didn't make it, but went down in the jungle en route. A Special Forces team had gone in immediately, finding the wrecked Beaver but no sign of Michaels or the pilot except spent brass from a firefight and a cupful of blood; dark red as from a muscle wound, not bright arterial and frothy as from a lung. There was a good chance Michaels and the pilot had shot their way clear and were making their way to Langhorn on foot, the captain opined.

"But at least one of them's wounded?" Tyler asked.

"That's the word I got," said McElroy.

"How much ground will they have to cover?"

"Eighteen miles in a direct line, but twice that due to the terrain," the captain answered.

Tyler sat on his bunk, lost in troubled thought.

McElroy said, "I'm sorry."

"No need," said Tyler, "he'll make it."

McElroy nodded and said, "You bet, I'll keep you posted."

"Thanks," Ty said as McElroy left.

Tyler slept not a wink that night.

Nor did Dave Michaels, half a continent away.

But each thought of the other.

Where are you when I need you, spud?

Where am I when you need me, Rocketman?

It made them both feel better.

• • •

Sook Moon was washing clothes in the river, slapping them against flat rocks, when Ty found her at the village the next morning. She knew instantly something was dreadfully amiss and went to him, ignoring her father's irritable stare. Ty explained about Dave, using his faltering Korean, the few English terms Sook knew, and their evolving sign language. She was sympathetic, consoling, reassuring, providing strength where his had waned, patience in the face of his anxiety, faith where his had grown thin, causing him shame at his display of lassitude. She brooked no such nonsense. No one can be brave and forthright at all times, she admonished. We all need someone to lean on when our resolve flags. She would be his buttress, as he'd been hers. I owe you, he said. Pay someone else, in their time of need, she replied. For now, I am here. Be silent.

He slept in the sun, brow in her lap, and dreamed of early, insouciant times, Dave and fishing poles, corks bobbing in the brilliant glare, the carefree breeze of youth. Of poor Emily . . .

Abruptly, the gilded waters turned crimson, the corks into twin skulls enswathed in red. Bloody, gaping holes . . .

He woke, sweating, gasping, inconsolable.

• • •

At that exact moment, Dave Michaels was jerked from a fitful sleep where he lay beneath a sheltering overhang of rock beside a babbling Cambodian brook. Something had disturbed him. A sound? No. A dream? Maybe. Something about fishing . . .

A pebble rattled down the slope off to his left. Another. Someone descending from the rocks above him . . . clatter . . . maybe two someones. Dave lifted the GI .45 from his lap; he was half sitting, half leaning against the rock face.

Waited.

A pair of boots appeared from above, dropped to the creek bank twenty feet away, nearly soundlessly, facing the water away from Dave. Plop, the second man, right beside the first, NVA regulars, little guys, AKs at the ready. *Tough luck I'm behind you, fellas.* As if turning at his thought, they spun, eyes popping with realization, rifles rising, safeties snapping off.

Dave's was already off. *Pow! pow!*—their bodies hit the water simultaneously, splashing the rocks, boots kicking and thrashing as they convulsed, drowning, bleeding, dying, their sucking chest wounds sucking water only yesterday tainted by a local villager's blood, a boy not yet twelve. Movement ceased. The bodies sank, slowly, floating gently to the bottom, eddied there, expressionless, staring with lifeless eyes. Soon vengeful residents would dredge them out, strip them of all worth keeping, savage the cadavers then feed the remains to the fish, except for those parts deemed interesting enough to be hung from tree limbs, on display.

By then Dave and the pilot were gone.

• • •

For the next twelve days, Tyler saw some slight evidence of KPA movement in the DMZ, but made no visual contact with any. Twelve days stretched into twenty-four. Tyler patrolled the 'Z half that time with little reward for his efforts. Maybe with fall coming on, things were slowing down. He'd gone once to visit Sook Moon, and she'd come to the base to see him. They'd had dinner at the NCO club, taken in a movie, visited the PX, where he'd treated her to such luxury items as soap, chocolate bars, shampoo, towels, and razor blades. She laughed, blushing, at her acquisitions; her parents would now be certain she was a demimonde. Such items were commonly used to barter for sex by GIs in the field, negotiating with adolescent pimps for the services of "field whores," those luckless ladies who were no longer sufficiently disease-free to obtain club cards, thus reduced to servicing randy GIs stuck on maneuvers. Ty apologized, trying to retract the gifts; he'd never do anything to besmirch her reputation. Nonsense, she told him. If her parents couldn't trust her at this late stage, they'd simply have to deal with their inquietude as best they could.

The pair walked the compound holding hands, enjoying the crisp night, the closeness, the physical contact. Their easy friendship, founded on a hideous incident no one else knew about, was blossoming into something special.

Sook Moon was falling in love.

• • •

After seeing her safely onto the last "kimchi bus" of the evening, Tyler returned to his billet to find a grinning Cpt. Rufus Earl McElroy waiting. "He's okay."

"Dave?" said Tyler, excited.

"Bingo. He made it to Langhorn, brought the flyboy

with him, gangrenous leg and all. Pilot lost the leg but kept his life. Said Michaels refused to leave him, no matter how bleak things looked."

"Dave's not hurt at all?"

"I didn't say that. He suffered a couple broken ribs in the crash, took a bullet low in his left side as they left the plane, no organs hit. Had to take a machete away from a pajama-wearing farmer, got nicked a time or two in that one, nothing serious. Can't say the same for the farmer. I don't have the complete details, or the entire body count, but Michaels's CO has put him up for the Silver Star for bringing the pilot in instead of leaving him, and for wasting a busful of VC while doing so. Most of the time with captured weapons, I might add, since he ran out of ammo for his .45 early on."

"He couldn't do that," Ty said, internalizing.

"What?"

"Leave the pilot. Not Dave. No matter what."

"Well, he sure as hell didn't. So it's at least a Silver for him, and Purple Heart number two. Who knows what else."

"I don't care about that stuff, just that he's intact. Dave deserves a Medal of Honor just for being Dave. The hero stuff is part of him. Expected. It's his safety I was worried about, not his bravery. Will he be going home now?"

"You bet. And this time he's ready to go. He could've rotated the last time he was hit, but he nixed that. Said that since he'd suffered all those damned shots, he was damned sure gonna stay awhile."

Ty grinned.

McElroy said, "Someday, I hope to meet the young man. Meanwhile, I'm turning in. Just thought you needed to know as soon as possible, and I couldn't simply leave you a note. Wanted to see your face."

"Thanks." Ty offered his hand. "Was it worth staying up late for?"

McElroy shook heartily. "You bet."

• • •

Two weeks later, patrolling the 'Z, Ty heard the thump of a mortar round and the distinctive rattle of AK fire, and ran a half mile at top speed for a look-see. Six KPA soldiers had blown one jeep apart and the following vehicle had run nose-first into a gully; its occupants were now pinned down in a pile of shale nearby, at least one of them returning fire futilely with a handgun. Must be a couple of officers.

Two of the North Koreans kept shoving projectiles into the mortar, then covering their ears and ducking; following each hollow *crump!* of firing, up they'd jump to fork another round down the tube. Vance took a quick reading for distance to the mortar forkers, then draped himself over a flat, table-sized rock, using his pack for a rest. Comfortable, he made his scope adjustments for 320 meters, leveled the crosswires between the shoulder blades of a corpulent specimen intent on feeding the mortar another dose, and squeezed the trigger. The man slid to the ground without a twitch, sure sign of a spine hit—unless of course Ty'd misjudged the range and gone high, to the brain stem. *Naw, three-twenty and not an inch closer,* he said to himself as the North Koreans looked frantically about, trying to figure where the shot had come from so they could hide from a second one. *Over here,* thought Tyler as he shot the next bushwhacker in the chest, saw blood fly out his back, the man stand up, turn, stumble backward, then fall to the ground, jerking like a beheaded chicken. *They've made me now,* Ty thought, as the four KPA troops swung the mortar his way. He waited until one of them rose to drop home a round and nailed the bastard on the rise. That one, too, engaged in unpleasant histrionics before yielding to unconsciousness and death. The good part was that it so unnerved the others they took off like broken-field runners, scurrying for safety. Vance careened a bullet off a rock, its angry whine intended to spur them on, which it did admirably.

He gathered up his brass, his pack, his hat, and went to see about the jeep. No need to check on the three KPA personnel; he knew exactly what he'd find. Their corpses would keep.

• • •

"Hello, the jeep! I'm coming in," Ty yelled, hoping not to get shot.

"Come on," someone yelled back from the sheltering shale.

Two men climbed to their feet. And one woman. One of the men was a captain, a chaplain to boot. The other, most likely the driver, was a Staff Sergeant; he stood with a pistol in one hand. The woman was a PFC. She looked like Jayne Mansfield.

The chaplain extended a hand. "I'm Chaplain Charles Smith. This is my assistant, PFC Lisa Craft, and Sergeant Ferguson."

"Pleased to meet you," said the PFC, giving Ty's hand a phallic squeeze. She smiled broadly, presenting slightly crooked teeth and a pair of exquisite dimples. Perky upturned nose, apple cheeks, skin eider soft. Really puffed out her uniform; Ty's too, different location.

Feet, don't fail me now.

The sergeant did not offer to shake hands, instead demanding, "What're you doing out here alone?"

Ignoring him, Tyler went to check out the damaged jeep. The mortar round had landed inside the vehicle, killing the driver and his passenger—another staff sergeant. Both were pretty well mangled. He said, "Bad luck, sir, getting hit while you were moving. Not usually the case with mortars."

"We weren't moving, Sergeant."

"Sir?"

"We weren't moving. We'd stopped for my assistant to snap a few pictures."

"Begging your pardon, sir," Vance said, "but it's not such a good idea stopping your vehicle alongside a road here in the 'Z. Gives the North Koreans an opportunity they aren't likely to pass up if they're in the neighborhood, as you can see." He waved an arm at the ruined jeep and its occupants.

"Well, we'd been warned. But Sergeant Ferguson thought it would be all right if we didn't—"

"Sergeant Ferguson was wrong, sir. His stupidity cost two men their lives. If I hadn't come along, maybe yours, too."

Ferguson stepped in front of Tyler, looking down from a moderate height advantage, and said, "I asked you what you were doing here alone, mac."

"Excuse me," Vance said, shouldering the bigger man aside to address the chaplain. "Sir, with your permission, I'll go radio this in, get you an escort out of here. In the future, may I suggest that you not stop en route to an

OP, either coming or going, and that you provide yourself with a more experienced advisor." He looked pointedly at Ferguson, who immediately got in his face again.

Ty was about to remedy that situation once and for all when the captain asked, "Sergeant Vance, just what are you doing alone in the DMZ?"

"That's classified, sir."

"You can't tell me anything?"

"No, sir."

Ferguson growled, "Well, he can damn sure tell me," then grabbed a handful of Tyler's shirt. He wound up under the jeep spitting dirt, which, at six-feet and 220, he was not used to. When he grabbed people, they cringed! Or so it had been all his life. He scrambled out from under the jeep intent on mayhem. The captain stopped his advance, and, unknown to the good sergeant, saved him a trip to the infirmary.

"I suspect," offered the chaplain, no fool, "that we should honor the soldier's orders and leave him alone." He turned to Vance. "If you could make that radio transmission, we'd be grateful."

"I'll go do it now, sir."

"Thanks again, Sergeant Vance. For everything. Come see me when you're on base. We'll talk."

"Sure, sir," said Vance, and left.

PFC Craft watched him all the way up the hill and out of sight. *There goes a man,* she thought, feeling his essence right down to her socks. *Come see me, too. We won't just talk.*

• • •

Sook Moon met him at the compound gate, since she had no entrance pass. They ate at the snack bar, then strolled aimlessly, hands clasped. She was pensive. After dark, near a little garden beneath a canopy of paperbark maples and a towering Asian white birch not yet shedding their leaves, she stopped. Took his right hand. Placed it on her breast. He was confused. She put her hand atop his, kneaded it, causing him in turn to knead her breast. Her dark eyes pleaded, intent obvious. In their special way of conversing, he started:

You should be in love the first time.

I love you.

But we can never be a couple, since I must return home.

I know, and I could never go with you, leave my family.

Then we must not do this.

On the contrary, we must. I want to remember you, the first. Someday I will marry, probably a marriage arranged by my parents. I want to love someone I choose, if only for one night, to keep in my heart forever. To keep you in my heart forever. I owe you my purity. I offer it to you as a gift of love. It is all I have to give. When I have entrusted it to you, it can never be taken from me. It will be in your safekeeping. I will always have it because you will always have it, and will cherish in your heart the spirit in which it was given. Do you see?

Yes. He saw.

So he took her to earth, and they kissed and caressed and fumbled, as young lovers do, making up in ardor and willingness for what they lacked in experience, and took of each other, and gave, and cared, and cried out in loving tenderness while the pale moon looked down and the nightbirds sang.

NINETEEN

SOOK MOON HAD TO SEE TY. HAD TO. SINCE THEIR LAST time together, that blissful, wonderful night, something had happened. She had arrived home late, so giddy, so filled with exultation, that her mother had become suspicious. Young women behaved like Sook was behaving for only one reason: She was in love with the American. *Eye-goo!* This was not good; a road with no future could not be allowed.

She approached her husband with some trepidation, justified. He ranted and cursed and kicked one of the chickens; started to kick the hog, but, since the creature weighed over one hundred kilos, thought better of it. Instead, he yelled at Mama Moon some more.

Directly, she'd had enough. Read him the riot act, Korean version. He throttled back on the invective, swallowed the bulk of his profanity, asked his wife what might be done. What else? she replied. Send her away. Do you not have a sister-in-law who speaks often of a well-to-do cousin in Yangyang, on the coast? Could you not arrange a visit? A long one? Until the American soldier had gone, back to the States, out of their daughter's life? Yes, he said, he supposed he could do that. Then let it be done, his wife commanded.

Ah, but how Choi Kyu would miss his beautiful daughter—the light of his eye, the spring in his step; her morning prayers, the lilting songs so dear to his heart. She's not dying, argued his wife, just leaving. For a while. Why don't I reason with the American soldier? pleaded Choi. Ha, Americans never do anything except please themselves. Yes, thought Choi, like covering our *koon-dingies* for twenty years, keeping the Communists out of our hair. But he said nothing; in this mood, his spouse was a viper.

It was settled. To Yangyang Sook would go, and not a moment to lose. Her heart was already filled to overflowing with this soldier. Soon maybe some other body part would be equally filled. She must go. Now!

So Sook Moon, apprised of her impending relocation, not knowing where her lover was at the moment, and not allowed on post to search for him—or even send him a message—went to the fence outside the DMZ, where they had picnicked. There she hid herself, waiting for her man.

The man she loved.

Three hundred meters away, unknown to her, just inside the fence, others waited.

For her man.

Love was the furthest thing from their minds.

• • •

Tyler, too, was unhappy. This "Hammer of Thor" business was getting old. Hadn't he learned in the second grade that one guy alone couldn't police society, right all wrongs, settle all scores? Obviously, he had not. Despite the fact that he had terminated North Koreans hither and yon, he didn't feel like he was accomplishing what he'd set out to accomplish.

Which was?

Showing the KPA they couldn't do what they did with equanimity. Had he done that? Yes. Had it stopped them? No. Was it likely to stop them? No.

Hammer of Thor. What a code name. At least he hadn't picked it; some shoulderboard at division headquarters had. At first he'd not minded, in fact thought it romantic, fitting. Tough sounding. So how tough was he?

Not very. Most of the firefights he'd been involved in he had set up, or the engagement was from a distance. These KPA troops seemed to him like Boy Scouts. Or Keystone Cops. Laurel and Hardy in Korea. Dave, on the other hand, had been wounded twice, nearly died in an airplane crash, fought his way back through enemy lines—carrying a wounded pilot—doing his fighting up close and dirty.

All I ever do, with one or two exceptions, is dial long distance, zap some sap four football fields away who never knows what hits him. His pals try madly to locate me before I zap them, but never do. Where's the valor in that?

He thought of Sook Moon.

She accepted him for what he was.

Which didn't appear to be much.

• • •

"They're sending you in a day early, Vance," said his platoon leader, closing the screen door behind him. Ty was on the floor beside his bunk doing leg raises, a Tootsie Pop in his mouth, breathing easy. "There're reports of tunneling explosions in a new sector. You're to check it out, now that you're a bona fide tunnel rat." The lieutenant smiled; caramel adhered to a tooth. He took another bite of Milky Way.

"Yes, sir," Ty responded, Lynyrd Skynyrd in the background, "Sweet Home Alabama" over Armed Forces Radio.

"Break your fast at 0430, ready to travel at 0500." Munch.

"Yes, sir," Skynyrd fading, the record spinner laying some vibes on his audience.

"Good luck, soldier," the words slurred from goo.

"Thank you, sir," to the looey's departing backside, Billy Preston wading in, "Nothing from Nothing."

That's me, Ty thought. *What I'm doing don't take nothing from nothing.*

• • •

The jeep dropped Tyler nearly a mile from his entrance point. He cut through the woods, brooding, only half paying attention to what he was about. As he neared the gate, he became more focused. Stopping at the edge of the road, he took up his binoculars and glassed the stretch as far as he could see, left and right. In both directions the road curved out of sight within two hundred meters. The gate was fifty meters to his right front, diagonally across the road. *Strange,* he thought. *Don't hear any birds.*

He moved into the open.

• • •

Sook Moon saw Tyler step into the road. She started to stand up, but something held her back. What? She swiveled her head. Quiet. Very quiet. She watched Ty approach the gate, dig in his pocket for a key.

Spotted something in her peripheral vision. Movement to her left, inside the fence.

There!

A KPA soldier shifted his position slightly, rifle at shoulder, waiting for the American to open the gate. Jumping up, she yelled to Ty in Korean while pointing frantically at the soldier, yelling again, "Look out!"

• • •

But there was not one North Korean. There were five. The one Sook Moon had seen also saw her when she hollered and stood, pointing at him. He swung his AK-47 toward her, took aim, and pulled the trigger.

• • •

Tyler Vance, key in hand, did not understand what Sook Moon was yelling, nor what she was pointing at. But he had a suspicion. Being of quick mind and agile body he wasted no time, but took three strides toward the other side of the road and dove for the ditch, hearing two AKs open up to his right rear, feeling the impact as six bullets smashed him from behind.

• • •

Sook Moon saw Ty move for the ditch, diving headlong. She also saw his movement speeded up by the multiple impacts of several bullets, even as she heard their siblings whiz past her ear to thwack into trees behind her. Her man was in trouble, had been hit, needed her. Now. He was thirty meters away, facedown in a ditch.

Committing herself, Sook ran low to the ground, twisting, dodging, making herself as small a target as possible, going to help, heedless of her own safety, bullets kicking up sod around her, pruning branches, showering bark in her eyes. She saw only Tyler, bleeding, lying in the ditch.

Fate dealt itself in.

Sook Moon would never see Yangyang.

• • •

Tyler, breath knocked out of him from five simultaneous hits to the PRC-10 on his back, heard Sook coming and looked up. She dove nearly on top of him, her hands running over his body, seeking wounds. Only one, the sixth bullet, through the top of the trapezius where it joined his neck on the right side. Bloody but not mortal.

"Where did you come from?" he said.

She just smiled joyously; her lover was okay.

Rat-tat-tat-rat-tat-tat-rat-tat-tat! came the distinctive AK rattle.

Maybe not okay for long.

Using sign, Tyler filled her in on his plan, all the while staying as low as possible and shouldering out of the ruined radio, patting it once for saving his life, and readying his Grease Gun. He helped her into his flak jacket, showed her quickly how to use a grenade—simple, just pull the pin and throw the motherfucker as far as you can—and stuck two in her hands.

The idea was this: they'd crawl as far forward as they could, as fast as they could, staying as low as they could, hoping to escape discovery by their assailants, who were still chewing up the landscape around them with their rifles. Soon the North Koreans would tire of this blazing-away-at-things-they-couldn't-see game, and it would be just a matter of time before they'd blow the gate somehow, come storming through to see what they'd wrought. When that happened, the two of them would be elsewhere, and as the KPA soldiers came across the road for a reconnoiter, Ty would pop up from a surprise vantage point and blast them to hell, or wherever North Koreans went. Sook must use the grenades in self-defense *only;* she was to keep her head *down,* no matter what.

Sure.

The pair had covered thirty meters or so when the guns quit barking. Twenty more when three explosions rattled the earth—poom! poom! poom!—one right behind another.

Grenades. There went the gate.

Get ready.

Heads down—being seen now would seriously rock the boat—they listened hard.

Pitter-patter of little feet, shod in combat boots manufactured north of the Imjin, no doubt.

It was time.

Ty came up out of the ditch, catching flat-footed three KPA troops who'd run through the gate, bayonets fixed, full magazines in place, itchy fingers on ready triggers, only to stand, dumbfounded, wondering where their prey went.

Over here.

They spotted Tyler as he opened up on them while charging like a madman, taking the immediate danger away from Sook Moon, his submachine gun stuttering in its slow-motion way, spitting 230-grain bullets in their direction, some biting flesh, others whining by, still too far for real effectiveness as they returned fire, one taking another hit, going down, then the second, Tyler catching a round through his thigh, near the bone, in and out, stumbling, replacing the magazine as the one Korean still standing continued to fire, divots rising and falling all around, magazine in, *click,* continue on, limping a little, firing, the Korean firing back from the hip (*why doesn't he raise the rifle? sight the thing; that's no way to shoot*), then watching the man take three rounds in the chest, two to the face, blood flying like in a Peckinpah movie, slow-motion, the tachypsychia effect a reality, Ty's mind assimilating so fast his body couldn't keep up, then spinning as his leg gave way, falling heavily, another soldier charging through the gateless fence, bandaged—Lee Jin Ku from Panmunjom, leering wild-eyed, not shooting, planning to skewer him with his bayonet, Ty's Grease Gun empty now, reaching for his pistol as the distance closed, lying on it, couldn't get it free, grey-green oblong streaking in from his left, like a baseball, Ku saw it too, dodging, too late, a grenade, air mail from Sook Moon, Ty ducking, covering his head, curling into a ball, back exposed as the grenade hit, exploded, separated Lee Jin Ku not only from his testicles, but from many other parts, several of them bouncing to earth nearby.

Well, he was a tough son of a bitch.

Held a grudge, though.

Vance rolled, coming up with the handgun as the last

soldier boiled through the opening the KPA had blasted in the fence. Sook Moon was running toward them, second grenade in hand, reaching for the pin. "Stay down!" Tyler yelled. Unheeded. The North Korean snapped off a shot at the woman; her blood spattered the rocks as she fell facedown.

"No!" Ty yelled, the .45 bucking in his fist, fat slugs striking home, the Korean not going down, returning fire, one round smashing into Ty's canteen at his hip, soaking him with water, then a second of Tyler's bullets sank deep, finding bone, turning the soldier away, deflecting his aim, the man's bullets kicking dirt and rocks into the air, a geyser of debris, Ty shooting again, again, to the neck, the shoulder, the Korean staggering, keeping his feet through extraordinary effort, rifle muzzle swinging around, spitting flame, then nothing, the weapon empty.

Ty's too.

The two stood, ten feet apart, chests heaving, bloodied bodies, enmity so intense it was palpable. The North Korean swayed, eyes glazing. He glanced at Sook Moon, prostrate, also bloody, and sneered. Ty hit him then, once, with all he had, extended-knuckle to the left eye. The man dropped like a stone, sneering no more. And died.

• • •

Ty limped to Sook Moon as fast as he could, after reloading his pistol. North Koreans usually operated in squads of six; he'd accounted for only five. Perhaps the other had sought a healthier clime. Or was lurking nearby.

He turned her gently, examining the wound. She

opened her eyes, brimming with pain. No tears.

It's over, he assured her. Let me look at you. She lay still. The bullet had quartered through her left arm from the front, piercing the muscles then exiting to graze her upper rib cage at the back. A lot of blood but no serious damage, assuming the flow could be stanched. He used a tourniquet on her arm, a pressure bandage on her side.

Worked fine.

He gave her an ampule of morphine for the pain, a little something McElroy had obtained for him since he worked alone, far from medical assistance. Thirty minutes later, he held her in his arms as she lay quietly, hurting no longer. Thirty-five minutes and she was asleep.

He hid her in a crevice, carefully wrapped, comfortably reclining, water at hand. Then he ran, bum leg and all, to the nearest OP, where he radioed McElroy, requesting that the captain come personally, bringing a medic and no one else, telling him where.

He then ran back to Sook Moon, explaining his actions to no one at the OP—vexing the OIC to no end—not even letting a medic examine his wounds.

Sook was still asleep, so he cradled her head in his lap and listened for McElroy's jeep.

• • •

"She saved my life, Captain."

McElroy was not happy. "How can I cover this up?"

"You'll think of a way, sir."

The medic was caring for Sook Moon, properly. He said over his shoulder, "Bullet cut an artery in the arm. If you hadn't applied the tourniquet, she'd be dead now."

"She need a transfusion?" Tyler asked.

"Probably not."

McElroy said, "Okay. I'll see she's attended to at the base. Then you can take her home. I'll find you a driver."

"Thanks. I mean it."

"Hell, boy, if she saved your bacon, she deserves it. Now let me see that leg."

• • •

A week later, Tyler visited Sook Moon at her home. She had explained everything to her parents. Everything. They treated him differently, now.

Using a translator from the base, Tyler told them the story from his viewpoint, leaving out the attempted rape. Told them how much he respected her, cared for her, admired her. They beamed with pride.

Sook Moon walked him to the jeep. It is best that we not see one another, she said. I understand, from Ty. You will live here, she declared, touching her heart. And you, he rubbed her cheek with a forefinger. You will not be sent to your cousin's? She shook her head. You are no danger now, she said, as far as they are concerned. One tear, at the corner of her eye, but trying not to. Do not forget me. Ever, so long as there is earth and sky. Promise. I promise, he said.

The sun was setting as he climbed into the jeep, profile limned by the dying light. The tear left her eye, tracking down her cheek, followed by many more as she watched him ride away.

For the last time.

TWENTY

WITH A HOLE HEALING IN HIS UPPER BACK, ANOTHER IN his leg, Tyler C. Vance, Sergeant E-5, Infantry, had been placed on light duty. It was driving him nuts. Bored with the inactivity, he saw every movie that came to base, often twice, spent considerable time in the library, consumed umpteen chocolate milk shakes (but no Moon Pies), and performed physical therapy in the gym, bathing in the whirlpool, swimming, jogging, lifting, performing katas. He was offered exercise of a different sort by PFC Lisa Craft.

"Hiya, stud," she greeted him the first day after his singular battle just outside the DMZ, he lying in bed in the infirmary, leg elevated, her heady perfume and brazen manner obviously intended to elevate another limb. It didn't work; he remained unaffected. She knew because she looked carefully at the targeted area. A second attempt was needed, little hands-on stimulation.

"How high were you hit?" she said, lifting the covers, placing a hot hand on his already warm body. He brushed it aside, resettled the covers, tucking them under his leg.

"Midthigh," he answered.

"Oh, good. The lower the better. When you gonna be up for a little exercise, pun intended?"

"When I'm sixty-five, maybe later."

"Sooner, I'll bet," she said, reaching again, tugging at the bedclothes.

He slapped her hand.

She withdrew it, rubbing the contact area ruefully. "What, you a Quaker or something?"

"No, just selective."

She was not easily put off, almost impossible to insult. "I don't want to marry you, stud, just enjoy you a little. Or a lot. You're far and away the best pickings I've seen since I got here."

"Thanks."

"I have nothing communicable."

"Besides a pushy manner?"

She smiled. "Don't put off 'til tomorrow what you can hump today."

"In this case, neither today nor tomorrow."

"I'm not pretty enough for you?"

"Sure you're pretty, sexy too, in a rough-hewn way, and filled out like you mean it."

"Then"—she again put her hand where it didn't belong—"what's the problem?"

"I'm just not into recreational sex, despite my having become glandularly functional in the sixties."

"Any kind of sex is recreational sex, unless it results in babies."

"Not so. Sex is for the mind, the spirit. It's just channeled there physically."

"What bullshit. You a virgin, that it?"

"It's really none of your business, but no, I'm not. But

I've never had sex with someone I didn't know well and have an emotional attachment to. Multiple sexual liaisons are not my bag. Sorry."

"I'm not multiple. There's just little ol' me." She leaned close to his ear. "But let me get hold of you, and you might think there's two or three. Or wish there were."

"No, thanks. Sex without emotional involvement is purely scatological. But I am flattered by your interest."

"Don't worry. It won't go away. We might even get emotionally involved, who knows?" She winked, then said, "Well, I told Chaplain Smith I'd look in on you. I'll be seeing more of you soon, I hope. Lots more." She started to leave.

"Will you explain something to me?"

"Anything, lover."

"The other day in the 'Z, none of you seemed especially upset over the casualties in the other jeep. I've wondered why."

"I grew up in Chicago. My brother was in a street gang. I held him in my arms while he died, his intestines lying beside him in the street, stomach cut wide open by a rival gang member. I was gashed, too, but not badly. As for Chaplain Smith, he did a tour in Vietnam in '69, Infantry Division near Gia Dinh. He held a lot of boys' hands as they died. I don't know about that big sergeant you tossed around like a bag of potatoes. Way I peg him is he doesn't give a fart about anything but acting macho. In my neighborhood, he'd have been reduced to a pile of sniveling viscera long before now."

"You don't sound like a PFC."

"Look who's talking, Mr. Scatological. For your information, and in hopes my proving to be a lady of quality will help land the two of us in a sleeping bag together, I attended the University of Illinois at Chicago for two years, until the money ran out. I'm not smart enough to nab a scholarship, and my family has less money than the Old Shoemaker, so I let Uncle Sam take advantage of my blossoming young body for four years in order to bleed him dry later in the form of the G. I. Bill."

"Incest." He grinned. "Disgusting."

"One takes what one can get. I'll administer favors to anyone who can either ring my chimes or boost me up the ladder, regardless of whether they do it with one hand on my rear. Other hands have been there before."

"Yours is a worldly attitude, and not without practicality. I like you better all the time."

She arched her brows several times, rapidly, up and down, knocking the ash from an imaginary cigar. "Just say the secret woids."

He laughed openly now. "Which are . . . ?"

" 'Spread 'em.' "

She left him shaking his head in wonder, smiling to herself. *Might snare him, yet.*

• • •

Two letters from Dave while Ty convalesced. The first went thus:

Dear what's-your-name,

I'm going home.
Naa-na, na-na-na.

Love,
Dave

The second, less succinct, said:

My dear Tyler,

I'm home. HURRAY!!!!!!! Are you? Is it cold there yet? Some guys I met in 'Nam told me it gets cold as hell in Korea about November, which my calendar says is coming up soon. Wear your long undies, Old Buddy.

What do you do over there, anyway? You never tell me in your letters and Odie says you never tell him and your mama neither. What gives? You top secret or something? Give us a break. We worry. Or at least they do. What do I care?

Keep your head down in the 'Z, And WRITE, you creep.

So long,
David (remember me?)

November arrived, and, as Dave had predicted, so did the chill, blowing down out of China as if it were welcome. It wasn't. Tyler was neither used to nor fond of really cold weather. But at least he was mending. He hounded McElroy unmercifully, wanting to return to active duty.

On November ninth, the captain relented. "How are you, really? No bullshit simply because you're bored from seeing movies and playing with yourself."

"My back's fine, and so's the leg. Just a wee bit stiff, is all."

" 'Stiff' ain't the same as 'well.' "

"That's not what Lisa Craft says."

"I notice her sniffing around you like a doe in estrus. You porking her?"

"Sir! I descend from Southern aristocracy! Besides, there's a letter from my mother on that footlocker, so please watch your fulsome metaphors."

"If I talked like you I'd be a colonel by now."

"Any day. I spoke to the general about you."

"I heard he stopped by. The man thinks you can take on the whole North Korean army by yourself."

"You mean I can't?"

"Probably not all of them. They've got a couple million troops."

"I could rest between engagements."

"You're full of shit as a Christmas goose. Okay. Take a run with me tomorrow. Keep up and I'll send you back in."

They ran and Ty did. Easily.

The following day, Sgt. Tyler C. Vance was dropped off for a three-day patrol of the Korean DMZ. It would be his last.

The date was November 11, 1974.

Veterans Day.

An omen.

TWENTY-ONE

"THE ZIPS HAVE BEEN ZIPPING ACROSS THE WIRE AND planting mines around the base of OP 17," McElroy had told him in the briefing room prior to his departure, "working only at night. Usually when seriously cold weather starts, clandestine activity grinds to a halt, but not in this case. A spec-4 from B Company lost his leg last week, and our boys up at 17 are spending the first two hours every morning sweeping for last night's implants. Not only is it irritating as hell, it's demoralizing."

"And you'd like for me to speak to the KPA? Ask them to give it a rest?"

"If you don't mind."

"With the Model '97 or the Grease Gun?"

"Your choice. Never tell a technician what tools to use."

"It's why I like working with you, Captain, you give me maneuvering room."

"How else could I keep a tiger under any semblance of control? But you be careful. Most of your patrolling has been in the daytime up 'til now. Night work's different."

"Half my field training in Thailand was done at night."

"I'll say no more."

So here Tyler was, sneaking around in the dark, looking for North Korean saboteurs without benefit of luminosity. Even the moon was against him, hiding its light under a bushel. For two nights he hunted, waited, circled, waited, listened, waited, tapped his foot to internal music, singing remembered lyrics in his head.

Nothing.

At 0400 on the morning of the third day, he was setting up a "cold" camp, one without a fire. He munched jerky, raisins, and Oreos, drank from his canteen until he became drowsy. Moving a hundred meters as silently as a ladybug on cotton bunting, he unrolled his sleeping bag, stripped off his boots, and slid into the bag's icy confines, then waited for his body heat to warm up the bag. He took with him into his nest a canteen and his .45 pistol, stuck his pack underhead as a pillow, and fell asleep in three minutes.

• • •

Lee Pyong San, a private in the Korean People's Army, had finished planting a mine on the road leading to an American observation post, the first he'd ever set for real, not in training. He was nineteen, a peasant from Sakcho, way up near the China border. Conscripted like many other soldiers in the KPA, he would perform his duty for an allotted time, then go home to work hard in a munitions plant from dawn to dusk, eking out a meager living.

Ah, but Lee had family—his mother and father, many

uncles and aunts, cousins, even a nephew, and his beautiful new wife, Ky. How he loved her. Though young—barely seventeen—she was with child. Lee hoped that with his army experience as a springboard, he might nab a better-paying job at the factory, move up the ladder more quickly, raise the living standard for his wife and child. One must work hard and hope.

He stopped at the edge of a clearing, the rendezvous point with Liu Biao, a crusty sergeant from Haeju. The sky was becoming light; they had best make their way back across the line before they were spotted, or worse yet, had to dig in and spend the day here. They'd brought no food along.

A slight rustling of leaves heralded the arrival of Biao, a cruel, arrogant, but competent man. "Did you finish?" asked the sergeant, Russian cigarette hanging from his lips, its smell enticing Lee, who could seldom afford cigarettes; Ky counted on his meager earnings for food and necessaries.

At Lee's timid nod, Biao sneered, "You are such an incompetent. You have no *iron*." He made a fist, clenching so tightly his hand shook. "I don't know why I let them saddle me with you. You are sure you set the mine properly?"

"Yes," Lee answered, tired of the constant badgering.

"I hope so. When they come to sweep, they will not look where it is hidden. One of them should trigger it, or perhaps one of the three that I set. Then we will see Imperialist entrails fly!" He smiled like a fox about to disrupt the henhouse.

You, I do not like very much, thought Lee as the pair moved off.

• • •

It was 0815. Ty was warm and snug in his sleeping bag, dreaming of back home, when he woke, bladder screaming. *I'm too warm to get out of this bag,* he thought, changing his position slightly, reaching for sleep. No good; his bladder was insistent, irritating, sleep-denying.

Shit.

He crawled halfway out of the bag, leaves crunching beneath him, checked the breeze, and aimed accordingly. No sense getting wet pissing against the wind.

• • •

Lee Pyong San heard leaves crunch nearby, despite the gusty breeze, and looked in Tyler's direction, spotting him just as the American soldier climbed to his knees to gain relief. Lee tapped his sergeant on the shoulder and pointed, saw the wicked grin form on Biao's face. The distance from them to the American was less than fifty meters.

"Should we circle around, go into that pine thicket?" he asked Biao.

"Why? Are you frightened?"

"I thought we were avoiding American patrols."

"He's not on patrol, you dolt. He is napping in his sleeping bag for warmth, the jellyfish."

"He must have friends nearby."

"Where?" the sergeant asked, lip curling. "Perhaps he is alone."

"So what do we do?"

"Circle, make absolutely certain no other soldiers are

in the immediate area. If not, then this may be the Killer Bee I have often heard of, the one who flies alone, stings so many, killing sometimes from the haven of distance, sometimes up close, spraying our comrades with bullets from ambush like the coward he is. If it is so—that he is alone and the Deadly One—then we will be hailed as heroes when we take with us his head."

"We are going to shoot him?"

"No, offal breath. First, we will check things out. Then, if he is alone, we will attack and slay him as he lies, asleep and unsuspecting. Remove the bayonet from your rifle or you might stick me with it."

"But what if—"

"Shut up! You circle that way. I will go this way. We'll meet," he pointed, "by that spruce. If you see we are outnumbered, slip away and cross the line alone. I'll meet you back at camp."

They parted, circled, and, since Ty was indeed alone and asleep and unsuspecting, they met at the spruce and made their final plans to kill him.

Lee Pyong San, unfamiliar with edged-weapon combat, did not like this business, but went along anyway.

He was, after all, a soldier in the People's Army . . .

Who had never killed a soul.

• • •

Dave's face was in his dream, screaming, *"Get up! Get up! Get up!"* when Tyler heard the swish of branches being brushed aside, the muted crunching of leaves underfoot, and came out of his bag in a hurry, to his knees, sleep-filled eyes blurry, .45 in hand, wiping off the safety as it came up, seeing a soldier running at him from the right, bayonet held high for a downward slash, like a novice. His pistol was swinging on target when a boot came from nowhere to kick it out of his hand; it landed at the opposite end of his sleeping bag with a dull thud. Springing to his feet, he spun counterclockwise, letting the attacker's own momentum carry him past, then elbowed Biao in the left kidney, sending him sprawling. Lee, still running straight in and now almost on top of Tyler, swung the blade down in a broad arc, which Ty merely helped along, leaning away slightly as the bayonet sliced downward past his head, grabbing his assailant's hand with both of his, forcing a change of the point's direction, now not only downward but inward, toward Lee's body, into it, the point sinking easily between two ribs, slicing into the right lung, hanging up on the ribs, staying, as the man's legs deserted him and he fell atop the bag. Ty'd had no choice but to dispatch this man as quickly as possible and return his attention to the other, who was now scrambling toward the .45 there on his bag. He kicked out swiftly, catching the diving man on the temple, knocking him rolling, senseless, to fetch up against a boulder. Vance was on him in a flash, to finish it.

In less than twelve seconds the fight was over.

It took Lee longer than that to die.

• • •

Tyler walked over to Lee Pyong San. The little Korean sat with his back to a lightning-killed tree, its branches swaying slightly in the wind. He held the bayonet—blade still buried deep in his chest—with both hands. Blood leaked between his fingers, threaded its scarlet way down his shirtfront, pooled in his navel. He breathed heavily, frightened to death, afraid of death, looking at death. Ty squatted on his heels beside him, pried one hand away from the blade, noted its entrance point, knew the man was dying. Started to stand. The soldier reached out his hand, grabbed Tyler's leg: Stay.

Ty stayed, again squatting on his heels.

The little Korean lifted his fingers to his mouth, miming taking a drag from a cigarette. Ty patted his pockets, spread his hands, shook his head: I don't smoke.

The Korean pointed to the dead sergeant Biao. Tyler went over, turning the body away so the young soldier wouldn't have to view the carnage, and found the smokes. Matches, only three left.

Ty'd never had a cigarette to his lips, but he lit one now, not inhaling, blowing out a mouthful of foul smoke and placing the butt carefully between the little soldier's lips.

Lee drew hard and long, then coughed hard and long, but seemed satisfied. His next puffs were shorter, produced no hacking. There was blood on his lips.

Tyler again started to stand, but the Korean stopped him. Making a gesture as if giving a shot, Ty pointed to his pack, then to the soldier's arm, made a horrible face as if pain-wracked, then relaxed it: I can take your pain away.

The soldier shook his head.

So Tyler squatted.

The Korean pointed to himself. "Lee," he said.

Tyler tried to smile, found that he couldn't.

The Korean pointed at Ty: And you are?

Ty couldn't respond for the constriction in his throat.

The soldier understood. He patted Ty's leg, as if saying: It's all right.

"Tyler," Ty managed to get out around the lump.

The small Korean tried it once, not doing badly for someone who had never spoken a word of English nor met a single American.

Until this one . . .

Who had killed him.

"Tyler," he said again, liking the feel of the word, the way it rolled off his tongue, then another puff on the cigarette.

"Lee," Tyler said.

Lee Pyong San smiled. "Lee," he admitted.

More blood from his lips, coughing deep, hoarse, and liquid.

Foamy blood now, spilling onto his chin.

Ty wiped it off carefully with a handkerchief.

Lee nodded his thanks.

They sat, Ty crossing his legs, the squat too uncomfortable to maintain indefinitely.

The Korean put a hand on Ty's knee, obviously needing human contact.

Ty sat helpless, not knowing what else to do. They were only boys, these men.

Lee touched the ring finger of Ty's left hand—where there was no ring—arching his brows: Are you married?

Ty shook his head.

Lee pointed at himself proudly.

Ty nodded in understanding.

Using his free right hand, the left still tightly clutching the bayonet that protruded from his thin body, Lee made a rounded motion at stomach level, then touched his ring finger.

Oh, God! His wife is pregnant, thought Ty, eyes filling. He didn't know what to say, what to do, how to comfort a man he had just killed. He was too far from home.

Like this North Korean . . .

Who would never see his again.

Lee grabbed Ty's hand, clutched it tightly, spasming, lids shut tightly against the pain, the anguish . . .

The certainty.

Then he relaxed, opened his eyes, pointed a quivering finger at himself, and said, "Lee."

Tyler nodded his head vehemently. "Lee," he said. "I'll remember." *Please forgive me.*

The Korean smiled weakly, squeezed Ty's hand once again, and died.

Gently, Tyler pulled the blood-soaked bayonet from the dead boy's chest, tears streaming, then threw it angrily, as far as he could. It clattered on some rocks, came to rest beneath a seedling fir.

There it lay.

Debased.

On the ground.

TWENTY-TWO

TYLER CARRIED LEE PYONG SAN THE HALF MILE TO THE MDL, in his arms. The small North Korean wasn't heavy; still, it was a trial. His arms ached from fatigue; his legs ached from the strain; his back ached from the effort. But, he never faltered, stopped not once to rest.

"Who the hell is that?" said the OIC of OP number 17.

"It's Sergeant Vance, carrying a chink, sir. Guy appears to be dead."

"Why the hell is he carrying him toward the MDL?" The lieutenant swung his glasses northward. Sure enough, some North Koreans had spotted Vance, were pointing at him, agitated. The lieutenant put his binoculars back on Vance. "The dumb bastard's not armed. Not even a pistol. Is he defecting?"

"Defecting, sir? Sergeant Vance? I doubt that, sir." *The lieutenant's gone nuts,* thought Specialist Tamarind.

"Someone yell down to him. Ask him what the hell he thinks he's doing. Right now!"

So, as Tyler Vance approached the MDL, a contingent

of KPA troops ran down the hill from their OP, rifles at port arms, while American soldiers atop OP 17 whooped and yelled and told Vance to Stop right there, or Come back, or Hit the deck.

Ty kept on walking, stumbling occasionally, tripping over a root or stone, never falling, one foot after the other, until he stopped, two feet this side of the wire.

Eight angry AK-47 rifles pointed at him, twenty feet away. He looked at them, unarmed, unafraid, but not unashamed.

On the hill above Ty and to his rear, two American M-60 machine guns were trained on his back. The lieutenant, chewing a cigar, said, "If he tries to cross the line, kill him."

"Sir?"

The lieutenant swung his head, glaring at Tamarind. "You heard me." Back at Vance through the binoculars. *Go ahead, asshole, try to cross that line.*

One of the North Koreans handed his rifle to a fellow soldier, straightened his cap, and walked over to Ty, stopping two feet north of the wire. Said something in Korean, face a granite mask. Ty, not understanding, just looked at him. The Korean glanced up at OP 17, noted the machine guns, back at Ty, then down at the small Korean soldier in the American's arms. His face softened. Not dramatically, just a blurring of hard lines, a slight lift at the corners of his mouth.

He'd known Lee Pyong San well. Liked him, where many of the others hadn't. Called him Little Lark, because he was tiny and loved to sing.

He looked into the American's eyes. Saw the pain. Held out his arms. The G.I. took a step, placed the small, still form in the big Korean's arms, biting his lip.

He has regret, the North Korean thought. *It took a huge heart to bring Lee Pyong San here. And such bravery. Several of those with me would as soon shoot this man as evacuate their bowels. He knows it; it's in his eyes. Yet he is unafraid. What manner of man is this?*

The North Korean turned away, trudged past his compatriots, up the hill, bearing Little Lark.

Tyler watched them go while machine guns were aimed at his back, though he neither knew nor cared. As soon as the big KPA and his small burden were out of sight, he spun on his heel, trekked back to his gear, ignoring repeated commands from the lieutenant: "Get up here, right now! Do you hear me? I'll have your ass, mister! You got that!"

Back at his campsite, Sergeant Vance radioed for an early pickup, and soon left the Korean DMZ forever.

TWENTY-THREE

"WHERE IN THE HELL DID YOU THINK YOU WERE TAKING him?"

"To someone who could get his body home to his family."

"We'd have seen to that," said McElroy.

"How would I know?" Vance argued. "You never told me how North Korean bodies are disposed of."

"You never asked!"

The man had a point. "I wanted to be certain Lee made it home, Captain."

"Lee? How do you know his name?"

"He told me."

"He *told* you. How nice. Did you hold his hand while he died?"

"As a matter of fact, I did."

McElroy goggled. Was he in the Twilight Zone? "Clue me in here," he said. "Didn't you tell me these two guys came at you while you were asleep? With bayonets? You think in retrospect they just wanted to show you their cutlery?"

"No. I think they were trying to kill me."

"Correct me if I'm wrong, but didn't you do to them what they were trying their damnedest to do to you, only you did it right?"

"That's what I said, Captain. But only one of them . . ."

"What? Only one of them what?"

"Only one was serious."

"Serious? Serious! How the hell do you try to kill someone and not be serious?" He *must* be in the Twilight Zone.

Ty shrugged. "I don't know. He was serious, but . . . inept."

"Inept? Good. If he weren't you'd be dead!"

"But there was no animosity."

"Oh, I get it. He was trying to kill you, but it was all in fun."

"You don't understand. Maybe you don't want to understand. I guess he had been told to kill me . . . well, not me, but Americans. So he tried because he had been told to, not because he wanted to, or had anything against me personally. He had been indoctrinated."

Do-do-do-do, do-do-do-do. Any minute he'd hear Rod fucking Serling's voice come out of the wall. "He was a soldier, Vance! Soldiers are fucking supposed to kill each other!"

"Because we're told to."

"Of course! Why else would you?"

"Because it's right!" Vance was heating up, too. "Or because of cruelty, like those first ones I shot to doll rags in the heat of the moment, in retribution for what they did to . . . they didn't have to do that. I doubt they'd been told to. Even if they had, who'd have known? They did it because they were junkyard-dog mean.

"Lee wasn't mean, just a soldier trying to do a job he didn't choose. So he could go home to his pregnant wife."

"How the hell do you know his wife was pregnant? What did you two do out there, exchange résumés while he was bleeding to death!" In his ten years in the military, McElroy had never run across anything like this. He'd seen men lose their nerve, plenty of times, especially In Country. This wasn't like that. He didn't think Vance had lost his nerve. Just his good sense.

"He had a child on the way, Captain. Just like Jas. Now that child will never see its daddy. Just like Jas's youngest daughter. And for what?"

"They're *the other side,* Vance! Get it?"

"So's the other team in a football game, but we don't kill them."

"You couldn't prove it by me watching NFL linemen going after a quarterback."

"They're wrong, too."

"Everybody in the world is wrong but *you,* right!"

"I don't know about that," Vance shouted, "but I do know this! I'm not going to kill for you anymore!"

"You're not going to what!" McElroy shouted back, a vein throbbing in his neck.

"Kill for you anymore!"

"Oh, you're not!"

"That's correct." Calmer now, passion ebbing.

"That's correct, *sir*!" Still pissed, McElroy.

"That's correct, *Captain.*"

"I'm not 'sir' to you anymore now that you don't want

to kill gooks, now that you're a conscientious fucking objector, is that it?"

"I don't respect what you stand for anymore!" Stormy weather again, just that quick. "If you want North Koreans dead, *you* kill them! Quit pulling kids off the street or out of school to do it for you! Wash your own fucking linen!"

In Tyler's face now, chin jutting like the prow of a schooner, McElroy gritted, "That sure as hell wasn't your attitude a few days ago. 'Please let me go kill more Commies, Captain, sir. I'm bored stiff watching movies and pinching little Korean gals' asses.' "

McElroy knew immediately he'd made an error in judgment. A major error in judgment. Vance looked at him as a bobcat might regard a mole, eyes aflame, as if deciding whether to maim him permanently or simply break an arm. Then the fire subsided. Embers though, glowing. Don't fan them again. McElroy stepped back, out of easy reach.

Vance said, speaking ever so slowly, picking his way through the rubble of their relationship, "You're right about that. And I was wrong. I've learned just how wrong. I won't make the same mistake again. Ever."

Still trying to find solid ground, McElroy said, "The KPA comes over the line, plants mines, machine-guns Americans on their own turf going about their jobs. You want them to get away with that kind of stuff?"

"No. But as long as the status remains quo, it'll never end. You follow your conscience; I'll follow mine. I've done my part a dozen times over. I'm not going to kill for you anymore. Period."

"We've got a lot of time and money tied up in you, Vance. You can't—"

"And you've received a sound return on your investment. But I have to live with the consequences, not you. No more killing. Not by me, anyway."

McElroy bristled again. "Soldier, you can't tell *me* what you will or won't do. Understood?"

"I've killed my last man for you, Captain."

"Then you're going to jail."

"We'll see."

"You're right. We will. Get the hell out of here. You're confined to quarters until further notice."

"Fine." Vance, starting to turn, stopped in midrotation. "Oh, Captain."

"What?"

He didn't get in McElroy's face, grimace when he said it, shake his fist, stab an angry finger. In fact, his voice was as well modulated as if he were asking for directions to the PX.

He wasn't.

What Tyler Vance said was this: "If you ever impugn Sook Moon in my presence again, you'll be eating soft food the rest of your life."

He meant every word.

Rufus McElroy believed him.

• • •

Before confining himself to quarters, Tyler made two phone calls from the orderly room, one to Lisa Craft, one to his former top sergeant, now about to rotate stateside.

An hour later, Chaplain Charles Smith was sitting on Ty's bunk listening attentively. Next morning, Top joined Ty for chow. He also listened attentively.

The chaplain phoned Odie Vance long-distance to suggest that he get in touch with his congressman immediately. Odie did.

Top called a friend of his, also long-distance. A command sergeant-major. At the Pentagon.

Two days later, the Division Commander, a one-star general, summoned Vance to his office, spoke with him for a half hour, released him from quarters confinement, and sent for Captain McElroy.

• • •

"I'm sending him home, McElroy."

"But, sir . . ."

"Four reasons. One, he's been here much longer than the obligatory thirteen months, and we've no official extension papers on him.

"Two, we've gotten plenty of use out of him. More than any five men, even if they were placed in the same situations he was.

"Three, I've got a chaplain with clout, a top sergeant who seems to know everyone in the Pacific and has served with half the brass in the Pentagon—not to mention a Southern congressman who sits on the Budget Committee—up my ass sideways. Any one of them might be able to take me on. Against all three I'm a gone goose.

"Finally, I like Vance. That soldier did all we asked, and more. This last situation is eating him up. No bullshit. Eating him up.

"By the way, do I need to remind you of the repercussions if he goes to the press with this?"

"Sir, he'd be in violation of the—"

"I know that, McElroy. Won't help us much what we

do to him after the fact, will it? You know the mood this country is in over Vietnam. They'd roast us on a slow spit."

"Yes, sir."

"Send him home. No disciplinary measures whatsoever. His folks want him at Fort Bragg. Assign him there. Captain Smith is arranging for an MOS change to chaplain's assistant. Expedite it. I want Vance home the day before Thanksgiving, earlier if possible. With all the leave time he's accumulated, he won't need to report for duty until after the first of the year."

"Yes, sir. I'll get right on it."

"Captain?"

"Yes, sir?"

"No disciplinary action. Whatsoever."

"Sir."

The meeting adjourned.

• • •

The next day, Tyler took spec-4 Lisa Craft to a movie in celebration of her bump in rank. Chocolate shakes after.

"Chaplain Smith will be back from Seoul tomorrow," she said. "He'll be tickled pink that things went well for you with the general."

"I'm tickled pink. I'll thank him personally for all his help."

"How about thanking me?"

"I am," he said. "Drink up."

"Oh, whoopee. Did you notice I said he'll be returning *tomorrow*?"

"I did notice that, yes."

"Means no one'll be in the chapel tonight."

"Lisa . . ."

"Never mind. Can't blame a girl for trying. Besides, you're leaving soon. I'll be stuck here for six months with only a battery-operated device."

"Lisa!"

"Besides, I want to tell you about my days with the Angels."

Aghast, Tyler said, "You were a . . ."

"Biker's old lady? Yeah. Well, not so old, fifteen. It was fun." She leaned forward and took his arm, hand hot on his skin. "I'll show you my tattoos. I have to take off some clothes, of course, but that's—"

"Lisa."

She grinned maliciously. "One's on my boob, easy to see and nice work, too. The second one is smaller, and lower down. Much lower down."

"Thanks for sharing."

She laughed good-naturedly. "You are such a prude." Then, lowering her voice, "But such a hunk."

"Can we change the subject?"

"Sure." And they did. But after a few moments, Ty stood and shoved back his chair, indicating a readiness to leave. So she sighed heavily, let him pay, and they decamped.

Three days later he departed Pusan, looking out one of the airliner's portside portholes a few moments before falling asleep, having his last look at the Land of the Morning Calm.

• • •

A day of processing in Fort Lewis, Washington, then standby flights cross-country to Richmond, Virginia, where Dave picked Tyler up, literally, and swung him around and around right there in the airline terminal, eleven o'clock at night, grinning like a six-year-old on Christmas morning. Ty hugged him back.

After baggage retrieval, they climbed into Dave's Challenger and headed south, for Greensboro. Dave was effusive, but the conversation soon lagged; it was obvious that Tyler was troubled.

Which would make what Dave had to tell him that much worse.

Dave told him anyway.

• • •

It seemed that Counselor Strobe Roundtree had been smoldering ever since Odie Vance had colluded with that bastard Judge Parker to finesse young Tyler out of a jam. And not only had the Vance spawn gone free, but far out of Strobe's vindicative reach—into the *army,* if you could believe that! So Strobe had sat up late of a night, plotting.

And arguing. With only son, Eldon—star high school fullback, golden-haired lad with the square jaw, 3.87 GPA, and an all-expense football scholarship to State. But unruly Eldon didn't want to *go* to State, nor even to continue playing football. No indeed. The hulking hunk had been so humiliated by the public licking administered by the undernourished Vance shaveling, that all he wanted was to become a tough guy too. A tough *fighting* guy. Then he could smack that undersized putz around like a Ping-Pong ball. But how to do that? Why, join the

Marines, that's how; the Corps made men out of boys. *Semper fi,* and all that crap. Just let him go off to boot camp for a couple months, learn some hand-to-hand, maybe a little training with the blades. Then when Vance was home on leave Eldon could fly up from Lejeune for a weekender and stomp the jerk into a mud pie, maybe carve him up a little.

No, no, no, his father had insisted. Better that Eldon go on off to college, play football, ravage coeds, smoke some pot, have fun, maybe do karate on the side if he wanted to learn to fight. But leave Vance to Daddy.

And so, pretty much, the arguments went, night after night. Nothing was settled; each side was equally obdurate.

So Papa Strobe plotted. Odie Vance made his living running a commercial lake—swimming and fishing—and trained hunting dogs as a sideline. He had many friends in high places—like that damned Judge Parker, not to mention the sheriff, Odie's longtime softball buddy—so any move on Vance had to be clandestine in the extreme or it might come around and bite Strobe in the ass. Better tactically, he decided—at least until the Vance kid returned to roost—would be a strike against Emily Jansen's family. Being a criminal lawyer, Strobe knew plenty of lowlife trash; it would be easy and cheap to have a few such roust the girl, slap her around, maybe molest her a bit for fun. But how much fun could that be? The girl had the brains of a sponge.

No, better to take it out on her family.

At the time Tyler entered the service, Abner Jansen ran a greasy spoon over on Tate, patronized by the college crowd for breakfast and lunch, blue-collar workers for dinner. Mama Jansen worked there too, and Emily's high-school-aged brother, who bused tables or some such. And so Strobe Roundtree, attorney-at-law, decided that he'd punish the entire Jenson family in one swoop, make them wish that their little girl hadn't been so damned standoffish to his playful son. And so he had, right before Christmas of 1972, while E-2 Tyler Vance was knee-deep in basic training at Fort Polk, Louisiana.

• • •

Dave was relating the story: ". . . they came through the front door like customers, but in the middle of the afternoon. When Mr. Jansen told them the place was closed until five, they pulled ball bats out from under long coats and took the place apart. Then Jansen. And Emily's brother, Amos. Mrs. Jansen and Emily had just left to take the day's receipts to the bank, so were spared a beating, or worse." He glanced at Ty as an oncoming car bathed them in light. Tyler's jaw muscles writhed with tension.

Dave continued. "The old man pulled through, but lost his hearing in one ear. Amos lapsed into a coma and died. After, Emily and her mom tried to make a go of it for a few months, fixing the place up with insurance money, but their hearts weren't in it. They sold out and moved to Danville to live with a relative. Old man Jansen stayed to run his other business, a junkyard out Burlington Road. Last I heard, he was still there."

Tyler said, "They ever find the guys who did it?"

"No. Everybody knew who was behind it, but there was no proof of course. The guys got away clean."

Silence for a spell, then Ty asked, "You reckon Roundtree is still pissed?"

Dave nodded. "You bet. And it gets worse." Tyler closed his eyes and listened.

• • •

Eldon Roundtree, immediately after hearing of the carnage at the Jansen eatery, had bearded his dad at the office. "The Jansens had nothing to do with it!"

"Don't yell at me, boy," warned Strobe.

"I want *Vance,* not the Jansens!"

"I understand that, and if that retarded bitch hadn't rebuffed you—"

"She had every right to act like she did, we were out of line. It was Vance who had no business—"

"And he'll get his, don't worry. But for now he's out of reach."

But Eldon had already spun on his heels and was slamming the door on his way out. That afternoon he joined the Marines. Seven months later, he was well trained, in great physical condition, and In Country.

• • •

"So Eldon was in 'Nam the same time you were?" Ty asked Dave as they crossed into North Carolina.

Dave nodded.

"What's the Marine enlistment, three years?"

"Doesn't matter," said Dave.

Tyler looked at him.

"He was killed before half his tour was up. Bouncin' Betty. He was lead man for a recon squad when the mine got him. Pretty much could have shipped him home in a number two can, I understand."

Ty rubbed his face with both hands.

"It's not your fault, bud. You didn't make him pick on Emily, didn't ask him to take a swing at you, didn't tell him to join the Corps, didn't cut his orders to Vietnam."

"I'll bet his daddy doesn't look at it quite that way."

"That's why I only took a week's leave when I got back to the World. Saved the rest for your triumphant return, so you'd have someone to watch your back. Since you still got a year left on your enlistment, and will likely be hieing off to some distant post, I figure ol' Strobe will be hot to move as soon as he hears you're back in town."

"When does your leave start?"

"Tomorrow."

Ty nodded and they motored on.

• • •

Over breakfast waffles and coffee at a Toddle House in Durham, Tyler said: "I don't need this."

After a steaming sip, "What?" from Dave.

"This Roundtree business."

"We'll take care of it, old son. After we scarf up lots of Thanksgiving chow then shoot us a brace of deer, or a mess of rabbits for one of your momma's stews—"

"No."

After another sip and a forkful of waffle, Dave chewingly asked, "No what?"

"Hunting."

Both brows up, Dave swallowed the mouthful. "Why not?"

"All I've been doing the past six months is hunting. That's enough for a lifetime. No more for me. Ever."

"Tell me about it."

So Vance did, leaving out some, here and there, but reliving most of it. Especially Lee Pyong San, Little Lark.

At the conclusion Ty had trouble looking Dave in the eye.

"So what's the problem, ace? That was war."

"Yeah? Whose?"

Big Dave Michaels shrugged his shoulders philosophically. "Ours not to reason why . . ."

"Horseshit. I don't even know for sure how many men I killed, and for what?"

"Democracy? Freedom? The right to drink Pepsi from your choice of can or bottle?"

Despite Dave's attempt at levity, Tyler remained grim.

"Good buddy," counseled David, "I laid more than a few low myself, and it doesn't bother me one whit. Relax, why don't you. Cut yourself some slack."

"Were all of them trying to kill you?"

"Near's I could tell at the time."

"Right. Not so with me. I whacked guys who didn't even know I was in the world. One minute they were easing along, breathing deep of the cool spring air, and the next they were coughing up blood."

There was little Dave could say to that, but after a moment he made one last stab. "Who knows where those guys were headed, Tyler? To slip over the line and shoot up a mess hall? To plant a batch of mines, ambush a patrol, gun down some poor jeep jockey from Pawtucket? How can you possibly know how many American or South Koreans lives you may have saved? Ease up, now, what's done is done. The North Koreans are the bad guys, pard. We're the ones in the white hats."

Ty just shook his head despairingly. "It's not so pat for me anymore, so clearly delineated between black and white. Lately I spend all my time dwelling in the gray."

• • •

While Tyler and Dave were finishing breakfast, a little more than an hour's drive west a man named Tabor was saying: "He hasn't come in via plane, bus, or choo-choo. We have them all covered. A private car, and all bets are off."

Strobe Roundtree sat behind an enormous mahogany desk, a tic at one corner of his mouth, a toothpick at the other. He was big and bluff and well-dressed and rich and fulminous. Everyone who spent much time in his shadow was fearful of him. Except Tabor. Tabor didn't fear anyone.

Roundtree's red-rimmed eyes gleamed coal-like. Speaking around the toothpick he said, "You got someone on his family?"

Tabor didn't bother to answer.

"Of course you do. It's why I pay you so much. How about Jansen's?"

"Why there?"

"Because Vance is a do-gooder. It's probable that his family has kept him apprised of the Jansen situation. Perhaps the boy will go by to pay his respects once he's home."

"Long shot." Tabor's cryptic assessment.

"Humor me."

"Sure. It's why you pay me so much," quipped the laconic ex-cop, and let himself out.

HOME

MULLIGRUBS

IT WAS THANKSGIVING, WITH ITS RICH TRADITION, CEL-ebration, herd of relatives—and oh, such splendiferous fragrances: ham and turkey with corn bread dressing, fried okra, potato salad, pies and peas and homemade black bread, and the uniquely seasonal wine "jelly." Laughter too, for the most part, and ribbing, practical jokes, football talk. Tyler Vance alone seemed to be suffering the mulligrubs, but the arrival of his sister, Anne, freshly down from Pennsylvania with five-year-old scion Mikey in tow, seemed to cheer him up. "Well, you're certainly no taller," she said as Ty folded her into his arms.

(Anne hovered near six feet, nearly four inches taller than her brother. No one in the family had a clue where the altitude came from, though Odie hinted at a milkman in her lineage. Whenever he did so, his wife would wink conspiratorily at those present and proclaim, "Pshaw, an embassy attaché from Tierra del Fuego, during one of my summer trips to D.C. I was staying at the home of a pregnant college friend, eating chicken cacciatore while she upchucked in the bathroom, when in strolled this lean, handsome specimen wearing a tattersall vest and a watch fob straight out of O. Henry . . .")

"And you're no prettier," Ty remarked.

"Don't need to be. I've always been gorgeous. Mikey, this is your uncle Tyler." The boy peeped shyly out from behind his mother's skirt and proferred a freckled smile.

"Hi, Mike," said Uncle Tyler, smiling back.

Later, filled to the brim with food and banter, Tyler sought his sibling in the sitting room, where she sat writing a letter. "To whom doth yon missive wing?" he inquired, settling into a leather chair.

"Nunayer," answered Anne.

"Nunayer?"

"Nunayer business."

"Well, pardon me. By the way, have I mentioned how much older you look?"

"No, so don't." She sighed theatrically. "For your information, I'm writing to a lady by the name of Nancy Fleming, who I have never met and I'm pretty sure you have neither, for which good fortune she should be eternally grateful."

"Why do you think some lady you never met would want to receive an earful—excuse me, an eyeful—from a plebe like you?"

"Because, dear brother, a couple of months ago, Betty Jean and I drove to Wendover to attend a garage sale. There, high on a dusty shelf, sat a stack of even dustier *Jack and Jill* magazines from the late sixties. Corrine Gibbs, the lady who was hosting the sale, allowed as how a buck would buy the stack, so I dug deep, came up with a picture of George, and the deal was done."

"You paid too much. Maybe you should have tried

barter, offered to trade her your collection of Pat Boone 45s or—"

"Shut up. When I got home, I read some of the stories to Mikey at bedtime. He liked them all, but one in particular. He had me read it to him seven nights in a row, and he never fell asleep until after I'd finished. Not once. It's a nifty tale about a boy who loses his magic ring, and what happens when a group of kids help him look for it. It involves bottle caps, tickle ants, worms, a lost child—"

"Tickle ants?"

"And—you'll appreciate this—food."

"Food?"

"Yeah. Popsicles."

"Oh."

"Anyway, I thought I'd write a letter to the author, to let her know how much the story meant to my little honeysuckle."

"And the author was Nancy Fleming."

"Bingo. She lives in Philly, practically next door to me."

"Anne, Philadelphia is not next door to Sewickley, it's clear across the state."

"You've never been much for looks but you're hell for geography."

"It's because my brain is keen and my bloodline clean."

"No milkmen?"

"Nor unctuous South American diplomats."

They laughed together, a fine sound. Odie Vance heard it from the dining room and rejoiced. *Leave it to Annie. Maybe now the old Tyler is truly back,* he thought.

Not really.

• • •

"You ready, Ty?" asked Uncle Clyde from the doorway to the breakfast room.

"For what?" Tyler and Dave were on the back porch. Dave was carving a soap figure. Ty was offering him advice on how to do it.

"For what!" replied Clyde, amazed. "How long've the menfolk in this family been going rabbit huntin' on Thanksgivin' afternoon? Surely not more'n twenty years."

"I forgot, Uncle Clyde. Sorry."

"Well, get on your rabbit-seekin' duds, boy!"

Ty shook his head. "Think I'll pass this time if you don't mind."

"Hellfire, you ain't been in three years, what with the army and all. Don't you—"

"He's a little tired, is all," said David. "Give him a rain check." A sliver of soap dropped at his feet, adding to the pile already there.

Clyde stomped back into the house. "The hell's botherin' your son?" he barked at Leigh.

Leigh looked him square in the eye for maybe ten seconds. "Whatever it is, Clyde, I'm sure he can count on you for understanding. Now go shoot some rabbits, I'm sure they'll enjoy it."

Clyde huffed into the den, where Odie and Darryl waited, encased shotguns at their feet. "The hell's bothering your wife?" he snapped at Odie.

"Clyde," said Darryl warningly.

"What?"

"Her name's Leigh," Odie said mildly. "She's worried about Tyler."

"We're all worried about Tyler," Darryl concurred. "Except maybe one of us."

"Well, I didn't know nothing was—" objected Clyde.

Odie clapped a calloused hand on his elder sibling's shoulder. "We know, brother. You're not the most observant member of the clan, or the most tolerant, so forget it. Let's go stir up some rabbits. The dogs're chompin' at the bit, to split a 'finitive."

"I believe that's mix a metaphor." Darryl laughed.

"College boy," said Clyde. "Knows everything." And, camaraderie rekindled, the trio quit the house.

No rabbits did they find, just one old nutria. It tasted gamey.

JUNKYARD DOGS

INSIDE THE SMOKY OFFICE OF A. J.'S AUTO PARTS, ABNER Jansen walked with a limp so pronounced it made him list, but his grip was firm, his long face split by a grin. There was no gray in the hair, sparse though it was, and few seams in the coffee-colored face. Age indeterminate, visually at least. (Abner was fifty-seven.) "Here, sit, sit," he said, indicating a freestanding bench front seat expatriated from a 1959 Edsel. It was back against a wall, vinyl covering cracked and discolored. Tyler sat. Dave leaned against a doorjamb, arms folded.

"Always hoped to meet you." Abner Jansen was speaking to Tyler. "Sorry about all the trouble you went through on our account."

"Trouble?"

"I talked to Judge Parker, good Christian man that he is. He told me what happened, how that lawyer fellow, Roundtree, more or less forced you into the army. And this one"—he pointed his stubble at Dave. "All on account of your helping my little Emily."

"No trouble, Mr. Jansen."

Abner Jansen tapped out an unfiltered Camel, last from the pack, lit it with a kitchen match he struck on his zipper, tossed the still-smoking stick onto a cluttered desktop. "I hear you had trouble over there," he said. "Him too"—again tilting his chin at David. "Different countries, same kind of trouble. All on account of—"

"A pack of wolves and a sleazy lawyer, Mr. Jansen. Not Emily."

Abner Jansen nodded, once, twice, up and down, slowly, inhaling through his mouth—cigarette clenched in his teeth—exhaling through his nose. "So what can I do for you fellows?"

"Actually, I came to apologize to you."

"You mean 'bout the restaurant?"

"And your son, and you getting busted up. If I hadn't—"

"No way to know that, then. It was pure happenso. Besides, it was prob'ly the best for them, what you did. That Eldon and his crowd always were raising Cain." He grinned abruptly. "Then you come along and chastised them, you surely did."

"And look at the repercussions."

"Roundtree caused all that, not none of us." Abner Jansen began to search through his pockets, then the drawers of his desk, then those in a dilapidated file cabinet. "Well, fudge," he said, obviously dissatisfied with the fruits of his search. "Either of you boys smoke?"

"I'm out," answered Dave. "But if you like, I can make a quick run to the 7-Eleven for you. Or we can stay while you go."

"If you could, I'd appreciate it. Get flustrated when I ain't got my smokes."

"Be right back," Dave said, pushing away from the jamb.

Abner Jansen fished in his pockets again. "Here, let me give you some money."

"My treat," said Dave, and out the door he went. The low V-8 rumble from his Dodge still hung on the air when in strolled three men, tough looking, mean as junkyard dogs, all wearing frock coats. They spread out a little as they entered, and Abner Jansen's eyes grew large with recognition. Ty noticed, his stomach tightening as the realization hit: These were almost certainly the men from the restaurant, the ones who had beaten Abner into the hospital and his son into the ground. Jansen, frightened into immobility, sat petrified as baseball bats came out from under the long coats.

"You had this coming for a long time, kid," the lead dog said, and for an instant, a fleeting, molten moment, Tyler Vance saw a flash of red.

It receded as they came for him.

1069

TABOR SAID OVER THE PHONE, "YOU GOT THREE MEN IN the hospital."

Strobe Roundtree, ten miles away, took a deep breath, exhaling slowly. Today the tic manifested itself in his right eyelid, which flickered rapidly as he knelt by the fireplace, the pine kindling beginning to flare nicely. Soon a conflagration. He crossed the den heavily, sank into a Naugahyde sofa, and tossed off a bourbon. Kentucky. Single malt. After it had scorched its way down his gullet, he said, "Tell me."

"You won't like it. Got a call from our man on the sheriff's. They'd had a 1069 reported, out Burlington Road. Three on one at a junkyard. The one walked, the three were carted off. I checked with the hospital. Missing teeth, multiple lacerations, several broken bones, one guy will need pins in his wrist just to comb his hair. Think you should maybe have warned these guys about Vance?"

Following another shot, Roundtree said, "Hell, he's a punk. Can't weigh 160 pounds."

"Right. Must have got lucky."

Roundtree stared out the window, gaze intent, intense, internecine, his eyelid flickering ominously. "What did they say to the police?"

"The Three Stooges? Nothing, what do you expect?"

"We may have a chance at an assault charge against Vance."

"Oh, you bet. Kid picked a fight with three heavyweights carrying Louisville Sluggers. A jury'd swallow that, no problem."

Roundtree suddenly threw his glass across the room, where it dented the walnut-paneled wall and clattered to the floor unbroken. That made him even madder. He tromped across the room and stomped the glass, which refused to break. He stomped again, catching its edge, causing the glass to skitter away like a poorly hit golf ball. Both eyelids flickered now, like window shades, as in a Bugs Bunny cartoon. Giving up on the recalcitrant shot glass, he returned to the couch and flopped, tossing his big broganed feet onto the glass-topped coffee table. The top cracked, all the way across, with an inflammatory *crink.* Strobe jumped to his feet, grabbed the table by its edge, and overturned it. Since the table weighed more than ninety pounds, it made quite a racket. Retrieving the abandoned phone from where it had fallen to the rug, the big man sank once more into the sofa, breathing sibilantly through his nose.

"Finished with your tantrum?" said the phone.

"Don't," Roundtree growled.

"So, what about our Musketeers?"

"Were they charged?"

"You bet. And there was a witness. Jansen."

Roundtree slid closed his tremulant lids.

"But you needn't worry," Tabor continued. "They won't be out of the hospital any time soon. I'll arrange bail when they are."

"And see to it that they go far away," said Roundtree, covering his pale face with a sweaty palm. "No trial."

" 'Course not. Anything else?"

"Not now. I need to think."

"Don't strain anything. Bye-bye." And Tabor was gone.

Why do I put up with his insolence? thought Strobe Roundtree.

But he knew why.

THE SCARLET CURTAIN

"YOU DID WHAT YOU HAD TO DO, SON," ODIE COMMISerated.

Tyler, seated in his favored wing chair, stared at the carpet covering the sitting-room floor of the Vance ancestral home and said nothing.

"I'm sorry I wasn't there to take part in the festivities," said Dave Michaels, "but it's pretty obvious I wasn't needed."

Tyler continued to scrutinize the carpet.

"There were three of them, with bats," said Uncle Darryl. "They weren't there to play baseball."

The carpet was tightly woven—maroon and black and pale yellow in an intricate pattern.

"Jansen told me they were the ones did him and Amos, and wrecked the restaurant," offered Uncle Clyde.

Ty had never noticed how worn the carpet was.

"Son?" Leigh knelt in front of Tyler, placing her face between his and the floor so he couldn't avoid looking right into her understanding eyes.

"Ma'am?"

"Some right bad things happened in Korea, didn't they?"

He nodded.

"Hurt some folks, didn't you?"

His vision swam as he nodded.

"Pretty bad, I suspect. Maybe permanent."

Tortured nod.

"Haunts you, doesn't it?" Leigh said softly.

Nod.

"Those men today, they give you any say in the matter?"

Watery headshake.

"No conversation, list of demands?"

Shake.

"And Mr. Jansen claims they're the ones who beat him and his boy insensible with baseball bats?"

"Yes."

"Then I suspect they had it coming."

"That's not what's bothering me," whispered Tyler, so low the others in the room could barely hear him.

"Then what, son?"

"I lost control. When I realized who they were, what they'd done, I just . . . lost it. I was never scared, just mad. So mad I saw red. Literally. And before I knew it, there they were on the floor at my feet. Well, except for one. He was inside Mr. Jansen's soft drink box where I'd stuffed him."

"I know that feeling," said Darryl. "Once when I was boxing in a club-level meet, my opponent clipped me in the, ah, jewels. I thought it was intentional, but the ref only gave him a warning. Two rounds later, the schmuck hit me there again. Just as soon as the pain hit me, I flashed red. Next I knew I had broken his jaw, and as he was falling I deviated his septum. When he hit the canvas I dropped on his chest with a knee. They had to pull me off. I got a six-month suspension out of that. It's never happened since, but I can still visualize that scarlet curtain. . . ."

Ty looked over at his uncle. "Doesn't it scare you, knowing something like that is . . . inside you, waiting to . . ."

"Flare up again?"

"Yes."

"I've been in some tough scraps—not like what you've likely been through, of course, but they scared hell—excuse me, ladies—out of me. During some of them, I got plenty mad. But it's never come back."

"Ty?" interrupted Anne. "Maybe if you hadn't lost it, as you put it, you'd be the one in the hospital."

"Not much chance there. They came at me in a bunch, got in each other's way. If they'd taken their time, put two of them circling for an opening while one had my attention, I might have been in real trouble. But they were cocky and overconfident, plus each one of them wanted some of me."

Clyde said, "Well, they sure got their wish."

Odie stifled a smile. It would be inappropriate here; Tyler was deeply troubled. Not to mention frightened. Of himself.

Leigh patted her son's hands. "Sleep on this. Let it go for now."

Ty nodded, climbed to his feet, and went to bed. Everyone seemed relieved, and for the most part they were.

Except Dave.

He'd had a portent.

Which came to pass.

• • •

An uneventful couple of days followed. Dave and Tyler visited old high school chums, shopped early for Christmas presents, worked out in the Vance basement, shinnied up lofty cypress trees seeking mistletoe. They spent a day in the mountains at the farm of Lawrence Goodall, then brought back a freshly cut fraser fir eight and a half feet tall. The entire Vance family—aunts, uncles, nieces, nephews, inlaws and outlaws—decorated it, then went their separate ways. Sister Anne, too, headed back to Pennsylvania, leaving little Mikey with Gran'maw until she returned for Christmas. Before leaving she said to Tyler: "You okay now, little brother?"

He shook his head. "I just can't go on without you."

She grinned and slugged his arm. Pretty hard.

"Ouch," he said.

She grinned wider. "It would take a pickax to make you say ouch for real."

"Wrong. I used to dance with you, remember?"

Laughing now. "I did tend to step on your feet, didn't I?"

"I was the only guy in the neighborhood who had calluses on *top* of his feet."

"Come here, lug."

They hugged and she sniffled, then aimed her AMX north while three houses down, someone watched their every move with binoculars.

• • •

Brenda Ames came by the Vance place early one morning, a bit down in the mouth. Seemed she'd gone through several beaus while Tyler was away, but was currently untethered. More or less. There was this one guy—lived in High Point—she'd spent a weekend at Ocean Drive with, but hey, it was largely platonic, and what about all this Nixon mess?

Tyler listened politely, responded largely by rote, then was blessedly rescued by his mother. "Son, breakfast is ready."

When Brenda left, she was still down in the mouth.

• • •

Christmas was three weeks away, and David and Ty were looking at cars and discussing Tyler's next duty station. On January fifth, Tyler was to report to Fort Bragg for TDY with the XVIII Airborne Corps pistol team. (There'd been no open TO&E slot for chaplain's assistant on the entire base.)

"What a puss," chided Dave. "Shooting a .22 and a .45 every day, under a covered firing point. No formations, not even for pay or roll call. Report for work at seven-thirty, off by four. Eat wherever you want, no more mess-hall chow. Matches at Benning, Lejeune, then the Midwinter Swing down in Florida. You'll go soft. Get a man's job, soldier."

"You mean shoving around raw recruits like you do at Fort Dix, scrawny, shaggy-haired teeny-rockers right out of school, with the love of Boz Scaggs in their hearts and crying 'Mommy' whenever you speak crossly to them. No, thanks. It's the posh life for me. Wine, women, and song."

Dave harrumphed. "You don't drink enough wine to make a duck waddle, and you can't sing a lick."

"I mentioned women in there somewhere."

"You always were lucky in that regard. By the way, I hear Brenda Ames stopped by."

"Um-hmm."

"What'd she allow?"

"That you were cute as a button."

Dave's eyebrows shot up. "Me?"

"You're all she could talk about."

"But I thought—"

"What, that she was still after me? Naw. She and the kid here are history. Brenda wanted a line on you, buddy boy."

"No shit," Dave muttered under his breath.

"Did you just utter an excretory expletive?"

"I have no idea."

So Tyler gave Dave Brenda's number, and Dave used it that night, and one thing led to another, and Dave acquired something from Brenda that took penicillin to cure.

He blamed it on Ty.

ROCKY AND BULLWINKLE

"THAT DAMNED VANCE KID AIN'T NEVER ALONE," whined Feeney, in a house just down the street from "that damned Vance kid." Rocky the Flying Squirrel cavorted on a nineteen-inch B&W TV set atop the credenza. No Bullwinkle. Then no Rocky either; Sugar Pops instead.

"So?" Tabor sat next to Feeney at the dining room table, sucking a cigar and spewing like an Akron smoke-stack, which coincidentally was where he'd been born. A pair of Bushnell binoculars rested on the tabletop.

"You don't want no witnesses, right?" said Feeney, tall and bowed, freckle-faced and forty, with a thick head of straw-colored hair. He wore galluses and a bow tie, and had feet the size of gunboats.

"So follow Vance and whoever he's with and snag them both." Tabor was slightly shorter and much sturdier; coarse black hair covered his body except for the dome. He was manicured, newly washed, dapper in an Aber-crombie & Fitch way.

"Grabbing one's not so bad, long's I got a piece," in-sisted Feeney. "Two's a whole other situation."

The dining room needed wallpaper; the ceiling was water-spotted; who-knew-what kinds of stains sullied the shag carpet. The windows were dirty, the furniture scarred, and the place smelled of cat. Or had until Tabor lit up his stogey.

"You getting paid?" Tabor blew a smelly circle of smoke.

"Not enough." Rocky was back. And Bullwinkle! Feeney watched them.

"Then quit."

Feeney looked hard at Tabor.

Tabor shrugged. "Hey, you take a man's money, you do the man's job."

Feeney looked back at the TV.

Tabor clapped him on the shoulder. "He's only a kid. Besides, like you said, you got a gun. And help."

Feeney snorted and tossed a thumb toward the front room. "You call him help?"

"Cable's strong as a horse."

"Yeah, and almost as smart."

Climbing to his feet, Tabor puffed mightily for five seconds, then said, "Get it done. Soon. You don't, I'm afraid Strobe's gonna pop a gasket. The man's barely holding together now. If he blows, there goes our golden goose. You know about the golden goose?"

Feeney was insulted. "I ain't ingnerant, Tabor."

According to who? thought Tabor, but what he said was, "Soon, hear me?"

Feeney nodded and went back to Rocky.

NO ELECTRIC

"ARE YOU CRAZY?" ERUPTED DAVE MICHAELS.

It was eighteen days before Christmas. Dave and Tyler were sitting at the Vance breakfast room table, hot cocoa at hand, when Ty dropped his bombshell.

"I don't think so." Ty took a heated sip.

"Are you tired of living?"

Another sip. "Not yet."

"Then why this harebrained idea?"

"I feel bad for Mr. Roundtree. He lost his only son, and—"

"He also had Abner Jansen beat up, his son killed, his restaurant destroyed! Not to mention siccing the same guys on you."

"We don't know that, not for certain."

"Like hell we don't."

"David, *mi amigo,* I'd like to defuse this situation. I've had enough—no, far *more* than enough—fighting over the past year or so to last a lifetime. Maybe if I go apologize to Mr. Roundtree, he'll—"

"Shoot you!" Dave, despite a normally calm demeanor, was outraged.

"Or not."

"And where do you intend to make this apology?"

"At his home."

"At his *home*! Now there's a great idea. That way when he shoots you he can claim you were a burglar. Better yet, that you came to threaten him, then lost control of yourself and he shot you in self-defense. No witnesses, either. How tidy for him."

"You'll be a witness." Ty finished his chocolate. Dave's cup sat forgotten.

"So maybe he'll shoot me too."

"Then I'll rip his lip and stuff it behind his ear."

"I get it. You're going out to apologize to him, but if he doesn't accept it you'll put a boot up his butt."

"You aren't making this any easier for me."

"I don't *want* to make it easier for you. I want you not to go. Write him a letter."

"Not as good as face to face."

"Maybe not, but it's sure as hell *safer.*" Dave was anything but taciturn.

"I'm through with my hot chocolate."

"*There's* a bulletin."

"It means I'm ready to go."

"Now?"

"No reason to wait."

"How about longevity?"

"You coming?"

"Shit."

Ty smiled to himself, rinsed the cups, placed them on

the drainboard, and they climbed into the ancient Vance Beetle with David still fuming.

• • •

"Pull over when you turn the corner," Dave instructed before they'd gone a tenth of a mile.

"Why?"

"Just do it."

Tyler negotiated the corner and decelerated. Dave said, "Drive a bit further. . . . That's good." There were now several houses between the Volkswagen and the Vance place.

"Has anyone rented the Jones house?" Dave queried. "The sign's still up."

"I haven't noticed anyone moving in."

"What I thought."

"So?"

"When we passed the house just now, I spotted a bright reflection from one of the front windows."

"Hello. Ol' Sol's up. That's him over my left shoulder there, shining away."

Dave ignored the jibe. "The houses on the other side of your street face northeast, right?"

"They do."

"Then they wouldn't be reflecting direct sunlight, at least nothing like the intensity I just saw. What I saw was direct sunlight being tossed back, and from within the house. I think someone was following our progress with a pair of binocs."

Tyler mulled it over. "Who?"

"Captain Kangaroo. How the hell do I know, Tyler?

Wait a minute . . . those guys at Jansen's got there within ten minutes of our arrival, right?"

"You think we've been under observation?"

"Don't you?"

"Maybe. So, do we call the sheriff's department?"

"And what, report an unlawful light refraction? And what if our friends're gone when the law arrives? Ever hear about the little boy who cried wolf?"

"No, just the chicken who claimed the sky was falling. Okay, let's check it out ourselves."

"What if they've got guns?" Dave asked belatedly as they quit the car.

"Duck."

• • •

The back door was easy. Making it across the broken-glass-strewn kitchen floor without sound was not, but they managed. Mack Feeney and Cable Pogue were in the dining room watching *Lassie* reruns. Timmy was being scolded for something, and the pair was absorbed. Ty and Dave looked at each other, then stepped into the room.

"Whoa back," expleted Cable the Dull upon spotting the unexpected visitors.

Feeney knocked over his chair and jumped to his feet, cracking a knee against the heavy table on the way up. "Fuck me!" he shouted in combined alarm and discomfort.

"Hi, fellows," greeted Ty, stepping quickly across the room to stop beside Cable Pogue, who was busy fishing a revolver out of a side pocket, his tongue protruding from the mental effort. When the gun finally came free,

Ty grabbed it by the barrel and twisted it free of Cable's grasp, like taking candy from a gargoyle. "Whoa back," expleted Cable again, reaching for his weapon. Ty whacked him once, very hard, on the carotid artery with the edge of his hand and Cable said "Ackk!" and dropped to one knee. Ty whacked him again, same hand, and Cable said "Unkk!" and dropped to the second knee. Ty shook his head in disbelief and struck once more. Pogue, fresh out of knees, fell flat on his face without a sound.

"You can't just come in here and do that," Feeney maundered.

"Yeah, we saw how much you did to stop us," quipped Dave Michaels. "Who is that guy, anyway?"

Feeney looked down at the unconscious Cable Pogue in disgust. "His name's Virgil Brown. Ain't much, is he?"

"At least he tried," from Tyler, brandishing Cable's gun. "I see a bulge under your jacket. You don't plan to reach for it, do you?"

"No time soon," assured Feeney.

"Just the same, I'll feel better if you hand it over. Very carefully."

Feeney did, butt-first. Tyler handed the gun to Dave, who examined it briefly and tucked it out of sight.

"Now what?" asked Feeney.

"I assume you're Virgil's brother," said Ty, poking Virgil's firearm into his own waistband.

"Uh, right."

"Can you show me a lease on this house, maybe a bill from Duke Power?"

Feeney shivered despite his heavy coat. "Can't afford no electric."

"So you're just two vagrants, down on your luck?" said Ty.

"Not vagrants, farmworkers. From Texas."

"Waiting for the spring thaw, are you?" Dave chided.

"That's right," said Feeney, chin up. A poor man but proud, just trying to earn his keep.

Sure he was.

"Hand me your wallet," Ty ordered.

"Fat chance," Feeney objected.

"You can join Virgil on the floor."

"Hey, no need for that. Here." He reached for his wallet.

"Slowly," warned Dave.

Out came the wallet—slowly. When Ty received it he flipped it open, noted the contents, tossed it back. "Well, Mr. *Feeney*, you and your brother are pretty well heeled for migrant workers."

"We don't spend much on worldly pleasures."

"Or amenities, such as electricity. By the way, that television run on propane gas?" Ty asked.

"Uh . . . batteries."

"Sure, the cord's just for looks. Now listen up, friend. We're going to call the cops and report a burglary. It's up to you, of course, but if I were you I wouldn't be here when they come to investigate," Tyler advised, and turned to go.

"We get our guns back?"

"Buy new ones. You've got plenty of money."

Feeney puffed up like a tall, skinny, aromatic pouter pigeon. "It ain't right, you coming in here and decking . . . uh, Virgil, then stealing our guns."

Dave walked over to Feeney. "Don't push it. I could keep you here while he calls the fuzz."

Feeney said nothing.

"Oh, one other thing," said Ty from the kitchen doorway.

Feeney looked at him.

"Tell Mr. Roundtree I'm coming to see him."

And then everybody left, even Cable the Dull, though he had to be half carried to the car. The sheriff's men arrived eight minutes later, on an anonymous tip. Several of them paused to watch a segment of *I Love Lucy* on the B&W TV set, which was on when they arrived. They laughed and laughed.

GRIFFON'S LAIR

STROBE ROUNDTREE'S COUNTRY HOME WAS SMALLER than the Taj Mahal but fancier, and was set off by stately oaks, a few diseased elms, and an orderly stretch of pines that lined the graveled drive. For a backdrop, puffball clouds sailed, and a red-tailed hawk drifted languidly on a thermal updraft, casting for rodents. Or perhaps simply enjoying the crystalline morning. A Rolls-Royce reposed in the cobbled courtyard below, bronzely gleaming; gray granite griffons flanked a porte cochere; the rolling emerald grounds appeared blanketed in Astroturf.

Tyler halted the Vee-Dub, hiked the hand brake, whistled softly. "Wonder if he'll give me a job once I muster out of the army."

"Probably. Pruning the hedge. Two bucks an hour and you get to tell folks you work here."

"Look good on my résumé," said Ty, staring up at the edifice. "I feel like a postulant."

"Whatever that is. We going in, or they got curb service?"

The pair climbed out and approached the house.

• • •

A butler answered the chime, then butled them into a foyer the size of Cameron Indoor Stadium while asking, "May I take your coats, sirs?"

Off came the outer gear.

"Something to drink while you wait, sirs?" queried the butler after depositing their garb in a nearby coat closet.

"No, thanks," Tyler demurred, then, as the butler left them alone, he said to Dave, "Is there a plural of 'sir'?"

"You're asking me?"

Before Ty could reply, the butler returned and bade them follow, which they did, to a paneled study richly furnished and warmly serviced by a roaring fire.

"What, no spitted calf?" David quipped sotto voce.

"Fireplace is pretty big."

A soubrette direct from Hollywood central casting brought two mulled ciders on an inlaid ebony tray, set them on a cherry end table, and left without so much as a glance their way.

"Now she's hurt my feelings," said Dave. "I was all set to wink. Would I get to work with her?"

"I thought I was the one getting the job."

"You were 'til I saw her."

"What about Brenda?"

"Brenda who?"

And in walked Strobe Roundtree.

• • •

"What do you mean by coming here?" Roundtree was a huge man dressed in a red smoking jacket of such brilliance that he appeared to be in flames. His dark hair was long and thick, his nose was long and thick, his fingers were long and thick. Only the feet were small, almost dainty, his bedroom shoes a carmine velour.

"My name is Tyler Vance and this is—"

"I know who you are, and I don't care who he is. Why did you come here?"

"I wanted to apologize to you, in person."

The big man curled a lip. "Apologize for what? Humiliating my son in public? Being responsible for his death?"

"How is Ty responsible for your son's—" Dave began.

"Shut up, you don't exist! This conversation is between him and me!" barked Roundtree.

Suddenly aware of the futility of all this, Tyler said, "Thank you for your time. We'll be going now. Oh, I am sorry about your son—for having to fight him, for his premature death, and for his having to endure a father like you." As Roundtree's eyes burned into Tyler's, the butler appeared as if on cue, their jackets over one arm.

As they turned to go, Dave stopped, pointed at two large shards, and said, "Those glass-topped tables do break easy, don't they?"

Then they left.

• • •

"That went well," said Dave. "Want some pizza?"

"He does have a hate on, doesn't he?"

"Some folks hang on to their grief. There's a Pizza Hut about a half mile from here."

"So what'll he do next?"

"Don't know about him, but I may starve."

"I don't think he plans to give up on this."

"What makes you think so? Smell that? Pepperoni."

Tyler drove past the Pizza Hut.

"A burger'd be good," said Dave. "Probably too early for pizza, anyway."

"This disturbs me."

"It must, if you're not hungry. Doesn't disturb me, though. Krispy Kreme coming up. On the right. There, right . . . Chinese, now. I could go for Chinese. Not as filling."

But Tyler had other things on his mind.

THE DISCIPLINARY COMMITTEE

BEHIND THE WHEEL OF HIS ROLLS SILVER SHADOW, Roundtree simmered like a pot of boiled blood pudding, heavy brows beetled, his aggressive progress through traffic a clinic in offensive driving. Another fifteen minutes found him outside an apartment complex on North Church Street, not far from the city limit, pulling into a parking slot alongside Johnny Mack Feeney's blue Ford wagon. Tabor's racing-green TR6 was slanted into two spots, so no one would ding his car doors; Roundtree was tempted to take a key to it—from headlight bezel to keyhole—but through sheer force of will he resisted the urge. In through the front door of apartment D he walked, without knocking, sat heavily in the nearest chair, and said without preamble, "Tell me," his directive aimed at Feeney, across the room on a love seat. Feeney related the specifics of the unfortunate incident at the rental house, with Cable Pogue providing the punctuation. When Feeney's account had run its course, Roundtree asked Pogue if he concurred with the details of the story. Cable, his bulk on a hassock nearby, replied in the affirmative.

"So two punks not yet old enough to vote made an end run on you big-time toughies from Chicago, knocked one of you out, and took both your guns away," summed Strobe Roundtree.

The pair of big-time toughies bobbed their heads in unison as Tabor stood in the kitchen, drinking V-8 juice from the can and shaking his head, knowing what was likely to come and having no stomach for it. These poor creeps couldn't help it if they were dumb; Strobe should have anted up the dough for real hoods out of Jersey, not these squarehead stumblebums.

Silence then for a couple of minutes, Roundtree letting the stumblebums stew in their own juices. He produced a lighter from his cashmere topcoat and flicked open its lid, thumbed the flint wheel, then *pop,* up flashed a yellow flame, and *clink,* down flipped the top, extinguishing it. Repeat: *flick, skritch, pop, clink.* And again. Cable Pogue began to sweat. Johnny Mack Feeney had been sweating since Roundtree arrived.

"Either one of you fellows ever see *The Yakusa*?" Strobe asked conversationally. "With Robert Mitchum?"

The two shook their heads.

"In Japan, when someone screws up royally, he goes to his boss to beg forgiveness. Often he'll cut off one of his fingers, wrap it in a handkerchief, and offer it to the head man, to atone for the sin."

Serious perspiration now, beading on philtrums and foreheads.

Roundtree went on. "Sometimes the big cheese accepts the offer, sometimes he doesn't."

Johnny Mack Feeney was trembling all over. Cable Pogue was having a little trouble following the drift, but he was as nervous as Feeney, on principle.

Flick, skritch, pop, clink, the lighter sang.

"Oh God," breathed Feeney, fingers quaking.

Abruptly Roundtree dipped into the pocket again, withdrew a Buck lock-blade, tossed it to Feeney. Feeney fumbled the catch and the knife bounced on the carpet.

"Wha's the knife for?" said Cable Pogue.

"Thought you guys might wish to atone," Strobe answered.

"Wha'sat mean, atone?"

"It means cut one of our fingers off," said Feeney.

Flick, skritch, pop, clink.

"Or I could burn one off," said Roundtree.

Cable climbed to his feet, all 250 pounds of him. "I don' think so." He was bigger than Roundtree, and younger, and stronger. Not meaner, though. Strobe kicked him in the kneecap—very hard—with the pointed toe of a very expensive Italian shoe, and when Pogue reflexively bent to rub it, Strobe kicked him on the point of the chin, which straightened the hapless Cable up, then Strobe kicked him in the groin with the same Italian shoe, and Cable yelled "Whoa back" and buckled to the floor, where he lay trying to decide which body part to clutch. While doing so he bled from his mouth and moaned a lot.

Feeney kept his seat during all this, carefully observing the unpleasant application of expensive Italian footgear and weighing the likelihood of his retaining a full complement of digits. Now, as his partner lay prostrate and in extreme pain, Feeney made a suggestion: "I'd be happy to cut off one of his fingers for you, Mr. Roundtree."

Roundtree, still seated and breathing evenly, said, "I don't want you thinking that I don't appreciate your offer, Mr. Feeney, but that's not how it works. There's the knife."

As Feeney stared at the unopened Buck on the carpet, Tabor cleared his throat. "Enough."

"I beg your pardon?" from Roundtree.

"I said enough. They get your point, and this isn't Japan."

"This is a high-level decision, Tabor. It's out of your hands."

"Like hell. I hired these two. Dismemberment wasn't part of the bargain."

"You hired them on my behalf," Strobe insisted.

"But it was still me who hired them."

Roundtree's eyes burned into Tabor's. Tabor didn't flinch.

"All right," Strobe finally relented. "But if they commit another gaffe, it'll be your finger I'll require."

"That'll be the fucking day," Tabor responded.

"We'll see." Roundtree stood. "I'll leave now. In a day or so I'll call with instructions. I want those two here all the time. I may need them on a moment's notice. They can send out for food."

Tabor said, "Okay," and the meeting of the disciplinary committee was adjourned. Not long after Roundtree left, Cable Pogue lost his breakfast.

Scrapple and eggs.

The coffee had been largely absorbed.

JAZBO

"YOU SHOULD HOLD OUT FOR THE FOUR-BARREL," DAVE insisted.

"I have been, and have we found one?" Tyler Vance responded.

"Might tomorrow."

"Or when I'm forty."

"We'll be riding in electric cars by then."

So Ty went with the two-barrel carb, three-on-the-floor, medium blue exterior, black vinyl inside, red-line Tiger Paw radials.

"Red-line tires are passé," admonished Dave Michaels as they drove off the lot.

"In '67 they weren't."

"On GTOs. This ain't a GTO. Even on a GTO they're passé now."

"Only fifty-three thousand miles. Can you believe it?"

"Three grand was too much by half," Dave opined.

"You're nuts, you know what Anne's AMX cost her? And it's only a year newer."

"This is no AMX. It has no 390 mill, no four-speed box, no—"

"Shut up."

Dave grinned.

"You're just jealous," from Ty.

"Of this, when I have a 340 Challenger?"

"Who'd want a Mopar, except maybe a Road Runner? Three-eighty-three, limited slip—"

"—handles like the Titanic, looks like a taxi," Dave interrupted.

"Does not."

"Does too."

And they tooled along, enjoying Tyler's "new" 1967 Camaro. A dark Buick trolled in their wake, though they didn't know it.

• • •

Dave leaned an elbow on the roof above Ty's window, which was rolled down. "I'm uncomfortable about leaving you alone after yesterday. You got that guy's handgun with you?"

"No. I'm through shooting at people. Forever."

"Never say forever."

"Forever, forever, forever. You still got that piece I tossed you?"

Dave patted his jacket. "You bet."

"You ought to sell it. What was it, a Victory Model?"

"Yep, .38 S&W. When I'm twenty-one I'll trade it for something with more authority."

"A BB gun has more authority than the .38 S&W. Try not to shoot anyone with it, you'll just tick 'em off. See you tomorrow." And he sped away.

• • •

Tyler was following an ancient beige Corvair with a Jersey plate that read COR-1963. The car was badly in need of a ring job; oily smoke billowed from its tailpipe, reducing visibility to a few yards. Tyler coughed and backed off just in time to see a burlap sack come flying out the driver's window. The sack landed on the yellow line. Ty narrowly missed it, and upon passing thought he detected movement.

"Shit!" he said, and braked for a three-point turn and reversal of direction. A pink Mustang passed over the bag, straddling it safely, but a tractor-trailer rig was swiftly bearing down, its front tires riding the center line. Ty passed the bag for the second time—opposite direction—then stood on his brakes, sliding to a slithery stop athwart the wrong side of the road, in the path of the onrushing truck; if the semi was going to hit the bag, it would have to go through the Camaro. Praying that the used car salesman had remembered to call his insurer, Tyler jumped out of the car and scooped up the bag, then dove for the grassy verge as the giant truck hammered by in a blast of wind and noise, horn blaring, its irate pilot red-faced, the central finger of his right hand pointing skyward. The burlap sack squirmed mightily as Tyler clutched it, so he crouched in the mud at the side of the road and cautiously untied the knotted cord, then stepped back. Out popped a brindle pup maybe ten weeks old, black-spotted, lop-eared, and ugly. Mad, too. A growl rose from deep within its puppy throat as the mutt set itself foursquare, prepared to repel boarders. Tyler laughed at the show of canine hubris, and the puppy's ears pricked as if to say, *What's this, a friendly human?* Carefully, Ty picked up the dog, which promptly soaked them both, but did not sink sharp teeth. To the Camaro they went, wetly.

• • •

"Son, they won't let you keep a dog in the barracks at Bragg," groused Odie.

"So I'll rent a trailer in Spring Lake."

"But he's awful ugly."

"You mean to tell me Midnight Zep is pretty?"

Odie bristled at the jab. "At least she's purebred."

"So's this one. Purebred *dog*," insisted Ty. "Besides, we understand each other." The puppy, on Ty's lap as they sat on the back porch, wagged his tail in agreement.

"Well, he don't like *me*," Odie complained, rubbing the back of his hand where the puppy had bitten him.

"See? He'll make a great watchdog."

Leigh spoke through the kitchen window, from which vantage point she'd been kibitzing. "Oh, Odie, let him keep the dog. But you be sure to wash him. And dip for fleas."

And it came to pass that the Vance household had acquired a new dog.

• • •

The pup didn't appear partial to most adults, but he sure took to Mikey. And Mikey to him. Dave and Tyler sat in the porch swing that evening and watched the pair playing fetch with an old sock. "What's his name?" said David.

"Mikey. He's my sister's kid."

Dave didn't miss a beat, just kept on swinging. "The pooch, wiseacre."

"Name's Jazbo, in honor of Charley Askins."

"The good colonel does tend to overuse that word, but I didn't think you admired Askins's stuff."

"I don't especially. But Askins is unique. And colorful."

"Like the cur."

"Don't call my dog a cur."

"I apologize. *You're* the cur."

"And you're a lemur."

They railed thus well into the gloaming, until Mikey fell asleep with his head on Jazbo's chest. The pup lay very still. Soon he too was asleep. After a few minutes, Tyler gently lifted Mikey and carried him to bed.

• • •

While Ty and Dave Michaels were on the back porch monitoring Mikey, the elder Vances gathered in the living room for a conference. Present were Odie and brothers Clyde and Darryl, and Leigh, of course. Clyde asked Darryl, "How much longer can your company run itself?"

"It isn't. Minnie's there every day, and she knows it as well as I do."

"Will them ol' boys take orders from the owner's wife indefinitely?"

"Minnie? Shoot, *I* take orders from her, and we've been married twenty years. The business is fine, no worry there."

"Okay," said Odie. "So what do we do about this situation? Ty won't say much about what's goin' on, but the ruckus at Jansen's junkyard won't be the last of this. I know Strobe Roundtree. He's no quitter."

"You talk to the sheriff?" Clyde said.

"You bet. And to Judge Parker. They can't do much except wait, just like us. Try and catch 'em in the act. What worries me most is if Strobe don't give a dang what happens to himself after he gets Tyler. His son's dead and his wife run off and he's got all the money in the world. I figure when the deed's done, he'll either hightail it with all his dough or go to jail, won't matter much which it is."

"He blames all his problems on Tyler?" asked Clyde.

Odie nodded. "Ever since that incident at the ice-cream parlor, things been goin' downhill for Strobe."

"How about a first strike?" Darryl suggested.

"Whip his butt?" Odie shook his head. "Won't matter none. Wouldn't deter me neither, was I him."

"So what do we do?" Clyde said.

"I was countin' on us to come up with something," Odie answered. But they talked for an hour and never did.

Soon it wouldn't matter.

• • •

Ty made a snack run around eleven o'clock, right before Johnny Carson, with a dark Buick sedan in his wake. He paid little attention to it, just distant lights in his rearview.

The Buick's driver paid attention to him, though.

DREAMS

BLESSED OBLITERATING SLEEP. AND DREAMS:

When the boy was scarcely two, Mama and Daddy at the lake teaching the delightful toddler how to swim, or what passed for swimming, no fear in the child, total trust in Daddy, jumping from the pier into his arms, slick little body all agleam with pride, splashing and giggling, swelling Daddy's heart to bursting, Mama's too as she watched from under the beach umbrella, she always burned so easily, then scrumptious ice cream as a reward for such bravery and trust, strawberry, running down the cone onto the little hand, tongue licking at the cascading sweetness, chuckling and chewing the frosty bits, residue at the corners of his mouth—a Cupid's bow like in the children's books. How his heart sang with delight and love for this child. . . .

Turning over brought him momentarily back, or partially so, enough to lose the drift, and then once again, deeply in:

Schooltime now, first grade, Mrs. Lambert, with the pink bow in her hair, ever smiling, how the boy adored her, and how he delighted her, watching and absorbing everything she offered, the smartest in the class, and the sweetest she claimed when no one else was around—lest she offend—and it was the same throughout elementary school, and summers by the water, swimming with such grace and precision, his fine hair blowing in the wind as they powerboated, spray off the bow glistening on everyone and everything, and laughter like the tinkling of bells, his son, his center, and then the terrifying brush with pneumonia, how it had squeezed his heart like an iron fist, the chance of losing his son, his universe, and his wife could see his fear, and resented it because he'd never feared for her *like that, not even during that horrific hemorrhaging right after giving birth, though she'd hovered like a windborne chrysalis on the cusp of death. . . .*

Turning again, pummeling the pillow into a more comfortable shape, then down once more into the murk:

Fourteenth birthday party, noticing girls now, including that Ames twat, all sullen and sexy and blatantly on the make, causing their first serious rift—he's always believed in Daddy, no doubts, but not now with hormones rampant, awakening the prowler within, every father's deepest fear, alienation from his son, his only *son, none other to turn to, though his wife sought solace, no time for her, had to repair the father-son cleft by whatever means—sports clinics, a new convertible, a larger place at the lake, then a beach house, but what his boy wanted was to go alone there with a girl, or friends, not Daddy like it used to be. . . .*

And it was killing him. . . .

Strobe Roundtree woke with a start, sheets soaked from briny memories and remorse, and slept no more that night. But oh, how he keened and wailed and heaped scorching vituperation upon Tyler Vance.

MIKEY

TYLER WAS COOKING. MIKEY WAS HELPING.

"Here," said Tyler, handing the boy a serving spoon. "Scoop out a couple of spoonfuls of butter from that crock."

Mikey, the epitome of concentration, shoveled up a baseball-sized dollop. "Where's it go?" he queried.

Tyler lifted a frying pan, held it out toward the boy, instructed, "Right there."

Plop went the dollop. "I think that's enough, little sweetie," said Ty, moving to the stove.

"You said 'couple.' That's two," Mikey pointed out.

"I sure did, but your one would make three of mine, so let's go with one."

"Okay." Mikey started to get down from his perch on the counter, where Ty had placed him, out of range of the range.

"You stay right there, bud, so if the butter sputters you'll be far away."

"You made a rhyme," exclaimed Mikey, delighted.

"You're right, little friend. Should I do it again?"

"Hey! You did!"

"Close enough. Pay attention now. I've already turned the oven on, so—"

"What degrees is it?"

"Five hundred."

"That's a lot of degrees. Mommy cooks the brownies at four or three hundred."

"You're right. Now watch, so you can tell her how to do this."

Ty trimmed and discarded the outside leaves from two heads of cabbage, then quartered the heads, cut out and threw the cores away. He then sliced the cabbage into half-inch strips, placing the strips into a large bowl. After drizzling the now-melted butter over the cabbage, he tossed everything to ensure a fairly even coating. In a large baking dish, he arranged the strips in a single layer, sprinkled salt and pepper, and put the dish on the upper rack of the oven. After fifteen minutes he removed the dish and rearranged the strips, moving pieces from the center out to the edge, and vice versa. Back in the oven they went for fifteen minutes more, then out again and back into the large bowl for another tossing.

Later, eating the result, Mikey said, "This doesn't taste much like cabbage."

"The flavor's different from that of steamed or boiled cabbage, but it's every bit as good," Ty assessed, chewing.

Mikey wasn't so sure, but he ate most of his anyway. "It's lots of trouble, though," he suggested.

"And much to clean up. But I think it's worth it. Want to go to the park, play on the big slide?"

And, after cleaning up the residue, they went to the park.

So did the shadowy Buick.

• • •

Mikey was hanging upside down from the monkey bars and Ty was sitting on a picnic table watching; Feeney could see them clearly through his 10X Bushnells. "Too many folks in the park," he said to Cable Pogue, beside him on the front seat.

"Don' care. I owe him. Le's do it," said Cable.

Feeney looked at him. "There are at least a dozen witnesses."

"We'll bluff. Shove our guns at him, in our pockets o'course, so's no one sees."

Feeney sighed. "What if he won't come?"

"He will," insisted Pogue.

"I dunno. Strobe's not the most patient man in the world."

"So le's make this work," said Cable the Devious as he climbed out of the car.

Feeney followed, two fingers of his left hand crossed for luck. Inside a coat pocket, his new revolver. Out of sight, but not out of mind.

He was going to need it.

• • •

Ty saw the Feeney faction approaching from fifty yards away, but there was nowhere to run and nowhere to hide. So he sat where he was and tried for nonchalant, though his brain was on fast forward.

"Well, fancy meeting you here," greeted Feeney, one hand in a pocket.

"Yeah," seconded Cable, ten feet from where Vance sat on the picnic table.

"Hiya, Virgil," Ty said to Cable.

"Who?" said Cable, whose brain was on slow forward.

"Never mind," snapped Johnny Mack Feeney. "See that Ford wagon over there?"

"By golly, I do," answered Tyler, turning his head to look.

Feeney poked his gun barrel forward, against the lining of his pocket, and said, "Head for it. Right now."

"Nah," Tyler refused.

"The hell you mean, 'nah'?" said Cable the Dull, moving a step closer and trying to poke his own gun forward, but it was in his trouser pocket, along with his hand, of course, and his hand was big, and the pocket was not, especially with the gun in there too, and so he couldn't poke it very far, but he tried, and the gun went off and shot him in the foot, whereupon he yelled "Whoa back" just before Tyler hit him in the throat with a straight hard right, and followed with a jarring left hook that sat Cable on his ample keister. The straight right to the throat had robbed Cable of his ability to speak, so he simply moaned and pulled the trigger of his gun, deliberately this time, but it was an automatic and the spent cartridge case hadn't cleared the ejection port—due to the tight confines of the pocket—and the gun was jammed and wouldn't fire, so Cable simply sat and tugged on the useless trigger, with a .25-caliber hole in his foot and a frog in his throat the size of a softball and his nose aching where Tyler had broken it.

Feeney said, "Try that with me and I'll blast you," and he meant it, but just as he said it Mikey ran up and kicked him on the shinbone so hard Feeney's eyes instantly teared over and he couldn't see Tyler to blast him. Ty took advantage of the situation and covered the distance between him and Feeney, grabbed the pocketful of six-gun with his left hand, and twisted it inward toward Feeney's body, and—nose to nose—growled, "Go ahead. Shoot."

Feeney didn't, so Tyler reached up with his right hand, took hold of Feeney's Adam's apple, and promised, "If you don't let go of the gun, I'm going to jerk this out of your neck."

"You tell 'im, Uncle Ty!" shouted Mikey. "I'll go get the other one!"

Cable the Tortured was trying to get to his feet, having rolled into a horselike position on all fours, when Mikey leaped onto Cable's broad back, grabbed a handful of fleshy Cable ears, and yelled, "Whoa back," hauling in on the reins. Cable, his ears on fire from the tightly clutching little fingers, bucked and heaved, trying desperately to dislodge his tormentor. Ty, afraid for Mikey—still gamely attached, little fists full of ears and his heels dug in—danced over quickly and sidekicked Cable in the temple. Abruptly Mikey's bronco crashed to earth.

Unfortunately, while Ty was taking care of Cable Pogue, Johnny Mack Feeney was drawing his gun. He pointed it straight at Mikey—effectively immobilizing everyone in the park—and backed away. Once at his car, he jumped inside and tore out of the parking lot, leaving Cable the Hapless to his fate.

The dark Buick pulled away a moment later.

• • •

"Pull him off, pull him off!" shouted Mikey. When Cable Pogue had imploded, his thick arms had folded in against his sides, trapping one of Mikey's feet. Mikey was shoving against Pogue's inert bulk with his free foot, to no avail.

"I gotcha," Tyler said, and hurried over to roll Cable to one side, freeing the foot. Mikey, convinced that poor Cable had entrapped his foot intentionally, bounded onto the unconcious figure and began to flail with his fists. Tyler pulled him off. "That's enough, little man. I think he's out cold."

"He did that on purpose!" Mikey protested, his sense of fair play diluted by rage.

"I don't think so," Ty soothed, holding the lad firmly. "He accidentally fell on your foot when I decked him."

The earnest little face turned to his. "You think so?"

"I think so."

The boy's rage drained away almost as quickly as it had come. *Genetic,* Tyler thought. And then the police arrived.

INTERROGATION

THE LADY AT THE PARK WAS ALMOST APOLOGETIC. "AS soon as I saw a gun, I ran to that house"—she paused to point—"and called the police. Was it a real gun?"

"Yes," Tyler assured. "You did the right thing."

The lady—short and stout and seventy-something—was relieved. "I was afraid for my grandniece . . . oh, and for your child too, what is he, a brother, you're too young to have a boy his age . . . I don't mean to say that you shouldn't, only . . ." She wound down.

Ty touched her shoulder. "You kept your cool, and did exactly the right thing. And Mikey's my nephew."

The short, stout lady tried for a smile, but her lips were trembling. "I was so frightened."

Tyler hugged her to him, somewhat awkwardly, for he was not yet of sufficient age to embrace older women comfortably.

"Mind if I cut in?" asked a voice at his ear.

"Dear me," replied the lady, turning her head toward a uniformed policeman, then stepping away from Tyler.

"Excuse me, ma'am, but I've got some questions for macho man, here," said the cop.

Macho man? Ty looked over at Mikey, sitting on his heels atop the picnic table watching a medic's efforts to revive Cable the Out Cold.

"Let's go talk in my car," said the cop.

"I can talk fine right here," Tyler responded.

The cop took Ty's arm, not gently. "I said in the car."

Vance looked down at the hand on his arm, then into the cop's eyes. "If you don't let go of my arm, that medic will be reviving you."

The cop stepped back, put a hand to his nightstick. "You threatening me?"

"Am I under arrest, officer?"

"Not yet."

"Then keep your hands off me."

Out came the stick. "Or what?"

Faster than the eye could follow, Tyler's hand flicked out and the nightstick was his. "Hey!" yelled the officer, reaching for his sidearm, but another voice sounded: *"Franklin!"*

The cop turned toward the voice.

"What's going on?" said a tall man wearing sergeant's stripes.

"This jerk threatened me."

The second cop, stepping between the combatants, looked at Ty. "Is that true? Did you threaten this officer?"

"Not exactly, sir."

"Boy says he didn't threaten you, Franklin."

"He's a liar!"

"You a liar, son?"

"Not normally, sir. Besides, I said I didn't *exactly*

threaten him. I did tell him not to touch me unless I was under arrest."

"The kids's right." The tall policeman turned his head toward the uniformed officer. "Go find something to do."

"But, Sarge—"

"Franklin?"

Away stomped an unhappy Officer Franklin.

"My name's Sergeant Street. You willing to tell me what happened here?"

"Sure," said Tyler, and told him. By the end of his story, they had joined Mikey at the picnic table.

"So as far as you know, what they wanted was to talk to you elsewhere, and they insisted by producing guns," Street said at the end of Ty's account. "Why would they need to talk to you somewhere else?"

"I suspect they planned to harm me."

"Why would they want to do that?"

"Money."

Street arched a brow. "You have a lot?"

"No, but whoever's paying them does, or so I would surmise."

"Surmise? Interesting word. You a college boy?"

"I'm home on leave from the army."

"Where're you stationed?"

"Bragg, beginning next month. I just got back from overseas."

"Vietnam?"

"Korea."

"What'd you do in Korea?"

"Do you have any more questions germane to this situation?"

"Germane, wow. As a matter of fact, I do have."

"Shoot."

"You're what . . . twenty?" Street asked.

"And a half."

"Weigh 155 or so?"

"Little over."

"So, Mr. Vance, how'd a young sprout like you go through that big guy and his pal"—Street snapped his fingers for emphasis—"just like that? And them with hardware, too?"

"Just lucky, I guess," from Tyler.

"And 'cause I helped him," said Mikey.

Ty tousled the child's hair. "You bet. Without you, I'd have been salted meat."

Mikey grinned at the praise, although uncertain exactly what it meant.

"Well," said Sergeant Street, stretching his back and pointing at Pogue. "We'll take that one off to the slammer, he seems to be coming around. Maybe he'll clue us in. Oh, one final question. You got any thoughts as to who might have hired these gents?"

"Can't say I have."

"Can't say, or won't say?"

"You choose."

Sergeant Street nodded his curly head. "That's what I figured. I'll keep in touch."

I'll bet you will, Ty thought, then took Mikey home.

• • •

"This is gettin' out of hand!" Odie griped to Darryl, pounding a fist on the kitchen counter. He'd been called and filled in by the chief of police while Ty was still being questioned at the park, and was stewing pretty good. "I'm goin' to see Strobe myownself!"

"And do what?" Darryl argued. "The man'll figure a way to slap you in jail, brother. We've no proof he's behind any of this. He's plain and simple got the move on us."

Odie continued to rant, but he knew Darryl was right.

• • •

"I'm never there for you when you need me," said Dave Michaels.

"I've noticed that. Quite a break for me that Mikey was." Jazbo was curled up in Ty's lap, getting his ears stroked. If he'd been a cat, he would have purred.

"We can't keep giving them all these opportunities at you. Sooner or later, they're gonna hit pay dirt. From now on, I'm sleeping, eating, and bathing with you."

"Bathing?"

"Saturdays, right?"

"Every other."

"Right."

For an hour they conspired, trying to come up with a plan, but everything they discussed was illegal.

And while they plotted, the caliginous Buick lurked.

THE BUICK

THE DRIVER OF THE DARK BUICK STOPPED TO DROP A dime. Strobe Roundtree picked up on the first ring.

"It's me," said the driver, a sallow man with a raptor's presence—the beaklike nose, keen vision, head constantly moving, restless eyes taking in everything, everyone, always searching for prey. And no conscience, not a vestige, but blessed with the patience of a vulture.

"What the hell's taking you so long?" Strobe snapped.

"I told you I'd need thirty minutes. Thirty unobstructed, unobserved minutes. I haven't gotten them yet."

"What about at night?"

"They have dogs. Pens of them. I doubt I can do it at the house."

"Where then?"

"I'll find a time, sooner or later."

"I prefer sooner."

"Who doesn't. I want out of here. The longer I stay, the better chance of being spotted. Not to mention getting a ticket. That Vance kid drives fast. Following him's not easy. The cops would love looking in my trunk. If I get stopped, it's fireworks." The Buick driver spoke in short, sporadic bursts, spitting slightly as he talked, the result of a childhood mishap that had reshaped his lower lip.

"You've nothing that can lead to me?"

"I'm not an idiot, Roundtree. I've got a reputation to protect. If I got folks in trouble, I couldn't get fifty gees a pop. I won't call again until the job's done."

"You mean when it's installed."

"That's my job."

"What comes *after* is part of the job."

"No deal. Once I've done my magic, I'm gone. The outcome is certain, at least so far as it goes. I have no control over who triggers it. When I call the next time, be ready to wire the money. You don't, I'll be around to see you."

"Don't threaten me," growled Strobe Roundtree, the tic in his left cheek driving him crazy.

"Wire the money, I won't have to," finished the Buick driver, and hung up.

TOOT

LUTHER J. SICKENBERGER, HIGH SHERIFF FOR GUILFORD County, North Carolina, sat in Leigh Vance's favorite Kennedy rocker and rocked; smoke leaked from his nose and rose ceilingward. Luther was called L. J. by the voters and "Toot" by his friends, a sobriquet earned in childhood due to his amazing ability to flatulate on command, with not only redolence but resonance. He was speaking now: "The man's name is Cable Horace Milton Pogue, currently hailing from Chicago, though San Diego's his home port. He's thirty-two, was in the army for a short stint, dishonorably discharged after driving his deuce-and-a-half into a colonel's mint 1955 Corvette. Twice. Seems Mr. Pogue had a personal grievance against the colonel. Since 1968, Pogue has been arrested five times—mostly for strong-arm stuff—in three states. He's been in stir twice, once for two years, but nothing really serious. He's big and mean and aggressive, and dumb as a potter's wheel."

"What makes you say that?" Tyler mumbled.

The sheriff took a drag from his Chesterfield, removed

an index card from a shirt pocket, looked at it, and continued. "He usually partners with a seedy grasshopper named Johnny Mack Feeney, or so I get off the network. Feeney is the brains of the team, or at least the shifty one. He hasn't been arrested as often as Pogue, and has never served time except on a shoplifting beef. He warmed a county bed for thirty days on that one."

"What's a grasshopper?" asked Leigh.

"A regular user of marijuana," Odie answered.

Leigh hiked a brow. "Is that right, Toot?"

The sheriff nodded and exhaled, then flicked ash off his tie. A neat, cheerful man of average height, though a bit heavier than his doctor preferred, L. J. Sickenberger was fair-minded and popular. Odie told newcomers to Greensboro that Toot had been sheriff since the war—the Revolutionary War.

Leigh Vance looked back at her husband. "How did you know that?"

Odie rolled his eyes. Tyler said, "Mom, everybody knows that."

"I didn't," Leigh informed the group.

Darryl Vance asked the sheriff: "You think Pogue will rat on Feeney, if that's who the second man was?"

"That's who the second guy was, all right. Tyler ID'd him from a mug shot. As to Pogue ratting, I'd say no way."

"Why not?" said Leigh.

"Why should he? All they have him on is simple assault, carrying a concealed weapon—a misdemeanor in this state—and discharging a weapon inside the city limits. He claims Ty made him do that. They might threaten him with an attempted kidnapping—that's a federal rap—

but it would just be his word against your son's. Pogue says he never tried to take Ty anywhere."

"But the man's a known criminal," Leigh argued, "and Tyler—"

"Beat an assault charge himself, and not so long ago," reminded the sheriff.

"Doesn't show on his record," from Odie.

"But the whole town knows. Besides, a jury'd never convict Pogue on attempted kidnap based on one man's word, especially since Ty whupped him pretty good anyway," Sickenberger insisted, then looked at Tyler. "Your dad and I have discussed this mess. We concluded that when you leave for Bragg maybe it'll all die down. Strobe's boy hasn't been dead long. After he's had another year to consider it, perhaps he'll let it go. Besides, unless Pogue turns state's evidence—and as I said, on these minor charges he's not likely to do that—there's nothing much else we can do."

"Can't you pressure Strobe?" Clyde queried.

"Remember the movie *Cape Fear*?" asked the sheriff, lighting another Chesterfield.

Odie said, "With Gregory Peck?"

"Right. The way it went in that movie is pretty accurate. And remember, the character Mitchum played was an ex-con. But he had a residence, and enough money so a vagrancy charge wouldn't stick. All they could do was wait it out. Well, that's us."

"Unless Ty wants to go live on a houseboat in the Cape Fear River," Dave said.

"Right," Toot laughed. "Did Gregory Peck a lot of good, didn't it?"

But Leigh Vance wasn't laughing. She was worried. She hadn't forgotten her customary hospitality, however.

"Will you stay for supper?" she asked the sheriff.

"No thanks. Got a date on the softball field."

"In December?" asked Odie.

"It's a pickup game. His Honor and some of the councilmen against a bunch of my youthful deputies and these old bones."

"Whip his tail good," Clyde prompted.

"I'll just be happy not to drop my teeth."

"How's that?" Leigh said.

Sickenberger grinned, displaying the items under discussion. "Last week I was playing against a ragtag group from Winston-Salem, old college buddies mostly, from Wake. We played baseball together, back when Hiawatha was a kid. I was at bat, had a two-and-two count, and for some reason I was laughing and cutting up when old Mark Barkwell tried to shoot one by me and I swung as hard as I could, and out popped my uppers. They plopped at my feet, right in front of home plate."

"What'd you do?" Darryl asked.

"Nothing I could do but pick 'em up and stick 'em back in."

"Oh, my . . . with the dirt still on them?" Leigh asked, grimacing.

"I wiped 'em off on my britches," said Toot, standing now.

"Were you embarrassed?" Dave said.

"Naw, but it shamed my daughter Jean to death. She's ten."

As Odie was showing him to the door, Sickenberger turned to Leigh. "Don't you worry about Feeney, hon. Now that we know who to look for, we'll grab him."

But they wouldn't, because at that moment Johnny

Mack Feeney was three hundred miles from Chicago, and closing. He wouldn't return to North Carolina until the following summer.

By then all the dead were buried.

POSSUM POISON

AFTER TOOT SICKENBERGER LEFT, LEIGH TURNED THE living room over to the menfolk. Odie began without preamble: "Son, I understand you kept the pistol you took off'n those thugs."

Tyler nodded assent.

"I also understand you won't carry it."

"No, I won't."

Darryl said, "Why not? Feeney has a gun, and whoever Strobe gets to replace Pogue will likely have one. So far you've been fortunate, they've been up close and personal. What if they just decide to shoot you next time, instead of spiriting you away?"

Ty shrugged.

"Don't shrug at us, son," Odie demanded, exasperated.

Dave said, "Ty won't tell you, Mr. Vance. So I'll tell you. He's never going to shoot anyone again."

"Again? When has he ever?" Clyde exclaimed.

Ty just looked at the floor.

Dave said: "I told you, he won't say. Nonetheless, it's a problem we're going to have to deal with. Ty'll fight with his fists to save himself, but he won't fight with a gun."

Clyde said, "We heard that. What we don't understand is why."

"Maybe the boy was forced to do something in Korea he doesn't like looking back on," Darryl hazarded, "and if he has to do anything like it again, it'd be too much for him to handle."

Ty looked into his uncle's eyes, and they all knew.

"Well, crap," said Clyde. "What now?"

"Obviously he can't be left alone. One of us, armed of course, will have to be with him around the clock," Darryl reasoned.

"Dang right," Odie agreed. "I got my M-1 carbine, and my old .32. Darryl?"

Darryl shook his head. "When I left Virginia, I didn't think I'd be needing a gun other than my rabbit-getter, and it's right hard to conceal that old Parker twelve-bore."

"Ty can give him the gun he took from Pogue," suggested Dave. "It's a Dan Wesson. Not exactly petite, but more concealable than a Parker double."

"Clyde?" Odie said, glancing at his older brother.

"I don't own a handgun myself, but my next-door neighbor has a Walther .380 he'll probably let me use. Hell, he borrows my lawnmower often enough, so he better. I can tote that little popper in my shoe."

"A pocket's better," said David. "You might need it quick."

On that ominous note, the Tyler Protection Coalition adjourned to the kitchen for supper.

• • •

Across town, Strobe Roundtree was watching a home movie he'd made many years before. On the screen were his infant son, his radiant wife, the sands of Myrtle Beach on a brisk March day, kites airborne in the background, a few intrepid swimmers, one kid with long hair and a surfboard, no sound from the screen, just silent laughter and gaity, his son grinning his baby grin, showing a baby tooth, little legs pumping, as if saying, "Lemme down, Mommy, onto that big sandbox," and she did, kneeling beside him as he sat in wonder, his baby grin widening as if saying, "Look, Daddy, crawly things," and he pointed at the sand crabs, rolled onto all fours, went after them, his plump little diaper-clad bottom swaying from side to side in his haste. . . .

But Strobe could no longer see the screen, for his eyes were filled with tears.

• • •

Jazbo chased the tennis ball back and forth inside the large fenced area to the rear of the Vance home. He'd pounce on it, shake it mightily, then release his toothy grip, slinging the sphere away then bounding gleefully after it as it bounced erratically.

He was a happy pup.

Not for long.

• • •

The driver of the murky Buick, parked under a row of sheltering trees, spotted a shadowy figure and trained his binoculars on it. *Now what is* he *up to?* the driver thought.

Soon he had his answer.

• • •

Strobe Roundtree had taken leave of his senses, but not his innate stealth. He kept low, moved quietly, stopped frequently to scan the area, then moved slowly on. So far, so good. At the chain-link fence, he paused, looked around, squatted on his heels. From a coat pocket came a bag filled with raw hamburger; from another pocket, a glass vial. He opened the vial, poured the contents onto the meat, cupped now in his left palm, then formed the patty into a lump and tossed it over the fence. Back into the pocket went the vial, a drop or two of its contents staining his coat. The stain was green, of course, having been caused by ethylene glycol.

• • •

Clyde Vance was on his way to his car when he spotted Jazbo vomiting in the backyard. He hurried over, noted a large dollop of green-tinged meat in the waste, quickly scooped the dog up and jogged to the house. "Odie!" he yelled from the backsteps.

"Yeah," said his brother.

"You been feedin' Jazbo hamburger?"

"No, why?"

Twenty minutes later a vet was purging the puppy's stomach.

• • •

"That son of a bitch!" Odie proclaimed.

"We don't know for a fact it was one of Strobe's hoods," warned Uncle Darryl.

"Like hell we don't! Soon's we hear from the vet, I'm going over to Strobe's and stomp his raunchy red ass!"

Tyler took his father by the shoulders. "You try that, Pop, and he can probably shoot you and get away with it."

"I don't give a flamin' fart!"

"I do," Tyler said grimly.

"So what do we do?"

"Same as ever," said Clyde. "Report it to the law."

Just then the vet came through the swinging doors into the waiting room.

• • •

"Antifreeze," said the veterinarian.

"Son of a *bitch!*" said Odie.

"Bastard!" said Clyde.

"I might go stomp his rear myself," said Darryl.

"Get in line," said Dave Michaels.

Tyler said nothing.

"Someone obviously laced ground beef with the stuff, which is what saved the pup's life," said the vet.

"How's that?" said Clyde.

"If they'd put it in soup, like some folks do to get rid of troublesome possums, the dog probably would have lapped it all up. That would've been curtains. This way, a lot of the liquid drained off before the dog ate it, and the meat itself helped prevent rapid absorption. That's a lucky pup in there."

"Right. Lucky," said Dave.

"Well," said the vet, "at least he'll pull through. I want to keep him overnight, keep an eye on him. But I think he's out of the woods."

"How does antifreeze kill, anyway?" asked Clyde.

"Same way it kills possums—slowly, excrutiatingly, by shutting down kidney function. Takes just a capful to kill an average-sized dog. Lot less on a puppy that size. Lucky you spotted him. If he hadn't been found until morning . . ." The vet let it hang.

"Son of a bitch!" Odie repeated.

• • •

The man in the Buick watched all the comings and goings and, after the Vance sedan departed for the veterinarian's, sat reflecting: *There's nobody at home except Mama, and the hounds didn't strike up the band when Roundtree slipped in and out. Wonder why. Maybe tonight's my night. Let's find out.* So he slipped out of the secluded Buick—a package under one arm, tools under the other—and made his move.

• • •

"This is getting out of hand," Darryl said from the front seat. "We can't guard against such collateral damage. Strobe is free to sic his goons on anyone—or anything—close to Tyler, and all we do is play defensive ball. Perhaps it's time to go on offense."

"Great idea," said Dave Michaels from the backseat. "But how do we do that without running afoul of the poleece? If one or more of us gets tossed in jail, Strobe'll laugh up his sleeve."

They discussed the situation all the way home, but could reach no consensus.

Which was most unfortunate.

• • •

"Feeney's vamoosed," Tabor informed Strobe Roundtree over the phone. "I just got a call from Chicago. He says stuff it in your ear. Want me to find someone else?"

Strobe said no.

"So what's the plan?"

"I've got it covered," Strobe replied.

"The guy in the Buick?"

"How do you know about him?" barked Strobe.

"I spotted him tailing Vance."

"What were you doing at the time?"

"Keeping an eye on things. It's what you pay me to do, remember? Oversee?"

"Well, hold off. And don't interfere with the Buick. In fact, steer clear of the whole thing for a day or two. Take a vacation."

"Why?"

"Never mind why. Just do it!" And Roundtree slammed down the receiver.

Tabor stroked his chin in thought.

• • •

Tyler C. Vance lay on his bed and huddled with himself, legs crossed at the ankles, his fingers laced beneath his head. The house was quiet; only the electric hum of a bedside clock disturbed the stillness. What a dilemma. Tyler, more than most people, knew exactly what he was capable of.

Knew that he could easily access Roundtree's palatial

home to slit his throat, then ghost out again with no one the wiser. . . .

Or take Strobe out when he stopped for a signal light, the engine of his Rolls rumbling in concert . . .

Or when the man went jogging . . . or came out of a movie . . . or stopped at a 7-Eleven to take a leak . . .

There'd be no more Strobe, no more looking over his shoulder, no more problems. . . .

But Vance knew he couldn't do it. Never, never, *never!* Nothing could make him go back to . . .

that. . . .

Nothing.

It would destroy him.

Nonetheless, he felt terrible about Jazbo, even worse about the rest of the situation. Uncle Darryl wouldn't go home to spend Christmas with his own family—and he had two kids—and Uncle Clyde was neglecting his own business, and Mom and Dad were worried sick. . . .

Maybe the sheriff was right; maybe when Ty reported to Bragg, this would all just fade away. . . .

Sure it would.

It would just be so easy, taking Strobe out, snapping his neck. . . .

No! He had to squelch those thoughts. They would only transport him back to the dark place . . . where men were merely cardboard figures, the destruction of which fueled his hate, his despair. . . .

But Dave was right, that had been war, and he wouldn't go back—couldn't go back. . . .

It would destroy him as certainly as a bullet, though not as quickly, as mercifully. . . .

His fingers ached from the pressure; he'd unconsciously tensed his hands. He eased off, though his jaw was still set, stonelike, as the morass of his guilt tugged him down, down, under, into troubled, fitful slumber. . . .

HUNTSMAN

THE RAPTOROUS DRIVER OF THE DARK BUICK HOVERED over his suitcase, open before him on the motel bed. Packed neatly within were three pairs of Corbin slacks; five Gant shirts, one Sero; an alligator belt; a pair of red suspenders; six pairs of dark Gold Cups; a pair of ox-blood Weejuns; six pairs of Fruit of the Loom jockeys; his toiletry kit; a Colt Huntsman .22 with silencer; two extra magazines loaded with CCI Mini-Mag hollow points. He looked around, hawklike eyes scanning the room. Leave the Gideon? Nah, let them replace it. He tossed the Bible into the Samsonite, closed and snapped and started to lock, but a rap came at his door, so he popped the lid and removed the Huntsman. It was after midnight, misty and cold out, and there was no peephole. Who knew he was here? No one. Could it be the cops? How? He'd been very careful. Was it the hooker he'd spent two hours with last night, wanting some more of his special kind of action? Let's go see. With the gun in his right hand—alongside his leg, safety off—he opened the door just a crack, chain still hooked, and examined a face he didn't recognize. "Yeah?" he said.

The face said, "I called Roundtree. Told him you finally got it planted."

"Got what planted?"

"Now that's a good one," said the face. "By the way, that was pretty slick."

"What was pretty slick?"

"Slipping in while the men were away with the dog."

"What dog?"

"Roundtree was happy to hear it."

"Who's Roundtree?"

"The guy who gave me ten large to bring you as a bonus."

The silence of speculation. "I'll close the door. Just slip it under."

"How about I just keep it?"

The narrow eyes narrowed. "How about you don't and say you did?"

"It's cold out here. Damp. I'll catch my death."

"That's why they make thermal underwear."

"Look," said the face. "I've got to get a note from you. Otherwise Strobe'll figure I pocketed the dough. After all, he won't be hearing from you again, so he can't very well ask you about it."

More speculation. "Wait," said the birdman, and he slipped the lock.

• • •

"Hello?"

"Guess where I'm calling from."

"I don't have time for games."

"Humor me."

"The sound you're about to hear is me hanging up."

"He planted the bomb."

"Not over the phone!"

"Up yours, Strobe. I didn't sign on for a bombing."

"Who gives a shit what you—"

"Your Buick-driving employee gives a shit."

"I told you to stay away from—"

"I know, but I didn't. He's right here beside me. Want to speak to him?"

"No. And I don't want to speak to *you*, not now."

"Don't hang up, here he is. . . . Oops, sorry, he can't come to the phone."

"Good, I didn't—"

"Know why?"

"Why *what?*"

"He can't come to the phone."

"I couldn't care less. Now if—"

"He's indisposed."

"Indisposed?"

"Well, I think so. Wouldn't you consider yourself to be indisposed if you had an ice pick in your neck?"

Silence from Mr. Roundtree.

"Well, I sure would. And he seems to agree. He's sitting real still, holding the pick handle with one hand and a bloody motel towel with the other. I guess he's afraid to pull it out. It'll just bleed worse. He's starting to look peaked, if you ask me . . . yep, indisposed."

"What are you talking about?"

"See, Strobe, old-buddy-old-pal, your Buick-driving bomber popped me with a freaking .22. Nicked me good, too. He's pretty fast, but, hey, the bleeding's already stopped. Just a flesh wound. Now him, I don't know. I stuck that pick in pretty deep . . . whoops, you're looking mighty white, friend . . . ach, he just fell over . . . wait, he's trying to get up . . . nope, there he goes again. Glad I'm not cleaning this room, never saw so much blood. You don't reckon there's anything here to trace him to you, do you? Well, gotta go. I was up all night. Bye."

"Wait. . . ."

But Tabor was gone.

• • •

Strobe Roundtree lay wide awake by his police scanner until the word broke.

It was a long time coming.

DISASTER

"UNCLE TY?" MIKEY STOOD SLEEPY-EYED IN THE kitchen doorway. "Why are you up so early?"

"Actually, I'm up late. I haven't been to bed yet."

Mikey came over and climbed onto Tyler's lap, his Lone Ranger bedroom slippers slapping the floor as he walked. "Whatsamatter?" he asked after nestling in.

To tell or not to tell? Yes.

"Jazbo's sick. Someone fed him some poisoned meat last night. We took him to the vet, so he'll be okay, but I haven't been able to go to sleep."

"It too scarisome to you? You afraid they'll poison Paw-paw's dogs, too?"

"Or worse."

"What's worse?"

Tyler kissed the tousled crown of Mikey's head. "Not to worry, little man."

"If you're gonna worry, I am too."

So they sat there quietly. After a couple minutes: "Enough worrying. Anyone for French toast?" said Tyler.

And they cooked and ate and cleaned until false dawn.

• • •

"Why's the phone off the hook, O nephew of mine?" asked Darryl, tighting his belt then brushing his hair into place with a palm.

"Everyone went to bed so late, I didn't want a ringy-dingy phone waking folks up," Ty answered.

"Thoughtful boy, always have been," said Darryl.

"Me too?" from Mikey over in front of the TV.

"By all means."

Mikey turned back to Popeye.

"And how much sleep did you get last night?" Darryl asked Ty.

"Young bucks like me need very little sleep."

"Me too," said the even younger buck by the TV.

"Yeah, well, Leigh said we all need some milk. Unfortunately, I'm low on gas," said Darryl, looking at Ty expectantly.

"The Bug's full of gas. No one's driven it all week."

Darryl grinned. "I couldn't drive some foreign car. It'd be un-American."

"But you *could* drive my squeaky clean, almost-new-with-barely-fifty-three-thousand-miles-on-it hotrod 327 Camaro."

"In a New York minute."

"And you'll drive it very sedately."

"Absolutely."

"Won't ride the clutch . . ."

"Of course not."

"Won't bald a tire . . ."

"I'm way too mature for that."

Tyler grinned back at his favorite uncle and tossed him

the keys. "Don't forgot where you got those."

As Darryl turned to go, Mikey said, "Can I come? I need Tootsie Pops."

"Sure," said his granduncle Darryl. "My treat."

And out the door they went.

• • •

As Mikey climbed into the front seat of the Camaro, Darryl looked over at him. "It's too cold for not wearing a coat, spud. Your grandma would lynch me."

"Un-uh," objected the boy.

"Better go get it."

"But the heat'll be on." Slight whine to the voice.

"Mikey?"

"Oh, awright," said Mikey, opening the door to get out.

"Atta boy," said Darryl. "Now you be careful going up those stairs."

"Okaayyy," Mikey called over a shoulder, his short legs zipping him along the grass toward the house, as Darryl inserted the key into the ignition.

• • •

Ty was just hanging up the phone when it jangled under his hand. "Vance residence," he said into it.

"Who the hell has been on the phone?" demanded a muffled voice.

Ty glanced at the clock: 6:07. "Who the hell wants to know?"

"Is this Tyler Vance?" said the voice.

"It is. You going to identify yourself, or is this a game?"

"Better check under the hood before you drive that Camaro. Gremlins lurk." *Click.*

Oh God! Ty dropped the phone and bolted for the back door.

• • •

Mikey was almost to the house when the blast knocked him flat.

SACRIFICIAL LAMB

THE CHURCH WAS FULL OF VANCES AND ATKINS (LEIGH'S family) and more than twenty law enforcement officers, come to pay their respects. Anne had flown in from Pennsylvania two days before; although Mikey was only mildly concussed from the explosion, he was in such an agitated state, no one but his mother could console him.

Darryl's wife, Minnie, was present, though so heavily sedated she moved as if she had no joints, her face wooden. Her children were at Clyde's house, being presided over by Aunt Dora, herself under the effects of Valium. Clyde, clear-eyed but stoical, greeted visitors as they entered the church fellowship hall. The viewing and funeral had gone fairly well, and without undue drama. The burial service would be held in Virginia; Darryl's body would soon be on its way there.

Odie, bleary from no sleep, was seated at a round table in the dining area, talking to the sheriff. Sickenberger was saying, ". . . used dynamite, just like you and I can buy at Southside Hardware for removing stumps from the yard. We may have a lead, though.

"Yesterday a John Doe was brought into the morgue from a motel out near Sixteenth Street. Homicide. Guy got an ice pick stuck through his carotid and bled out like a sacrifical lamb. In the trunk of a '69 LeSabre parked at his door were all kinds of nasty stuff: dynamite, C-4, blasting caps, fuses, electronic gizmos I don't understand, a Thompson submachine gun—no tax stamp—plus a cannister of .45 ball, case of K rations, five gallon cans of water, sleeping bag, tool kit, burglar's tools, you name it. Beside the body was a Colt .22, stolen, silenced, fired once. We found an expanded hollow point slug in the drywall, some traces of blood that didn't match the stiff. We figure this was our bomber, and that instead of getting paid he got dead. At least he seems to have gotten in a blow of his own, but probably not a lethal one. Twenty-twos aren't much on penetration. The killer was probably hit around the edges or the bullet would still be in him."

"Any ID?" Odie asked.

"Sure. Stolen credit cards, bogus driver's license—Vermont, if you can believe it. The LeSabre was boosted. The plate too, and there were three extras under the front seat."

"So you've drawn a blank," Odie said.

"We're running his prints through everyone but the Vatican. At first blush, I thought it might be Feeney. Physically, they're a decent match. But no dice. We got Feeney's latents through his service record, and they're not even close. So he's still John Doe. My guess is that he won't be connectable to anyone local, especially you-know-who. Pro like this is too smart for that. It would kill his reputation. No one would hire him."

Leigh came over and sat down. She put a hand on Odie's. "You doing okay, sugar?"

"Hell, no, I ain't, and Sickenberger ain't helpin' none."

The sheriff shrugged, understanding and unoffended. "Doing the best I can."

Odie patted his arm. "I know you are, Toot. Your best just ain't very damned good."

"How's Tyler?" the sheriff shifted neatly.

Odie shook his head. "Not good."

"He's not likely to go off half-cocked, is he?"

Odie looked his old friend in the eye. "No. But he might go off *full*-cocked."

"I'll count on you to see he doesn't."

Odie slammed a fist on the table. A saltshaker fell over, rolled, and hit the floor, spilling salt. "Yeah? Seems to me you been looking to *us* Vances for too long. When are we gonna be able to look to *you*? When we're all dead?" With that he kicked over his folding chair and strode away.

Sickenberger looked at Leigh. "Getting mad isn't going to do anybody any good."

"So what is? Darryl's dead. The last time we talked with you he wasn't. Who's next? Tyler?" She leaned forward, eyes filling. "Do you know how close Mikey came? Two or three seconds, Toot. That's all. And he's five, and never hurt a soul. So don't warn us; do your job. Or maybe my men will have to do it for you. We don't plan to bury any more of our own."

Then she followed Odie.

Luther J. Sickenberger put his elbows on the table and ran his hands through his hair. Things were out of control, and there seemed to be little he could do about it.

Except go to funerals.

• • •

Tyler and Dave Michaels were sitting on folding chairs in the Vance basement gym, surrounded by barbells and martial trappings. Ty was morose, seething, barely able to cope. David said to him, "You realize there was nothing you could do."

Ty looked at him. "Yeah? When Strobe sent his goons to Jansen's junkyard, right afterward I should have gone after him."

"Right. Now you'd be in jail."

"And Uncle Darryl would be *alive*!" Ty jumped to his feet, grabbed his chair, slung it across the room with a metallic crash.

"Tyler."

"What!"

"You don't know that. Strobe may have put the bomber on your tail as soon as you got back. In fact, he probably did. It just took the guy a while to think of poisoning the dog as a means of being alone with your car. Before you bought the Camaro, you sometimes drove the VeeDub, sometimes your mom's Dodge, or Odie's International. He couldn't booby-trap them all. So he likely waited and watched."

Ty sank to his haunches, forearms on his ears, head down, his arms over his head, fists clenched in anguish. *"I didn't have to give him the keys!"*

"If you hadn't, *you'd* be dead. Probably Mikey, too. Who knows why Darryl sent him back to the house, but you might not have. Would that be better? Two of you dead instead of one?"

"But it wasn't Uncle Darryl's fight!"

"Tyler. When one Vance is in trouble, they all are, you know that. This situation is nobody's fault."

Up came the eyes again, steely gray. "Oh, yes it is. It's Strobe Roundtree's fault."

• • •

Jab, jab, hook. Jab, jab, hook. Left, left, right, dancing and punching, jawbone set, eyes grim, Tyler pounded the heavy bag, catching it on the swing, the smell of leather deep in his nostrils, face saturated. He danced away for a side kick, and again, then chest to the bag he pummeled, left, right, left, right, glide away, kick, again, over and over, seeking catharsis.

None of it helped. It did, however, blunt the anger. Ty's pulse, though, assaulted his temples, a three-Excedrin headache. Dave sat watching, waiting for the angst to run its course. It didn't. It couldn't. Tyler knew what was coming, like pestilence, and he couldn't stop it.

Anne came into the basement and said to Dave, "May I talk to Ty?"

"Sure."

"Alone?"

"You bet." Dave relinquished his chair and left the room.

"Brother?" Anne said.

Ty, back in his own chair, which he'd retrieved from across the room, looked at her. "Yes?"

"What are you going to do about this situation?"

"Take care of it."

"How?"

"You don't want to know."

"When?"

"Almost immediately."

She nodded. "What do you want me to do?"

"Keep Mikey safe."

"What if Strobe has someone in the wings to take another stab at you?"

"He does. Feeney. But I don't think Feeney's smart enough to blow his nose, let alone a bomb."

"Can you find him?"

"Depends. If he's deep underground, it might take longer than I have left of my leave time. If I don't report to Bragg in a couple weeks, they'll send MPs after me and I'll end up in Leavenworth."

"So what options does that leave you?"

"Strobe and I are going to have a chat."

"Will he tell you if there are others, I mean besides Feeney?"

"He'll tell me."

"I don't want to have to come visit you in jail, brother, but . . . it could have been Mom. Or Daddy."

"Think I need you to tell me that? And how close it came to being Mikey in that car?"

"You taking any help?"

"No. I could get caught after; I won't take someone down with me."

"Not even Dave?"

"No one."

"Can you handle it by yourself?"

He nodded.

"You seem so certain," she said.

"I am."

"How can you be?"

He shook his head.

She kissed him then. "Be careful."

He nodded his agreement. "Keep Mikey safe. Dad's in no state. I'll talk to Dave, get him to cover you. You call Clyde. He can help."

"Will this be over by Christmas?"

"By tomorrow, unless Strobe's gone to the Bahamas, and I doubt he's worried that they'll trace this to him. But he has no idea . . . Yeah, I'll be able to find him."

"He has no idea about what?" Anne pressed.

"What he's gotten himself into."

A FALLING OUT AMONG FRIENDS

TYLER WAS UPSTAIRS SLIPPING INTO SOME LOOSE, DARK clothing.

"We gonna shoot a few hoops?" Dave asked him.

"I don't think so," Ty said, tossing a black nylon jacket onto the bed.

"What's up, Tybo?" Dave asked.

Tucking in his shirt, Tyler said, "I'm going to remove a cancer."

"As in remove how?"

"Permanent."

"You can't do that."

Ty stopped to look at his friend. "Why not?"

"It'll mess your mind up."

"Better than burying another family member. We can't go on like this, playing a waiting game. The attrition rate is too high."

"You've got a mad on," Dave countered. "It's keeping you from thinking straight."

"How so?"

Dave flexed his arms and stuck out his chest. "I'm the man for this job."

Ty sat down on the edge of the bed. "You can certainly do it. But not like I can."

"You're lots tougher than me, right?"

Ty shook his head. "Not tougher; more experienced."

"What do you think I did over in 'Nam, pussycat, play mah-jongg all day? Now, I don't want to get into a pissing contest with a real bad-ass like you, but they don't give out Silver Stars as consolation prizes. Besides, I thought you were a changed man, Mr. Pacifist himself."

"I thought so, too. But I can't let this continue. Roundtree will keep throwing folks at us, or have his minions continue to plant explosives, maybe take potshots at us whenever any of us go for a walk in the woods. I won't subject my family to that kind of terrorism."

"And you're the great righter of wrongs, like in Korea. That really helped your psyche, didn't it?"

"No one else can do this."

"What an ego."

"David, the cops aren't doing anything constructive. They can't at this point. My dad could handle Strobe, all right, with his fists. And he can take care of himself with that old carbine of his, in some kind of shoot-out. But Roundtree doesn't play fair. He'll have help. This won't be a cakewalk, and when Roundtree goes down, the law will look pretty hard for his killer, what with him being such a prominent citizen. My mom couldn't live with Pop in jail. There's also the fact that I created this situation two years ago, nobody else."

"Wonder if the Jansen family would agree that you created the situation."

"Doesn't matter. This is where I am, not where I'd like to be."

"But Tyler old pal, this is a no-win situation for you. If you take Strobe out, your mind will be liver pudding, or you'll move to Montana and shack up with a sheep. And if you lose you'll be dead, and your family will be devastated, and I'll have to mow your lawn."

"I've got no choice," Tyler said.

"Well, I have a choice. I'm not going to let you do it."

"How'll you stop me?"

Dave smiled grimly. "I whipped your hinder the first time we met. I reckon I still can."

Ty stood up from the bed. "I love you, Dave, and God knows I don't want to fight you. But I will. And this isn't third grade."

Dave sighed. "Hell, it was worth a try. I guess I should have known better. Here, hand me your jacket. Least I can do is carry it to the car for you."

Ty turned to reach for his jacket. While his attention was diverted Dave Michaels hit him a sucker punch to the side of the neck, very fast and very hard. Tyler collapsed in a heap beside the bed, with Dave catching his head before it cracked into the floor, then handcuffing Ty's hands behind his back and duct-taping his legs together. Tossing his unconscious friend over his left shoulder, Dave went down the stairs, out the door, and over to his Challenger, where he eased Ty into the front seat then drove to Clyde Vance's home. Clyde answered the door to a very strange sight, but didn't say a word, just stood back to allow entry.

"Don't ask," Dave said.

"I won't," Clyde assured.

Gently laying Tyler on the floral couch, Dave said, "I gave him a sleepy-time shot a short while ago. Before that I had to smack him in the neck, so there'll be a bruise. His pulse and breathing are normal, and he'll be out maybe four hours. That should be long enough."

"For what?"

Dave raised a hand.

Clyde said, "Never mind," then, as Dave turned to go, asked, "Can I uncuff him?"

Dave tossed Clyde the key. "Your decision, but I wouldn't recommend it. He'll be in a really foul mood. It was me, I'd lock him in a closet until morning and go to sleep with the television on. Loud." Then he crossed the room and slipped into the night.

• • •

The Vance and Atkins contingent was at Tex and Shirley's Pancake House, spread over several tables. Anne sat on one side of Odie, Leigh on the other. Mikey was at Anne's left, sleepily nibbling crackers. Anne leaned toward her father to ask, "Where's Ty?"

"Dunno. Probably out with Dave."

Ty was out all right. Out cold. And not with Dave, but in the basement of Clyde Vance's home, lying peacefully with his head on a down pillow. His uncle was upstairs watching ACC basketball on Channel Two, a pretty close game.

The volume was turned up real loud.

Eleven miles away Dave Michaels was stepping into the breach, alone.

Well.

Not entirely alone.

STROBE

OVERHEAD, A SMOOTH CHUNK OF MOON, NOT FULL, SAshayed amongst a herd of patchwork clouds, its pale glow illuminating the Roundtree manse. *No security lights,* thought Dave Michaels, *not even a porch lamp. Well, that's fitting. There are no porches. Or even Porsches. Ha-ha. Not funny.* He swallowed. *Why am I nervous? There're probably only ten or twelve guys waiting to puncture my hide, or beat me to death with baseball bats.* The Rolls-Royce hibernated on the cobblestone turnaround near the front door. No movement. Anywhere. Except for Dave, approaching the house from the west, weaving his way through the sickly stand of elms, stopping frequently to scan for visual or audible signals of danger. Naught. So on he moved, the crisp night air chilling the nape of his neck. Or *was* it the air? At the back door now. Was there an alarm? Certainly. The man was as rich as Bob Hope; of course he'd have an alarm. But there was no help for it, and no time to circumvent. *Let's see what happens,* Dave thought, and the knob turned under his hand. A short hallway, pantry to the right, then a small bathroom, and the kitchen, clean as an operating theater, fresh fruit in a large bowl on the counter, the floor an interesting parquet—*ceramic inlay? Who gives a flip! Pay attention, boy! Screw the floor, or pretty soon you may be lying on it, bleeding*—so he moved on, into an interior hall with a lengthy runner, Persian no doubt, and thick underfoot, but no windows here so he couldn't discern color. The hall took him past several open doors: library, study . . . he stopped at the study. Through a large window the arrant moon cast its glow on a walnut desk upon which were piled heaps of photographs, mostly of a boy-child, occasionally in the company of his mother, never with his father, the child well fed and seemingly happy, the woman less so, but obviously enamored of the child. The backgrounds were eclectic: beach, mountain, woodland, domestic gardens; some secluded shots, some peopled by passersby; not only loose photos but filled albums; boxes stacked and spilling over; framed shots; a collage, professionally done. Room by room, Dave determined that no one was on the ground floor. Except him. If there was an alarm, it was of the silent type, and if so, at any moment uniformed officers would descend. *Then I'll have to make like a tree and leave. Ha-ha. Quit stalling. One floor to go. Be a shame if I came all the way out here and Strobe's in Poughkeepsie. Guess I could wait, but for how long? Once Ty wakes up, he'll come straight here.* That thought galvanized him. Up the stairs, down a hall to his left, and the first door Dave came to was an upstairs study. And inside that study, behind an enormous desk, in near-total darkness, sat Strobe Roundtree.

"Where's Vance?" said Strobe, a gun visible on the desk near his hand.

Dave didn't answer.

He simply stepped into the room.

INTRUSION

ALL THE WAY OVER TO THE DESK DAVE STRODE. AS HE drew near, Strobe Roundtree's right hand moved toward the gun on the desk. Dave said, "You touch that piece and I'll tear off your arm and slap you with the wet end."

Strobe's hand stopped. He looked up at Dave Michaels, a tic playing along one cheek, his eyes burning with an alarming intensity. "I was expecting Vance."

"Which Vance? You blew one of them up."

The tic flickered. "*Tyler* Vance." Oozing scorn.

"Sorry, he's tied up. Priorities, you know, what with the wake and all. He asked me to come in his place."

"I have no quarrel with you."

"You will. I came here to discuss arrangements for your burial. Or do you prefer an urn? You know, to avoid the worms."

The heated gaze intensified. "Maybe I do have a quarrel with you after all."

Dave smiled pleasantly. "You better be damn quick with that sidearm, then, because I'll be all over your sorry self in about one second. Maybe less. But, hey, give it a shot, if you'll pardon the pun."

"You're goading me. Why?"

"I'm not goading you, I'm challenging you. If I were goading you, I'd point out how really ugly you are."

The tic bounced beneath Strobe's right eye. He said, "I can shoot you into chum and get away with it. You're an intruder. I'd never even be charged."

"Only one problem with that logic."

"And that is?"

"First you gotta do it."

Suddenly Strobe Roundtree broke into a slow grin, the worry line between his brows erasing itself. Dave sensed a shift in momentum. Could he really make it over the desk in time to get the gun?

He'd never find out. . . .

There was a slight whoosh of air just before the cosh took him in the back of the head and he thudded to the floor.

• • •

"Is one blow enough?"

"To do what?"

"Finish him."

"Who wants to finish him?"

"I do."

"Tough shit."

Roundtree's eyes sizzled. "What did you say?"

"I said tough shit. He's done nothing to you."

"He came here to kill me. He told me so."

Rough hands ran over Dave's prostrate form, searching. "Then he planned to do it with his hands. No gun, no knife, not even a pair of wire cutters."

"Kill him anyway."

"No."

Strobe stood and picked up his revolver and came around the front of the desk to stand over Dave Michaels. "Then I will." And he would have if Tabor hadn't jerked the gun from Strobe's hand and tossed it across the room. It landed with a thunk and skidded against the cold stone fireplace.

"What are you doing?"

"I've been working for you eight years, Strobe, but I didn't sign on for a killing. Your guy in the Buick blew an innocent man to smithereens, and still that didn't satisfy you. Now you want to grease this kid. You're out of control, and when you go down you'll implicate me in a murder, sure as God made little green apples."

"There's no way to trace anything to me."

"I'm not convinced. The cops, both city and county, already have your name at the top of their list. They'll find a way to make things stick, especially now that they found your mystery Buick driver and his carful of gadgets."

Strobe went back around his desk and sat down. "So what? They have no proof. I went through three intermediaries with him, and only you know about Feeney and Pogue. You won't talk, Feeney's long gone, and Pogue's been assured of a fat bundle waiting for him when he gets out. They can prove nothing against me, and I don't give a damn about their suspicions."

"Blowing up Vance's uncle wasn't kosher, Strobe. Plus a little boy nearly went up with him."

"What about *my* son?" Strobe spoke through clenched teeth.

"I don't think Vance's uncle had anything to do with that."

"Screw the whole fucking Vance family!" Strobe screamed, his facial tic quivering out of control.

"That's what I thought you'd say. Too bad. You always did pay well," said Tabor, moving to the side of the desk. Strobe shucked a drawer, pulled out a second gun, and was bringing it to bear when Tabor slapped it from his hand then leaped behind Strobe's chair, encircled the man's neck with his arms, and secured a solid sleeper hold. After just a few struggling seconds, Roundtree was out.

• • •

First Tabor trussed Dave Michaels with nylon cord, then he retrieved the revolver from across the room and, wiping it free of prints, placed it in a desk drawer. Then he took a straight razor from a coat pocket and slashed both of Roundtree's wrists, in line with the axis of his forearms. Blood spurted all over. Strobe was beginning to stir, so Tabor slid thick arms around his neck once again and put him back to sleep. Onto the desk Tabor placed a can of Sterno, then lit it, piling newspaper on top. The papers lit, burning brightly. Some fell to the floor. Lighter fluid enhanced the conflagration and ignited the carpet; more papers atop the blazing pile and the fire began to run amuck. Tabor next doused Roundtree's clothes and chair with the lighter fluid; within a minute, spreading flame turned the unconscious barrister into a human torch as Tabor carried Dave Michaels through the study doorway. Behind them the room was an inferno.

• • •

The fire department saved much of the house, especially the lower floor, but two-thirds of the top story was demolished.

Dave Michaels awoke in the bushes outside his parents' home. He smelled like smoke, which did not make him happy, though he was unsure why. With his head seeping and aching, he sneaked into the basement, put his clothes in a plastic garbage bag, took a shower, then drove ten miles and weighted the bag down with rocks and tossed it into Lake Brandt.

A homeless man observed Dave and immediately recovered the bag and its contents with a long pole, washed the clothes thoroughly using an old bar of Dial soap, then wore them for several weeks until he was arrested for trespass in Granville, West Virginia. He never did get back to North Carolina.

REMEMBERING DARRYL

LUTHER J. "TOOT" SICKENBERGER, DAPPER AS USUAL and freshly shaved, his brown fedora resting on his left knee, was saying, ". . . obviously a suicide. Not only was he badly burned, but both wrists were slashed to the bone. The fire was initiated by a can of Sterno, and helped along by lighter fluid. The scorched cans were found on his desk, along with a straight razor. The ME thinks he waited until he was nearly unconscious from blood loss to light the Sterno, because he was still seated in his chair—what was left of it. Normally, burning to death causes folks to, ah, move around a bit. That didn't seem to be the case here."

Leigh Vance said, "Was the house destroyed?"

"No. Most of the top story, though. In a downstairs study we found hundreds of photos of his wife and child, mostly the child, lying on a desk. He was obviously still grieving over his son's death."

"The poor man," Leigh commiserated.

Odie looked at her. "That 'poor man' was responsible for my brother being splattered all over the yard."

Leigh took her husband's hand. "I know. Still . . ."

"Still what?"

"Never mind."

An awkward silence then, into which Sickenberger stepped gingerly: "No offense, Odie, but I have to ask. It's my job. Where—"

"Right here. Leigh and I both, and Anne. Mikey too," Odie said sarcastically.

"See? Everyone gets mad."

Leigh smiled dimly, to mitigate Odie's harsh reaction.

"How about Ty?" asked the sheriff.

Odie's chin came up.

"I have to ask."

"You didn't do this much asking when Darryl got blown up, or Ty was set upon, or—"

"Yes, I did. But you didn't have a chip on your shoulder."

Leigh said, "Tyler's at Clyde's house. He spent the night. Clyde and Dora can verify that. I spoke to them this morning, right after breakfast. Ty took a sleeping pill or something; he was still groggy from its effects."

"How about Dave Michaels?" Sickenberger pressed.

"I wouldn't know about Dave. I suspect he stayed at home. Why don't you call him and ask?" Leigh said.

"I will." The sheriff stood and put on his hat, running his thumb and forefinger along the brim. "Sorry to have troubled you folks, especially during your time of grief. But I thought you'd want to hear about Strobe from me, and be questioned by me, not one of my subordinates."

Leigh got up to pat his arm. "Of course. And don't let Odie offend you. He's upset."

Odie, still seated, simply grunted.

"Well, I'll show myself out," said L. J. Sickenberger, and he did.

When he had gone, Leigh turned to Odie. "Do you think it was Ty?"

"You bet. Strobe Roundtree wasn't the suicidal type."

"Would Clyde have helped?"

"Dang right. And Dora would provide the alibi."

"What about Dave?"

"He's not family. Ty wouldn't have let him stick his nose out."

"Will Toot figure all this out?"

"He'll suspect. But Ty was smart. He made it look like suicide, not to mention dang near burning the house down to cover any mistakes. My guess is that he beat hell out of Roundtree before he did him."

"And all that doesn't bother you?"

Odie looked at her. "Not . . . one . . . bit."

Leigh absorbed that. "You don't think Toot could have tied Darryl's death to Strobe, ever?"

Odie shook his head. "Strobe would have insulated himself too well. And he had too much wealth and position. There's not a chance in hell the sheriff would have nailed him."

Leigh sat pensive for a moment. "Then we have to face the fact that our son murdered a man."

"Easier for me than to have Roundtree get away with everything he's done."

"Yes, I suppose it is, for you," said Leigh. "I'm not so sure about me."

Then they sat for a long while, looking out the window and holding hands, leaning on one another, just as they had for twenty-eight years.

• • •

Clyde Vance said, “How you feeling?”

Tyler Vance said, “Like a Roman legion used my head for a soccer ball.”

Dora Vance said, “That good, huh?”

Clyde began, “You want to take the Gremlin? You can use it until your insurance replaces the . . . your car.” He averted his eyes for a moment, then had to leave the table.

“Sure. Thanks,” Ty said to the retreating back. He looked helplessly at his aunt Dora.

She said, “He’ll live. We all will. Especially now that that awful man has gone to his fiery reward.”

“I’m much obliged. For everything.”

“You mean letting you sleep over?” The picture of innocence.

“And forgetting how I got here.”

“How *did* you get here?” Dora smiled. Then: “The car keys are on a hook by the back door.”

“First let me help you with the dishes.”

“You’ll spoil me,” she complained. “Clyde’s never washed a dish in his life. I might come to expect it. Then we’d get divorced and I’d have to move to Fayetteville and work in a topless bar.”

Tyler laughed. All the Vance women had a terrific sense of humor.

They had to, to put up with the Vance men.

• • •

Anne was talking to her aunt Minnie. "I'm taking Mikey back to PA for the holidays."

Minnie Vance said, "Why in the world would you do that?"

Anne shifted on the sofa. "It just doesn't feel like Christmas. For as long as I can remember, Uncle Darryl would come down from Virginia a week early, and . . ." She couldn't continue. When she could, she said, "It just won't be Christmas."

Minnie smiled and said, "Pretend Darryl is sitting here listening to you planning to abandon something really special that he was a huge part of. What would he say?"

"He'd say, 'Chin up, girl. Life goes on.' That's what he told me when Jerome left."

"And he was right, wasn't he? Mikey's great; you have a nice house and a good job. Your family is supportive. You're young and beautiful and bright and sharp as a tack. And you want to abandon your most cherished time of the year, the season when you'll always feel closest to Darryl?"

Anne began to cry openly, deep, wrenching sobs, letting go. Minnie held her until most of it had run its course, her chin on Anne's head, sharing the pain. Then she said, "Remember the time we all went to Grandmother Vance's farm for Christmas? You were eight or nine. Ty was two, and no bigger than a button. You and he had to sleep in the music room, which had no heat, just a big fireplace. Odie piled on the wood, but it got really cold that night. The baby slept closest to the fireplace, of course, and in the wee hours you woke up freezing. Do you remember?"

Anne looked up, eyes glistening, but she couldn't help but smile. "Do I ever. I moved Ty away from the fireplace and lay down where he'd been. When Uncle Darryl came in to wake us Christmas morning, poor little Ty was blue from the cold. Uncle Darryl made me stand outside on the porch for five minutes, in my nightgown, barefoot, to show me how it felt. I'll never forget it. It was the longest five minutes I ever spent." She laughed at the memory. "When he finally came back to get me," she continued, "I was so frozen the *Titanic* would have sunk if it had run into me. He felt so sorry for me, he wrapped me up in an old army blanket, carried me in by the fire—roaring by now—and held me tight until my teeth quit chattering. I said, 'I won't ever do it again, Uncle Darryl,' and he cried and told me, 'I know, honey, I know.' I'd never seen a man cry before. And then, fifteen years later, he cried again when Jerome left me. He could see how devasted I was, and . . ." She teared up again. "He always told me that if he ever had a little girl, he'd want her to be just like me. That I was his favorite niece."

"And you were, he told me that many times. And he'd never have allowed you to give up Christmas, especially over him. It would have broken his heart."

"I know. But I miss him so." And the two rocked and hugged, remembering Darryl.

"I'LL NEVER FORGIVE YOU"

ANNE AND ODIE AND MINNIE AND LEIGH HAD GONE SHOPping and to see *Murder on the Orient Express*. (Leigh loved Sean Connery.) Mikey was napping in the front bedroom. Tyler and Dave were sitting on the screened-in back porch. In the wooden swing. Swinging.

Tyler said, "My neck still hurts."

"Sorry," said David.

"You sucker-punched me."

"You're damned right. Otherwise we'd have beaten each other to a pulp and Mikey would have had to go after Strobe." He reached into his jacket. "Mind if I do a jay?"

Ty looked at him. "You know what that does to your brain cells?"

Dave lit up. "I don't inhale."

"Oh, sure. Well, *exhale* the other way."

The swing creaked under their combined weight. Back and forth.

Tyler wrinkled his nose against the smell. "My neck *hurts,*" he said.

"Complain, why don't you."

"I'll never forgive you for the sucker punch."

"Never?"

"Well. Not for a couple months, anyway."

"Couple months?" said Dave, taking a drag and holding it.

"At least a week."

"A week?"

"Okay, I forgive you."

"Then I can count on you to return my Creedence Clearwater eight-track?"

"Forget it, I don't forgive you."

More swinging, feet on the floor, legs crossed. Buddies willing to go the distance. And then some. No matter what.

"So how'd you manage it?" Ty asked.

Inhale and hold, then a choked "What?"

"Don't play dumb with me, not that it'd be hard for you. How'd you take care of Strobe?"

Exhale. Dave was becoming very relaxed. "I have no idea."

"What do you mean, no idea?"

"Feel right there." Dave indicated the back of his head.

Ty felt.

"Ouch," said Dave. "Where do you think I got that goose egg?"

"Fighting Strobe?"

"He hit me in the *back* of the head? What was I doing at the time, running?"

"No offense."

"Well, I hope not." Inhale and hold. Exhale. *Very* relaxed was Dave Michaels. "No, right when old Strobe and I were getting better acquainted someone snuck up behind me and mistook my head for a golf ball."

Ty snorted. "You let someone creep up behind you?"

"I was focused on Strobe. Totally. He had a .44 Magnum about three centimeters from his right pinky, and I must confess it was making me nervous."

"You didn't have your gun on him?"

Dave looked through his friend in disbelief. "I didn't even *take* a gun."

Tyler, equally incredulous, said, "What!"

"How would I have explained a shooting to the fuzz? 'I dunno, Officer, I was just looking through his Lawrence Welk albums and he drew down on me.' "

"Then how—"

"I figured I could get close enough to take him if I was surreptitious."

"Surreptitious?"

"It means—"

"I *know* what it means, it just doesn't sound right coming out of your mouth."

"Hey, I read."

"Yeah, when your lips aren't chapped."

"You want to hear this or not?"

"Sure. Tell me more about how you went unarmed after a known murderer, then, while in the enemy camp, let someone sneak up and donner you. Wait, let me take notes for my future book—*Surreptitious Clandestiny.*"

"You are a major-league smart-ass, Tyler Vance."

"It's been said. So continue."

"Well, there I was, intimidating Mr. Roundtree, and all of a sudden the lights went out."

"Really?"

"Figuratively, not literally. Next I knew, I was looking

up at my father's prized azalea bushes. I noticed they could stand a pruning, and—"

"How did you get there?"

"I guess the guy who popped me decided against barbecuing me alongside Strobe."

They stopped talking to swing for a while, deep in thought. Dave finished his joint and dipped a hand inside his coat, but Tyler said, "Please, not another. I'm beginning to hallucinate."

"That's LSD. I don't do that."

"Thank heavens. You're so mellow now you're about to melt."

"But my head no longer hurts."

"Well, my neck does."

"Don't start."

"To recap, person or persons unknown conked you on the bonnet, carried your sorry carcass to safety, then slipped away into the night."

"That's it."

"And you expect me to believe that?"

Dave feigned offense. "Why would I lie?"

"So I wouldn't have to fib to the police when they come interrogate me after they arrest you."

"Ha! You're a crackerjack liar. It would scarcely challenge you."

"Thanks." Tyler stopped swinging to turn sideways. "Look me in the eye," he demanded.

David did so.

"Do you swear that the foregoing was the truth, the whole truth, and so forth?"

Dave raised his hand solemnly. "So help me God."

Ty just shook his head. "Who'da thunk it. Think we'll ever know who did Strobe?"

"Sure, someday."

But they never did.

ROMEO

AT 6:16 P.M. ON CHRISTMAS EVE, GRANTHAM TABOR stopped into the Phillips 66 on Summit Avenue to top off his Triumph's tank. He also purchased a bag of M&M Peanuts, a pack of Nekots, some Spearmint gum, a Mountain Dew, and six prophylactics from a coin-operated vending machine in the men's room. He paid his tab with a twenty-dollar bill, one of many in his wallet. Hundreds more were in a couple of entaped shoe boxes in the trunk of his car, along with most of his clothes and a six-pack of Bud. On the bucket seat beside him, hidden beneath a green sweater, was a Colt Trooper .357 Magnum. At 6:25, the retired Dade County cop pulled back onto the nearly deserted street and tooled toward Highway 29, which conjoined with I-40 at the bottom edge of town. In less than four hours, his car was guzzling premium on the far side of Asheville. From there it was northwest, toward Leicester on Route 63, drinking Sanka from a paper cup and thinking about his girlfriend in Romeo, Tennessee, until the driver of an eastbound tractor trailer rig, falling asleep after seventeen hours at the wheel, crossed the yellow line and tagged Tabor's TR6 near the rear wheel on the driver's side, knocking the vehicle into a spin at seventy miles per hour, then off the road to collide with a concrete cistern. The trucker walked away from the crash, but Tabor was ambulanced to a hospital where he clung tenuously to life for more than a week. At three minutes after midnight on January 1, 1975, he died as a result of internal injuries, and no mortal soul would ever know what really happened to Strobe Roundtree. In a year—after a postmortem feeding frenzy within Strobe's law firm had subsided—no one gave a shit.

EPILOGUE

A FULL HOUSE WAS THE VANCE DOMICILE ON CHRISTMAS Day, 1974, filled with camaraderie and holiday spirit, a Yule log roasting in the fireplace, spitting and twinkling, its colors dancing like merry elves, spreading warmth and cheer. The Jansens also were there, all three, the two womenfolk fresh off a bus from Danville. Emily, awkward and troubled, talked with Tyler at length, with him trying to allay her feelings of causation. "I sorry," she said tearfully, and he hugged her and patted her head. Perhaps it worked, for she seemed calmer afterward to her daddy, watching from the living room doorway while she excitedly opened a gaily wrapped parcel from Tyler. Inside the box was a bright silk scarf, which wet her eyes, not from pain but delight, and brought a slow, shy smile. She immediately tied the scarf around her slender neck, to appreciative remarks from those gathered. What a beaming, beautiful girl!

Minnie Vance left not long after, for Virginia with her two children, to spend Christmas Day at her own family's. A subdued farewell, everyone proffering brave smiles and dry eyes, for the most part. Anne especially hated to see Minnie go, and the two clung for a long while, and released reluctantly, then, long after Minnie had driven off down the silent street, Anne stood alone in the yard waving, the tears now unrestrained. The wind rosied her cheeks before she at last turned to go in, shivering, not only from cold.

Except for Mikey—chomping at the bit, but playing with Jazbo for diversion—the family had waited patiently for Anne to rejoin them before ripping into the resplendent packages. Santa first: Mikey received an electric train, and Lincoln Logs, and an inflated clown punching bag that popped upright after you socked it, and a truck that went *boop-boop-boop* when backing up. (Jazbo got three rubber bones and a collar.) Then, following Vance tradition, each adult would wait while another opened their gift, not only to voice suitable admiration but to make the morning last as long as possible. Music wafted from the organ stereo: Bing Crosby doing "Adeste Fidelis" and "O Little Town of Bethlehem," followed by Julie Andrews's crystal elocutions. Then, after presents but before lunch, the entire assembly—surrounded by happily discarded wrapping paper—sang in chorus. Leigh sat at the organ, with Mikey beside her on the bench vocalizing "Angels We Have Heard On High" at the top of his voice, and Emily stood behind Mikey, her voice lilting.

• • •

And looking down upon it all, from high atop the Christmas tree, was Uncle Darryl's framed photograph, smiling, in the angel's place.